Mitch Engel

Noble Windmills

iUniverse, Inc.
New York   Bloomington

iUniverse books may be ordered through booksellers or by contacting:

iUniverse
1663 Liberty Drive
Bloomington, IN 47403
www.iuniverse.com
1-800-Authors (1-800-288-4677)

Because of the dynamic nature of the Internet, any Web addresses or links contained in this
book may have changed since publication and may no longer be valid. The views expressed
in this work are solely those of the author and do not necessarily reflect the views of the
publisher, and the publisher hereby disclaims any responsibility for them.

ISBN: 978-1-4502-4328-5 (sc)
ISBN: 978-1-4502-4329-2 (hc)
ISBN: 978-1-4502-4330-8 (ebook)

Library of Congress Control Number: 2010909994

Printed in the United States of America

iUniverse rev. date: 07/29/2010

In memory of my father, a man of modest means and immense wealth.

Prologue

The spindly filament likes to give the illusion there's no hurry. Day after day, month after month, that second hand pauses almost imperceptibly at sixty different checkpoints, bumping ever onward with its circular accounting. It may pretend to be nonjudgmental, but it mocks us by trying to draw our attention to the preciousness, the wasted opportunities and fleeting nature. With each hesitation, reproach for the irretrievable moments, for our failure to make life more momentous.

This place begs everyone who enters to monitor time's progression more closely and ponder what could have been. Next lap around, the second hand will again join forces with the imperial twelve that sits atop the large wall clock and together they'll unleash a shrill to signal visiting hour is over.

The room is cavernous, the surroundings seemingly designed to discourage happy thoughts—unless one happens to be sado-monochromatic. The cinder block walls are gray, as are the heavy metal doors. The linoleum floor appears to have been white at some point, probably during one of Eisenhower's terms, but long since faded gray. Some twenty-five feet overhead is a labyrinth of ductwork and water pipes, all color-coded in their respective shades of gray. The walls on both ends are interrupted by long narrow windows at least fifteen feet above floor level. Reinforced steel screens are bolted inside and out, apparently so squeegees or rags don't ever make actual contact with the filthy glass between—assuring that even sunlight gets filtered into gray.

Nonetheless, the clusters of friends and family members assigned to eighteen gray steel tables have imbued this colorless space with needed warmth for nearly an hour. Warmth that must sustain hopes and spirits until next visitation. The final minutes are toughest, as the despotic wall clock regains control. Eyes are drawn to that damned second hand during an unspoken countdown. The cacophony of joyful reunions gradually is displaced by a murmur of teary encouragements, and lastly there's the ominous quietude. God, how I hate the silent separations.

As soon as that dreaded buzzer goes off, the unmistakable sound of cellblock doors will echo through adjacent corridors. "Residents" immediately line up at the door to be shepherded back to their assigned homes-away-from-home. The loud speaker will start barking a litany of exit procedures in an authoritarian tone that seems to rebuke visitors for bothering to maintain bonds with convicted felons. And like all the times before, I'll keep thinking about how differently things might have turned out.

With so much to reflect upon, my story could take a while—so I hope you'll be patient. Every now and then, stretch or something … maybe pour yourself an iced tea, or a cocktail if you're inclined. Take a whiff of the roses. With a great deal more time on my hands, I've finally discovered the benefits of slowing down, of not stressing so much over past mistakes. Believe me, there were plenty and we'll get to some of the more blatant ones. I've also learned not to judge people too quickly. Good or bad. Sometimes folks just end up being different than you thought they were—even those you felt closest to, the ones you were most sure about. At least that's what happened with me. It's amazing how much perspectives change; in fact, your whole life can change in the matter of a few short months.

I guess we could say this is my Enron, but then you might wonder why a guy needs his own personal Enron. Well, such comparisons just seem to be in vogue these days. Some foreign nation gets hit with an act of terrorism and its leaders are obliged to proclaim that this is their 9/11. One of our cities suffers a rash of tornadoes or floods and the local populace automatically declares that this is their Katrina. Escalating cultural standards are conditioning us not to view life's various calamities as adequately serious unless they can hold their own with other, more notorious events. I'll grant that "my Enron" may seem a bit far-reaching to some. But not to me. You see, I previously hadn't found myself in the center of a federal investigation. So it probably goes without saying that this was the first time I'd been the cause of one.

For over two decades I'd been tethered to the convenient tenets of a free market system, worshipping daily at the altar of upward mobility. I would have been the last person that anyone should have expected to cross over to the other side. Even as I'd heard the reports of the fiscal atrocities committed at Enron, WorldCom, Tyco, and elsewhere, intermingled among my reactions was a twinge of contempt for the insiders who actually blew those corporate whistles. They'd broken rank, ratted out their capitalist brethren ... behaved in a way that was so un-American. How could I have known I was destined to become one of them? I'd never envisioned myself as a traitor to the bonds of executive silence. And certainly I wouldn't have considered myself any sort of ethical champion, as some later would attempt to label me. However, I'd be lying if I pretended that I hadn't worried about being a little crazy from time to time.

In the final analysis, we might disagree on whether I initiated the whole ordeal out of vengeance or virtue. Or what might have happened if others hadn't intervened. Even after this time to reflect, I still admit to not knowing for sure. But definitely we can agree that I had to be nuts to do what I did. Hell, all the outside experts agreed on that.

Chapter One

At six thirty on a frigid Saturday morning in Chicago, even the sun has the good sense not to be up yet. My third full week back in town already had been enough of a blur, but then came the tapas, tequila, and more tequila at Friday night's festivities. As a card-carrying captain of industry, I couldn't allow myself to succumb entirely to human frailty. I figured I at least should muster the energy to crawl out of bed and tackle a week's worth of unread *Wall Street Journal*s. Of course, I chose Ashton's. Sliding onto the red vinyl of that window booth under the "L" tracks on Franklin meant I really was home where I belonged. There I could enjoy some time alone with a couple of over-easy, bacon grease, and another hangover. Ashton's always had been the perfect place to pull myself together.

At such an ungodly hour, I hadn't expected any familiar faces, especially not Luke's. It had been four, maybe five or six years; I'd lost track of the time since I last saw him. But there he sat at our table, the table where our mongrel gang had gathered so often in college. The table where Carly and I first had realized we were becoming more than just friends. The table where Luke would join me a few years later, after Carly had told me we should try to remain good friends. The table where the others had joined me on the morning after my father's funeral. I always could count on this table to help bring clarity to my life, so it was only fitting that Luke be sitting there when not much of anything seemed clear anymore.

"Peters, I'd heard you were back in Chicago and figured if I ever wanted to see you again, coming here was my best shot."

"Luke, I was planning to call you next week, I promise. It's been way too long and that's my fault … but, man, you look awesome."

"Don't sweat it. You've been busy doing the Lord's work ... you know, single-handedly ridding the world of sloth."

Then he flashed that grin of his and I knew I'd been forgiven. Once more. Years of built-up guilt, instantly absolved by his welcoming eye contact. Since grade school, Loukas Alexio Papadakis had been cutting me slack. After all this time I still couldn't hold up my end of a lifelong friendship. When he and Natalie had celebrated their big Greek wedding twenty years earlier, Luke could have asked any one of his numerous close friends or relatives to stand up as best man. Instead, the privilege had been mine—and still I managed to shirk almost every responsibility by not arriving until the day before the ceremony. I'd allowed the latest round of important meetings in my life to take precedence. At the reception I at least did remember to make a toast, though I hadn't bothered to prepare any comments in advance. I spoke what was in my heart and watched in amazement as Luke arose from his chair at the head of the bridal table so that everyone in attendance could see the tears streaming down his face like badges of honor. If I'd gotten around to marriage, Luke for sure would have been the best man, by every definition.

Age forty-four definitely looked better on him than on the narrow, sagging face I'd seen in the bathroom mirror that morning. His curly black hair might have been slightly thinner, with perhaps a hint of gray around the edges. The beaming smile probably exposed an extra crease or two. Otherwise, Luke looked the way he always had. Dark skin, hulky shoulders, shirt-sleeves rolled up above the elbows of his thick hairy arms. It was great to see him sitting there, even if his positive influence was sure to pull me out of the unprecedented level of self-disgust toward which I'd been working myself. I wasn't going to settle for a mere midlife crisis; I'd been gearing up for a midlife nuclear meltdown.

In theory, I should have been happy as a lark, or clam, or any of those other allegedly elated fauna. The latest promotion had put me on the executive committee of a $21-billion-dollar holding company, a respected publicly held corporation. I was one of only four direct reports to the CEO. My new responsibilities entailed a relocation to our vaunted corporate headquarters, which overlooked Grant Park and Lake Michigan. After more than two decades of chasing roadmaps, my mailing address finally was back in my hometown of Chicago. Not since college days at DePaul had I been able to experience the perennial disappointment of the Cubs and Bears in person. To top it off, I was making more money in a year than that skinny middle-class kid from the suburbs had thought he might earn in a lifetime. So where was all this fruit I was supposed to be reaping? The clover I was supposed to be rolling in? Where was the faintest twinge of satisfaction for what I'd accomplished?

Throughout the years I'd convinced myself. The hard work, the sacrifices would pay off. The compromises and misplaced allegiances. The manipulation. The disingenuousness. On the way up the mountain, the trade-offs had seemed such a natural and integral part of the climb. But a steady erosion of principles can lay one barren. It's no surprise that so little grows above the tree line.

I should have been gratified that my new corporate staff had hosted a welcoming bash the night before. But it wasn't like any of them had been forced to dig into their own pockets; the company picked up the tab and the costs would get thrown against my P&L. All the officers and managers who now reported to me had gotten a free dinner and drinks out of the deal. Sure, some of them might have given up a Friday night with their wives or families. But what choice did they have? I was their new boss. It was my turn to place unrealistic demands on each and every one of them and then freeze their salaries at the first sign of a tough year. I'd be the next forked tongue in their lives to spew whatever was necessary to justify another inane approval procedure or the next round of cost cutting. They knew it and I knew it, yet with each tray of shooters we'd high-fived and fist-pumped like we really intended to perform like some cohesive team. I abhorred such hypocrisy ... and really abhorred being one of its poster boys.

I should have been touched by the glowing tributes included in Wilson Delaney's remarks. After all, he was our CEO and the person most responsible for my swift ascent through the ranks of the corporation. Problem was, I no longer could stomach being in the same room with this Machiavellian snake. Nonetheless, I'd plastered on my best exaggerated smile and embraced him with my manliest man-hug.

I'd lost count of the empty shot glasses we lined up. I normally wouldn't drink that much with business associates ... I did my best drinking alone. But I'd needed to show them what a regular guy I could be. Teambuilding can be selfless on occasion, so I kept right on drinking until the last few stragglers crammed into a taxi. After they cleared out, I kept drinking purely for myself, trying to dislodge a disdain for everything I'd become.

Luke shoved a heaping stack of pancakes aside to offer me his full attention. "How's your mom doing, Milo?"

"Great ... gets around amazingly well for almost eighty. Still misses my dad, though."

"What's it been, eleven years?"

"You're something else, Luke. You never forget."

"Hey, your parents were like second family to me."

"Yeah, we had some amazing times growing up, didn't we?" My mind started drifting back to a treasure of memories, but he apparently wanted to keep me in the present.

"Please give your mom a hug for me."

"Sure ... I've promised to take her to dinner as soon as I get more settled in." I was tempted to pull out my BlackBerry and send myself an e-mail so I wouldn't forget. "So how'd you know I'd be here this morning?"

"Just a hunch and I decided to take the chance. We always ate breakfast here on Saturdays." He seemed eager to change subjects. "What do you hear from Hilpert or Jenkins?"

"Luke, you know me ... I'm lousy at keeping in touch."

I thought he might be a little relieved to learn that I hadn't been any better at staying connected with the others than I had with him. Instead, there was a trace of disappointment before he quickly moved on. "What about Carly?"

"Seems to be doing fantastic. Married, two kids, still living in Cincinnati. She jumped law firms last year as a senior partner. I knew she'd become one heckuva litigator."

Luke's attention perked up. "So at least you've been talking to her?"

"Nah, I Google her name every now and then. She's been featured in a few articles that always come up."

Carly was the kind of ex-girlfriend with whom a guy could maintain a genuinely amicable relationship and should want to. Yet somehow I'd never found or made the time to pick up the phone. My loss and I knew it. So did Luke, but he wasn't one to pile on.

Reunited for less than five minutes and already we'd whisked through some of the foremost individuals on my lengthy guilt list. But indeed, confession must have been healthy for the soul because even these feeble acknowledgments of my self-absorption were starting to assuage the angst I constantly lugged around. Luke was just plain good for me and always had been ... and I could use any available assistance to feel a little less shitty about myself.

The repugnance had built over years of career obsession. Despite repeated lofty intentions, I'd been unable to pull myself out of the spiral. Success in the business world was too intoxicating. Victories kept trumping virtues in the race to get ahead. With each passing month, the emotional burden had grown weightier from the pillars of my youth. My once deep-rooted convictions and the people most important to me now stood in stark, tortuous contrast to the shallow man I'd become. The foundation had been so rock solid. Those formative years were chock-full of principled loved ones and nurturing role models. I'd launched into adulthood with such dead aim on the sanctity of friendships and family and human compassions but then so carelessly misplaced my priorities. All these years later I was empty inside. I couldn't remember the last time I'd really put myself out for someone … or the last time I'd even had a genuinely good time. How had I allowed myself to veer so far off course?

Exiting Ashton's, I tossed the unread *Journals* into a trash can on the sidewalk, a symbolic act of my renewed commitment. Now that I was back in Chicago, I would bring my life into a proper balance. This time I could do it. In this city of broad shoulders and second chances, I'd be able to discover that born-again decency. Absolute faith in myself was a long way from being restored, but my oldest and closest friend had provided enough encouragements to help me believe I wasn't a lost cause quite yet. The atrophy wasn't total. Luke's presence and affirming personality had rekindled a long dormant optimism.

Chapter Two

Since childhood, Luke had insisted that our friendship was solely attributable to his beloved Greek ancestry. I could close my eyes and still hear him making his case in the school cafeteria. "Sure, those teachers can pretend English is based on some Latin alphabet if they want to, but any true scholar knows that the lousy Romans lifted most of their letters from us ... that the Greeks came up with the original alphabet."

As a point of fact, our tight friendship had been a direct result of the alphabet and a first-grade teacher in Park Ridge who seated us according to it. Back then I was Mikey rather than Milo, and one Michael Peters had been assigned the desk directly behind one Loukas Papadakis, who immediately turned and started talking to me. So naturally, I started talking to him, at least whenever I could get a word in. Only thirty minutes into our elementary education, that teacher already was threatening to separate the two of us. But for the next dozen years, Luke and I weren't separated very often. Even our decisions to attend different colleges hadn't kept us too far apart. We both chose to stay in town—Luke accepting his full academic scholarship to Northwestern, me graciously allowing my parents to foot the bill for DePaul.

As kids, if we caught the one traffic light correctly and ignored the two stop signs, we could travel the distance between our houses in under three minutes on bicycle. That trip was made thousands of times. We took up the same hobbies and played on the same sports teams. We registered for the same classes, watched the same TV shows, and dated the same kinds of girls. We were like brothers—except for the fact that his body reached maturity by summer of eighth grade, while my battle with puberty seemed to stretch on forever. Luke was five-ten, solid and stocky, dark-skinned, and able to sprout a full beard over a three-day weekend. I finally topped out at a lanky six-five with wispy blond hair and a mama's boy complexion. We rarely were mistaken for twins.

Ethnic heritage permeated each of our households and childhoods. Luke's grandparents had immigrated to Chicago from the Greek city of Larissa. Mine had left a small village in Serbia and ended up in Gary, Indiana. Growing up, we both were treated to authentic foods, massive holiday gatherings, and cherished stories about the old country. My visits to his house, or likewise his to mine, were greeted with a mandatory round of hugs and kisses from anyone in sight. In either home, the shows of affection were heartfelt and there was no such thing as inhibition.

The Papadakis bloodlines had remained purer since arriving in the States. Both of Luke's parents were Greek, and after dating dozens of all-American girls, Luke finally returned to the fold. Once we'd been old enough to journey out of Park Ridge on our own, he would drag a group of us into the city every spring for the Greek Independence Day Parade. Afterwards, we'd stop by his uncle's restaurant on Halsted, where IDs weren't required for friends of the family. To this day I still feel a need to keep an eye out for cops if I hear somebody order ouzo or Roditis.

During junior year of college, it had been love at first sight for Luke. The stunningly attractive Natalie Straka was waving from the last float of his beloved parade. Her embarrassment was obvious as she sat upon the towering throne, draped in robes, small children at her feet. It was a favor to her Greek father, an insurance agent who both designed and sponsored the tribute to Athena. Luke had been convinced that she was waving only at him and so struck up a conversation—or at least as much of a conversation as one can strike while jogging beside a flatbed truck for six-and-a-half blocks through Greektown. He somehow convinced her to meet us at his uncle's restaurant and the rest would be history. Like everyone else, Natalie was smitten by Luke's incorrigible charm and forevermore would be his Greek goddess.

On the other hand, I don't think I ever dated a girl with an ounce of Serbian blood—but in my defense, we Serbs didn't have the advantage of our own parade. In the Peters family, cross-pollinating wasn't unprecedented. My mother was a self-proclaimed "melting pot mutt"—part Italian, part German, part Norwegian, but no-part Serbian. However, she was all-parts devoted to my father and the family obligations that came as part of the marriage package.

Following their wedding, my mom moved into a household with my dad's mother and two brothers. My parents hadn't needed the family financial support that many newlyweds did in those days; it was the other way around. My dad had been supporting his family since he was seventeen years old, when his father, my grandfather, died during the overnight shift at a Gary steel mill. Speaking only broken English, my grandmother had taken in sewing and laundry but couldn't earn enough to feed and clothe three teenaged boys. My father was the eldest son of proud but uneducated immigrants, so in Balkan tradition he assumed the role of family patriarch and with it the responsibility of breadwinner. During his senior year of high school, he worked one job in the evenings, another on weekends, and still maintained high marks in the classroom. But any plans to enter college were scrapped because of the need to pursue full-time employment.

Once he'd earned his high school diploma, my father started catching the daily South Shore to Chicago before dawn. For most of the day he would pound the pavement, searching for a salaried position that might offer a career path. Then late in the afternoon, he would train it back to Gary for his night job. Nothing had materialized after more than a month; in fact, he'd rarely gotten past a receptionist. At the time, his name was Djorde Petrovic—and that time was 1947. Slavic stereotypes and prejudices being what they were, doors didn't open as easily as they might have. One morning he finally took the step he'd hoped to avoid. He marched himself and his two younger brothers down to Gary's City Hall and filed papers to legally change their names. With the stroke of his pen, each was officially anglicized. Eighteen-year-old Djorde Petrovic became George Peters, sixteen-year-old Tihomir became Timothy, and twelve-year-old Milorad became Michael.

Apparently as George Peters, potential employers were better able to appreciate my father's maturity and character. A year later he moved his mother and brothers to Chicago, where he'd been commuting as an invoice processor for Goldblatt's Department Stores. Two years after that, he proposed to my mother, Winnifred, whom he'd been dating since meeting her during the egg toss at a Goldblatt's company picnic. Following their honeymoon, a weekend in Milwaukee, she moved into the small house he was renting on the South Side. Uncle Tim and Uncle Mikey moved into the second bedroom and my grandmother, Baba Milka, took the couch in the living room. Children soon would follow, or so they thought. Ten years later, Mom finally became pregnant with my brother … five more before I officially was on the way. By then they'd bought their dream house in Park Ridge.

Growing up in George and Winnie Peters' household, the priorities were easy to grasp—family came first, second, and third. Everything else fell way down the list. The white house with green shutters was where the broader Peters clan gathered regularly—at least once a week, often more. My uncles, aunts, and cousins were a constant and welcomed presence in our home. They certainly had wanted to visit Baba Milka, who lived with my parents in every house they ever rented or owned. But mostly it was because of my dad, who always would be viewed as the Peters family patriarch. He was the one who had helped raise my uncles, who'd kept them focused on their schoolwork, who encouraged them to apply for the scholarships that paid for the college education he'd missed out on. By sacrificing countless times throughout his life, he was the one who had taught us all the importance of family. The entire family's devotion to my father was palpable, as was his to each and every one of us.

In terms of physical size, the two-story frame was relatively modest. On any other dimension, our house was enormous and filled to capacity. Filled with family and friends … filled with love and laughter … filled with life to its fullest. And forever filled with memories.

My older brother was named after our Uncle Tim, and I after our Uncle Michael, whom everyone still called Mikey. Of course, both of those uncles had named their firstborn sons, George, after my father. Being a namesake in our family made you feel special.

When I was almost sixteen, during a Sunday dinner, one of the younger cousins asked my dad to once again tell the story of how our family's name had been changed. Previously, I'd merely thought the whole episode fascinating. But this time, for some reason, the inherent bigotry and attendant emotions surrounding that decision finally had registered with me. For several days I reflected on what it must have been like for my dad, and the thousands of other immigrant families who'd found it necessary to alter their names to better fit in. The next time the Peters clan gathered, I surprised everyone with an announcement.

Out of respect for the family's proud Serbian heritage, I intended to start going by Uncle Mikey's original name. Henceforth, I wanted to be known as Milorad, or Milo, as my uncle had been called as a boy. I doubt my father figured such commitment would last long; so few of my commitments ever did. But the gesture alone had prompted him to hug me and shed a tear or two. It was at least ten minutes before Baba Milka got her sobbing under control. While this was going on, a horde of happily

Americanized cousins quickly dwindled from sight, fearing they might be encouraged to follow suit.

Looking back, that announcement may have been my crowning act of selfless decency … and, Lord knows, there haven't been many since. The first nonfamily member I informed was Luke, of course. He got busy, as only he could, and forty-eight hours later I forever would be called Milo by anyone who knew me. I even asked my dad if we legally could file for the name change, but he said that choice should be made when I turned eighteen. Despite my assurances at the time, I must have been too busy when that birthday rolled around a couple years later. But at least I never backpedaled from the name itself … and unto this world was born Milo Peters.

My many shared interests with Luke in high school did not include academic prowess or career aspirations. He enrolled at Northwestern with a laser determination to keep going right on through to law school and not stop until he was completely immersed in public service. Luke would light up when he talked about taking on one social injustice after another. No one ever questioned his resolve or the powerful impact he was sure to have.

My particular calling had been journalism—at least during freshman enrollment, when I'd been forced to write something down. Next there'd been computer science, which soon was followed by philosophy and then real estate. By the time I was done sampling majors, only a flurry of summer credit hours permitted me to squeeze out of DePaul University with a general business degree. But as I often reminded my parents, one's campus education should encompass a great deal more than pure academic curriculum. People too easily underestimate the significant role that all-night poker, beer chugging, and broom ball might play in future years.

Luke's ambitious timetable ran into a small detour. She was precisely five pounds, thirteen ounces, and they named her Alexandra. Luke and Natalie had been living together in a studio apartment during his second year at Northwestern Law School. They'd planned to be married once he earned his law degree. Natalie was working in a Gold Coast boutique and Luke was putting in twenty hours a week at his uncle's restaurant. Plus, he was loaded up with student loans. Together they could handle the expenses, but barely. In hindsight, one place to skimp might not have been the off-brand condoms. But the happy young couple never looked back or second-guessed. Baby Alexandra simply was meant to be.

No surprise, Natalie's parents adored Luke. They still popped for a traditional Greek wedding, and Luke's folks still sent them off to Mykonos for a honeymoon. Law school was shelved and Luke accepted a full-time position with the Chicago Region of the Minority Business Development Agency, which fell under the Commerce Department. With a career in public service underway, Luke was certain he soon would resume his law classes at night. But being the dutiful and loving character Luke was, those evenings became consumed with Natalie and Alexandra. Not to mention Vanessa and Gregory, who followed in close succession. There also were the countless hours he volunteered to the minority businesses that he helped organize, and the various community groups in which he took an active interest. To my knowledge, Luke never cracked another text book. Too bad … with Luke in the fold, the legal profession might have avoided a lot of derogatory jokes.

Once I had my coveted college degree in hand, I relocated to Macon, Georgia, and drew my first salary killing cockroaches the size of offensive linemen, along with a vast array of other Arthropoda Insecta that achieved sci-fi proportions in a southern clime. At a Chicago job fair during my final semester at DePaul, I'd stopped by a booth sponsored by Zero Bug Tolerance, "America's Fastest-Growing Pest Control Company." Granted, the clever name and impressive banner probably should have been alluring enough to an unemployed twenty-two-year-old with anemic academic credentials. But I have to admit it was the free packets of Gummi Worms that convinced me to step inside. Not that I wasn't further impressed when I noticed the praying mantis costume stretched tightly over a long-limbed and very buxom model … because, after all, spandex would have to be considered one of the modern marvels of textile science.

By the time I'd exited that booth, I was lugging a bag filled with Zero Bug Tolerance literature and paraphernalia. When I wasn't looking, someone must have slipped in a brochure on their branch manager training program. The description inside indicated that a college degree was mandatory, but there wasn't a space anywhere on the application that required me to disclose my actual grade point average. I hurriedly mailed my form that evening and was invited for an interview the following week.

"According to our OBP, ZBT is hiring thirty-seven BMTs for the current year." The "RRC" had provided this unintelligible response to my opening question during the interview. I simply was trying to get right to the point and assess the odds of getting hired. Before entering the real world, it became obvious that I needed to learn how to speak Acronyms. Amidst all my declared majors in college, I'd somehow missed seeing such a course listed in any of the registration catalogs.

Upon translation, the Regional Recruitment Coordinator (RRC) was telling me that the Operating Business Plan (OBP) for Zero Bug Tolerance (ZBT) had specified that thirty-seven Branch Management Trainees (BMTs) were to be hired in 1987. At the time, all I really heard or understood was "thirty-seven," which sounded like a heckuva lot of new hires and therefore a decent chance for landing an offer—even though I had no idea how many overly endowed praying mantises might have been working their magic across the continent. For all I knew, thousands of applicants might have succumbed to spandex and Gummi Worms. I couldn't worry about that … it was the only legitimate job interview I'd been able to wrangle.

Apparently college grads weren't pounding down the doors of the pest control industry, because ultimately I made the final cut. Boot camp, Macon. The proud, the few, the thirty-seven. Six months of merciless field training to become an elite killing machine. Chinch bugs. Barklouse. Earwigs. Fire ants. Stoneflies. Termites … subterranean or dry wood. By the time we were done, there wasn't an antenna-wielding thorax that we couldn't properly eradicate. One by one, they shipped us out—we, the newly commissioned assistant branch managers. When my orders came through, I'd pulled Tallahassee … where the war against bugs was waged twelve months a year. I packed my bags and prepared for combat. Selling pest control in Florida would have to suffice until I figured out what I really wanted to do when I grew up.

Over the ensuing twenty-two years, I would pack those bags many more times. What started as an available paycheck would evolve into a bona fide career. Before that first interview, I hadn't even realized that Zero Bug Tolerance was but a single division of a large corporate conglomerate which had taken shape in my very own hometown. With so many other interesting diversions in college, such matters hadn't merited my attention. In the years that followed, I would overcorrect.

Chapter Three

Before leaving Ashton's, Luke and I had agreed to meet for breakfast again on the following Saturday, but over the next few days I grew concerned about something he'd said as I was sliding out of the booth. It was a totally unexpected comment.

"Milo, I was hoping to bounce a few questions off you related to ASC."

The street long ago had dispensed with the full name. ASC stood for American Service Companies, the corporation to which I'd become indentured. From acquaintances at cocktail parties, to complete strangers sitting next to me on airplanes, I'd become wary of anyone who forewarned me that they had a question about ASC—it was a Darwinian reflex after being hit upon too many times.

"I was hoping to bounce a few questions off you" invariably was code for "*I need to find out if your company is hiring.*" When someone was preparing you for a yet-to-be-asked question with this prefatory statement, it could only mean one thing. This person was looking for a job. If not for himself or herself, then a position for a daughter or son ... a brother-in-law, a niece ... a neighbor's aunt ... maybe a favorite bagboy at the local grocery store.

I wasn't proud of the fact that I'd instinctively become suspicious of my oldest, dearest friend. If Luke was looking for a new job, I easily could find a place for him somewhere in one of our companies. God knows, I'd found jobs for plenty of other people. That part would be easy. No, what was eating at me was why Loukas Alexio Papadakis might want to jump over to the private sector. He couldn't possibly have lost that fire in his belly for public service. No damned way he would abandon his precious principles. Luke was the only friend I had left with any principles at all. *Please, not you, Luke.* He was my rock. I may have been negligent about staying in touch, but so often he'd continued to loom large in my thoughts. Luke represented everything I'd meant to be. He epitomized the values I still held high but was too gutless to adhere to. When doubts were darkest, he alone shined through as a beacon of hope that I still might salvage some part of my self-dignity.

⌒ノ⌒

American Service Companies was incorporated in 1982, a mere thirteen months after Ernie McCarthy and Norm Rosenthal first had met. The McCarthy family had owned and operated Overnight Janitors for half a century, dating back to when Ernie's grandfather started the business in Eureka, Kansas. Norm Rosenthal hadn't launched EverGreen Yards until 1973, in the suburbs of Louisville. However, both companies shared an intense commitment to customer service and, as a result, became the largest players in their respective industry sectors. The two gentlemen were so recognized at an awards dinner honoring the nation's best family-owned enterprises in1981. It was at this gala event where a mutual acquaintance had tossed out an idea … a seemingly spontaneous whim. This individual, who happened to be a rather savvy corporate attorney, conveniently wound up becoming the CEO of the combined company that was taken public as American Service Companies the very next year.

Within a year of the public offering, Messrs. McCarthy and Rosenthal were politely informed that their talents no longer would be required to run the legacy service operations. Each could hold onto his corporate board seat for a few more years, but otherwise they should busy themselves investing their newfound mega-millions in order to assure that future generations of McCarthys and Rosenthals be born with silver spoons.

By the time I signed on with Zero Bug Tolerance in 1987, American Service Companies was making substantial progress on its stated goal of assembling a stable of workhorse service brands. In addition to janitorial cleaning, lawn service, and pest extermination, ASC had acquired its way into roofing, home security systems, and car detailing. Then in the years after I joined ASC, the expansion continued into housecleaning, pet grooming, exterior painting, driveway installation, sprinkler systems, outdoor lighting, and other multifarious service lines. In total, ASC now owned recognized brands in twenty-nine different revenue segments, with the largest market share in most of them.

The strategic soundness of a corporate holding company specializing in these types of maintenance service operations had been hailed by Wall Street since the inception of American Service Companies. The synergies that could be gained by housing so many service brands under one corporate roof proved plentiful. From purchasing service vehicles and employee health care, to recruiting service technicians, to negotiating media advertising, ASC was able to flex more muscles more often than its many smaller competitors and thus derive marketplace advantage in each of the service categories it entered. By the time I moved to corporate headquarters at the beginning of 2009, ASC had fulfilled the expectations of industry analysts and shareholders for over a quarter of a century. Along the way, ASC had paid sizable sums to many families and independent operators in order to acquire their businesses. All and all, it was another great American success story. Unless, of course, one cared an iota about satisfying customers, reputable business practices, or respectful corporate cultures.

During the first couple years of my career, I was so busy ridding the planet of many-legged creatures that I didn't give much thought to the ASC umbrella I'd been toiling under. As the assistant manager of ZBT's Tallahassee branch, my primary responsibilities had included a sizable fleet of local service trucks, endless EPA paperwork related to the assorted chemicals we discharged into the universe on a daily basis, plus administering the work schedules and payroll for seventy-three associates. Not bad for a twenty-three-year-old adult male who still thought the best part of breakfast was lapping up the sugary residue from the bottom of his cereal bowl. Perhaps in my formative years I didn't know which body part I was supposed to put against a grindstone. It wouldn't have mattered, because I hadn't known what a grindstone was either. But now I possessed my very own work ethic. Who could have guessed?

No one had been more surprised than me when my one-year anniversary with the company rolled around and I received an exceptional performance review, accompanied by a salary increase. I was beginning to believe that in time I actually might function as a grown-up.

As I wrapped up a second full year with ZBT, the word "assistant" was dropped from my title. I was promoted into the branch manager slot. Not because of any particularly brilliant moves I'd made, but because of some particularly stupid ones made by my boss, the previous branch manager. The district supervisor to whom our branch reported had received a mysterious letter about how our certified technicians were providing free monthly service to a few of the branch manager's friends and relatives. Not two or three, mind you. Fifty-seven … and climbing. The man had deluded himself into thinking he was the Vito Corleone of pesticides for North Central Florida.

Fortunately for me, the end of a fiscal year was nearing and our district supervisor's annual performance incentive still hung in the balance. He didn't have money left in his budget to recruit or relocate a more experienced manager to the Tallahassee branch, so he elected to vest his unwavering faith in yours truly on an interim basis—at least for a few months, until the next budget cycle kicked in and he could hire someone more experienced and demote me back to assistant. I suppose I was hoping for just such a chance when I'd mailed that anonymous note to him, but I still needed to rise to the challenges ahead. I only had a short period of time to prove I was up to the responsibilities of a branch manager position. Once again, I surprised myself and pulled it off.

At the time I had this chicken-and-egg thing going on with my social life, which greatly contributed to the amount of time I was able to devote to my job. Carly and I were still together, though she was in law school back in Chicago. We would reunite for a weekend or two out of every month. During the intervening weeks, I became especially good at sulking over our separation during late night phone conversations. Then when we were together, my conduct would get even worse. Why couldn't she simply transfer law schools or consider alternative pursuits? After five years of dating Carly, my capacity for stubbornness had evolved into a continual source of amazement to us both. For some inexplicable reason, I chose to behave in a totally dysfunctional manner toward one of the most wonderful young ladies who ever graced the planet.

Until I completely could destroy what had once been a healthy and fulfilling relationship, I wasn't interested in meeting anyone new during my off-hours in Tallahassee. The practical solution was to minimize those off-hours. The more I avoided social life, the harder I worked. The harder I worked, the less time I had to worry about needing a social life. Presto: a workaholic. I, of all people, had developed a philosophy for getting ahead. *Arrive early, stay late, and act like there was no place else I'd rather be.* It helped in my case, of course, that I actually had no place else to be.

Darned if all the hard work didn't start generating measurable results with anything I touched … and with those results came acknowledgment.

A year after my first promotion, I was recognized as one of the top branch managers in the country. Not that he should recall, but that's when I had my first direct contact with Wilson Delaney. He was president of Zero Bug Tolerance at the time. I shook Delaney's hand during the awards ceremony at the company's annual convention in Las Vegas, right after he'd presented me with a rather unusual Seiko timepiece. Instead of numbers, there were twelve tiny hornets embossed on the watch's face to denote the hours— hardly the kind of keepsake one thinks to buy for oneself.

The middle-aged woman standing next to me on the auditorium's stage went a little teary during the presentation, overwhelmed with gratitude because it was her fourth such honor. I tried to convey proper enthusiasm when she pointed to the ten-karat gold cicada pin on her lapel ... the diamond chip eyes definitely were a nice touch. She also was kind enough to rummage through her purse and pull out her prized calculator—a silver-plated beauty shaped like a Japanese beetle. Unfortunately, I had to settle for a mere description of the Waterford millipede that she'd left back on a mantle in Albuquerque. True to her word though, she did remember to send me a picture as soon as she got home.

By the next annual convention, I'd relocated to Albany as district supervisor for upstate New York. When Wilson Delaney invited me to join him onstage again, it was because my district had been recognized as the most improved district in the Eastern half of the country. I closely monitored his reaction and was almost positive there'd been real-time facial recognition when he reached out to shake my hand. He even asked the company photographer to take a picture of us both holding the oversized gift certificate he presented me ... a romantic weekend getaway to Bermuda.

Ultimately, I gave the trip to a branch manager from Binghamton, with the clear stipulation that I expected to see pictures when he returned. He was married to a fox, so at least I might derive some vicarious pleasure from whatever shots he took of her while they were on the beach.

The timing hadn't been right for me to enjoy the award myself. In fact, Carly was rather surprised when I bothered to call and suggest three days alone in an oceanfront villa. She thought she'd been reasonably clear during our most recent and final weekend together in Chicago.

Another Saturday night had run hot and cold. Typically we'd been able to smooth things into a relative state of normalcy by the time I headed for the airport at the end of a visit. It wasn't all that unusual for her to be on the quiet side until we'd had our Sunday morning coffee.

But this last time, she'd waited until we were almost done with brunch at Ashton's before opening up. I wasn't even paying full attention when she started—assuming, I guess, that I'd heard it all before. I was wrong. She hit me with a new one. In fact, she hit me with a brick.

"Milo, the time has come for you to eliminate me as an unnecessary distraction from this shiny, new career obsession of yours."

Okay, maybe her uncharacteristic sarcasm should have been a wake-up call that I'd started to take myself a bit too seriously, or that I was headed around the bend with my job. But how could she relate? She was still sitting in law school classrooms, while I was busy tasting the fruits of real world success. How was it possible that Carly could have preferred that aimless, happy-go-lucky goofball I'd once been? How could she not appreciate what had been required for my transformation ... the redirected energies, the cultivated thirst for achievement? So what if I too often talked about work when I shouldn't ... or occasionally went a few days without remembering to phone her. Down deep I still was that guy who could be "funny" and "caring" and "sensitive" ... and all that other stuff she used to see in me. I figured she would change her mind. I was wrong again.

After a five-year relationship, Carly didn't even think I was worth a last shot at a fancy resort in Bermuda, all expenses paid. In hindsight, I'm astounded she gave me as many chances as she did. While dating in college, our friends, our families, and everyone around us had assumed that we'd someday get married. But by the time we broke up, not a soul other than me seemed surprised by her decision to hit the delete button.

Carly moved on with her life. I was ill-equipped to move on, so I channeled more and more energy toward moving up. After another record-setting year in Albany, Wilson Delaney asked me to tackle his most troubled district, the Ozarks. So the final ZBT rung on my ladder took me to Little Rock.

When Delaney was transferred out of Zero Bug Tolerance to become president of Overnight Janitors, ASC's flagship business, I knew it only would be a matter of time before he made a call to his proven bullpen. In six years with ZBT, I'd turned into Delaney's "go-to" guy. The signs were obvious that I'd achieved special status with this man who seemed destined for the top spot in the whole corporation. If we happened to be in the same city, we often conducted business over shrimp cocktails, steaks, and brandy, no less. On occasion, we even smoked cigars together. It was on one of those occasions that he'd counseled me on the importance of diversifying my experience within ASC's portfolio of companies. Coincidentally, he thought he might have just the right position for me inside Overnight Janitors.

If I was willing and emotionally prepared to take on a major overhaul, the Rocky Mountain Region would be mine. Six states and 594,000 square miles, chock-full of dirty office buildings and strip malls begging to be cleaned by underpaid janitors. All I had to do was commit to firing six of the nine district managers in the region and upward of a dozen local branch managers. For reasons Delaney wasn't compelled to share, he didn't sense adequate levels of intensity or loyalty coming from the region's existing leadership. Meanwhile, they continued to post sleepy results. For Overnight Janitors to make Delaney's aggressive three-year goals, a jumpstart was needed in the Rockies. Patience was for sissies. Ten days prior to my twenty-ninth birthday, I became a regional vice president. I promptly relocated to Denver with only a couple of suitcases. The company could pay for someone else to pack and ship the remainder of the earthly possessions that I'd begun to accumulate.

Sure, I had to fire a few long-term supervisors without giving them a fair chance, and reduce wages for hundreds of hourly workers who had no choice if they wanted to hold onto their green cards. To advance in business, one can't always consider the disrupted lives, marital complications, or missed tuition payments of others. In fact, it had been far easier not to consider the welfare of one's associates at all. Success required trade-offs. In this case, I was becoming a vice president—which meant stock options, a company car, and health club privileges. Not to mention all the major league points I'd be putting on the scoreboard with the corporate bigwigs in Chicago who were starting to take notice of me. The trade-offs obviously had been warranted; any discomfort would be temporary, at least for me.

I hadn't seen any of it coming … the whole blind ambition thing. The stages of my sell-out were so seamless over the ensuing fifteen years that by the time I was elevated into the rarified air of ASC's Chicago headquarters, I couldn't discern where the various points of no return had been crossed. But I did recognize what I'd become and what I hadn't. I was utterly sickened by the possibility of Luke jumping into the private sector and rubbing elbows with hollow creatures like me.

Chapter Four

"I'm just a humble public servant. You need to explain to me again what a president of corporate strategy and support services does."

"I'm telling you, Luke, there aren't any standard descriptions for my job title ... I don't know of another company besides ASC that has one. It's a classic Wilson Delaney move. He created the position just for me."

"You should be flattered."

"Why, because he wants to hold a Texas death match to determine who will succeed him as CEO? By the time he's done, all three of us may have destroyed each other's chances."

"Come on, Milo, you see right through this guy. You'll handle the situation just fine."

A week had passed and we were back having breakfast at Ashton's. The outside temperature was noticeably warmer than the previous Saturday. Already above zero ... downright tropic for late January. I'd forgotten just how much I missed those Chicago winters. Not that it mattered. During the intervening week, I hadn't been exposed to the elements for more than a minute or two at a time.

Only a half-block separated ASC headquarters from the overpriced hotel the company was paying for until I could find the time to buy a lakefront condo or something. I wasn't planning even to think about where to live until spring. Work needed to come first. I'd relocated plenty of times; the pattern was ingrained. I'd already established a daily routine for my newest staff to behold and admire. In the office by six in the morning, out by ten at night. Late dinners from room service while I surfed the cable news networks in the anteroom of my suite. Asleep by midnight so I could drag myself into the office before sunrise for another sixteen hours. But in the spirit of full disclosure, I usually did spend twenty minutes with my newspapers and coffee, ten minutes scarfing down a lunch, and upwards of six or seven minutes during the day tending to bodily functions. I don't want it to sound like I was one of those all-work-no-play creeps. Heck, one afternoon I even dropped by the employee lounge to make a quick appearance at a baby shower for one of our paralegals.

Whatever heartfelt resolutions I'd made about finding balance in my life after the previous Saturday breakfast with Luke, they quickly had been forgotten once I was back in the swing of another work week. I did remember to call my mother one morning, almost certain I'd get her answering machine. Between book group, Bible study, bowling league, and mahjongg, home was the last place I was likely to reach her. I'd promptly shoved the burden off to her by leaving a message that she should call me back so we could schedule our dinner. After a month in Chicago, it was time that I journeyed out to the suburbs for a visit in person.

During the cab ride to Ashton's, I realized that I'd fallen short on every one of my good intentions during the intervening week, which caused me to feel even lousier about myself. I desperately needed another dose of Luke. This time he'd been devouring a platter of french toast and sausage when I arrived. The man still possessed an empty leg. No matter how many of us might have gathered during our college days, as we all finished eating, we'd push our plates toward Luke so he could tend to whatever scraps remained.

Before I even could order a breakfast for myself, Luke started questioning me about the promotion that had brought me back to Chicago. "Milo, it would be nice to know whether this latest move will allow you to sink your roots back where you belong, or if it's just another stop on your climb into the corporate clouds."

Luke had a way of cutting to the quick. His question was loaded with many of the emotional landmines I'd purposely avoided for too long. Where was I headed with all these years that I kept shoveling into my career? I'd rarely taken time to contemplate a final destination; it was easier to keep barreling along in a state of oblivion, contented by the feeling of motion and the hypnotic hum of the track I was on. How good it might feel to finally slow down … or better yet, change courses.

For months I'd been pondering my journey more intensively. Accepting the latest promotion had meant moving back to a city where the route lines of my life intersected. My spacious corner office that faced the northern and western skylines of Chicago had placed me just steps away. For years

I'd been pushing myself along a path toward the other, more coveted corner of the executive floor at corporate headquarters. If my ambition was strong enough, Chicago was where all the sacrifices could pay off. The highest point on the ASC food chain, the office of the CEO, might be mine.

Retracing another, more distant path, took me back to happier days, to the people, memories, and values I most cherished. If my character was strong enough, Chicago was where I might be able to regain some part of that foundation. Perhaps contentment could be mine.

However, I knew from experience it wouldn't be possible to navigate some clever route that accomplished both. I'd been fooled by those naive fantasies before. No, fate was interceding to force a final showdown this time … high noon on State Street. My ambition versus my character, or what remained of it. Based on personal history, not even a fair fight.

I couldn't have fathomed the sense of liberation from finally telling someone the unvarnished truth about my career. Not once had I really let down my guard in twenty-two years. I'd carried too much masculine swagger to reveal my insecurities to Carly or the smattering of women since. I'd feasted on the pride and praise that my father showered upon me, so when he was alive I didn't dare expose him to the true pettiness and emptiness of my upward climb. And I certainly couldn't have shared my deepest personal feelings with a trusted co-worker—not that I ever had any. Generally, I'd tried to obscure the reality of my meaningless, superficial success even from myself. So I really wasn't planning to open up with Luke the way I did, but once he'd asked, it all came pouring out. More accurately, some of it oozed and parts of it slithered.

Wilson Delaney was sixty-two years old and set to retire in a little more than three years—not that he wanted to, but the governance policy established by our board of directors required it. He'd been the CEO and chairman of American Service Companies for five years, and he'd been on the top of his game for more than three decades, amassing a wealth and lifestyle that showcased his accomplishments. ASC stock had outperformed all the indexes and remained a favorite with the investment community. Even during the recent recession, our share price had held up because ASC was able to exploit weak market conditions to go on an acquisition binge at bargain basement prices. Delaney had won every game there was to play. Which is exactly why he still needed to create new ones. The man was addicted to the adrenaline of a hard-fought battle, especially when he could watch from above and force others to engage in it.

His latest brainchild had been the formation of an executive committee (the "EC") that consisted of the five most senior corporate officers. When he'd become CEO a half-decade earlier, he instituted his senior management committee, fondly dubbed the SMC, of course—which at the time consisted of the top dozen officers. For all practical purposes, that group had continued to function quite well together. But he'd grown bored. Suddenly Delaney had decided to establish an even narrower strip of power atop his corporate pyramid. With him presiding over the new EC, his elite little playgroup also would include our chief financial officer, T. Albert Guenther, who was a contemporary of Delaney and scheduled to retire at the same time.

In announcing his executive committee, Delaney also had decided to reorganize our operating companies. Previously, I'd been one of three group presidents that oversaw our service lines. Now he was consolidating all twenty-nine business units under the other two "Groupers" and they, too, were invited into his precious new power circle. That left me. As one of the three Groupers, I'd consistently posted the best numbers. My just reward was to be taken out of line operations and thrust into a corporate no-man's land with an albatross of a title stamped across my forehead— "president of corporate strategy and support services." To me it sounded like the kind of job that an organization created when one of its executive elephants was being sent out to the graveyard. But Delaney had assured me otherwise … just like he always did.

Delaney's flowery staff memo had announced that as the fifth member of his executive committee, I was being placed in charge of "the development and implementation of ASC's annual operating plans, as well as a new three-year strategic plan." Fine, I knew how to do plans. But he'd also bundled legal, human resources, information technology, and lots of other crap that I detested and then stuck them all under my name on the org chart. I was expected to be responsible for them. Insanity. I was an ops guy; I'd been trained to impugn and distrust all those costly overhead functions. I wasn't even sure what half these people did all day. The senior officers in charge of the various corporate departments now reporting to me couldn't have been any happier about the news than I was. But everyone kept their game faces on, knowing what the whole damned charade was really about anyway.

Since Wilson Delaney needed to step down before age sixty-six, he'd already announced that he would wait until the last day of his sixty-fifth year to do so. That meant three-plus years until his hand-picked successor would be handed the regal reins. Three-plus years of mind-numbing, dignity-stealing competition between me and my once fellow Groupers … each to be obsessed with our individual crusades to become the next CEO. If he had wanted to single me out, why not make me chief operating officer? The notion of one executive in charge of all the operating entities was hardly unprecedented. In fact, there wasn't another publicly held corporation of our size that didn't have a chief operating officer. Gosh knows, I'd proven myself worthy with every unreasonable assignment that had been thrown in my direction. But that wasn't the way Delaney's demented mind worked.

First off, Wilson Delaney didn't want any amount of meaningful authority concentrated in any one individual other than Wilson Delaney. He would hold onto as many puppet strings as he could for as long as possible. Second, naming an heir apparent too early would have spoiled the barbarian fun of it all. Then third was the fact that I was his favorite. I may or may not have been his favorite in terms of actual performance. With my track record of results, I should have been; but I didn't know how much weight that really carried with a sicko like Delaney. However, I was certain that I was his absolute favorite when it came to the sport of manipulation. He knew exactly how to get under my skin and toy with the nerve endings.

Wilson Delaney had found every one of my buttons and learned how to push them. How many times had he used me to get what he needed? How many times had I knowingly sold my soul to this conniving bastard? Yanking me up into corporate headquarters would provide him easier access. In his final three years as CEO, he could work all kinds of angles with me and through me. Another playful diversion to help Wilson Delaney overcome the boredom of his uncontested power. A ball of yarn, a rubber mouse, and Milo Peters.

When Luke had started our breakfast with his innocent questions, he couldn't have expected me to unload all this bile. But by the time I was done, I could feel myself sitting straighter from simply getting it out. I'd finally expressed what had been building for months related to my exalted new corporate position … for years related to Wilson Delaney.

"Milorad, if I didn't know better, I'd swear your admiration for Mr. Delaney might have slipped a notch or two since those early years when you constantly were raving about him." At times, Luke could be a master of the understatement.

After I'd changed my name to Milo back in high school, there were only two people that ever thought to use the longer form. Baba Milka had started calling me Milorad immediately and without exception. Luke would do it only when he was trying to tell me to calm down. My temper occasionally would get the best of me when we'd been growing up, and Luke often saw those storms on the horizon before I did. He possessed this innate ability to catch the signs and disarm me before I said or did anything I truly would regret later. If he called me Milorad, it usually meant one thing: I needed to lighten up.

"Loukas, I hate to admit it, but my opinion of Wilson Delaney probably hasn't slid that much during the whole time I've worked for him … deep down, I think I've always known the type of man he really is. No, it's my opinion of myself that's been dropping like a rock over those years. I forever am wondering why I allow myself to be manipulated … why I can't suppress my hunger for his affirmation … why I'm willing to tolerate so many devious and underhanded actions inside our company."

"Milo, my friend, I'm confident you'll find a way to do the right things."

"I'm not sure I even know the difference anymore."

"Well, maybe I can help with that."

I was waiting for him to continue, but Luke had completed his thought. He propped his elbows on the table, rested his chin on a cradle of interlocking fingers, and patiently stared at me. His pregnant statement hung in the air; the ball was in my court. I picked up the invitation, "Okay, Luke, what do you mean?"

"Last Saturday … do you remember me mentioning that I wanted to talk to you about ASC? Well, I owe you an explanation because I wasn't as forthcoming as I should have been."

He reached into an oversized briefcase on the booth seat next to him and pulled up an accordion file folder. It was more than six inches thick and secured with rubber bands due to the volume of paper jammed inside. He slowly shoved the bundle to the middle of the table, as if to punctuate the seriousness of the conversation to follow. Suddenly I had this funny feeling that Luke wasn't interested in asking about a job.

"Milo, believe me, ever since I heard you were moving back to Chicago I've been eager to get together. But last Saturday, I was seeking you out for professional reasons. I wasn't sure if you'd show up here or not, but I had a pretty good hunch you might and I needed to find a way to talk with you in private. Then once we started talking, it was just so great being with you again that I didn't get around to a rather delicate subject."

"And that subject would be?"

"An investigation into your corporation's business practices."

"Great, after I just told you that I'm carrying all this guilt about the questionable actions inside my company."

"Milo, this isn't about you … at least, based on everything we know so far."

"We?"

"Milo, for a number of years I've been employed by a different part of the federal government than you thought. As much as I loved working with an agency that addressed social needs, some very persuasive people were able to convince me that there were other vitally important ways to serve the public's interest."

"Don't tell me that Luke Papadakis is an FBI agent."

"No, I'm not … but what I do is not dissimilar. I'm sorry, but for now I can't disclose which agency I work for."

"Or who the people were that persuaded you to become a secret agent?"

"Milo, I'm nothing nearly as exciting as a secret agent … and you're correct that I can't divulge who recruited me. But I can tell you that we could use your assistance."

"Luke, my mouth's gone kinda dry … so why don't you just keep talking."

"This folder is one of dozens we've been compiling on American Service Companies. There are some very specific examples of what appear to be financial irregularities within your corporation. Unfortunately, the available facts have led us to believe that these mistakes aren't anomalies … that they may have been intentional and highly illegal. But the truth is, we still need a few more facts to make our case."

"You're the federal government … why don't you just come in and subpoena our files?"

"We could and eventually will, I'm sure. But sadly, in recent years the federal government has gained a lot more experience with investigating nefarious activities inside large, well-known, and once-revered companies. We've learned two important lessons about making our official presence known too soon. First, no matter how much we reinforce the absolute confidentiality, our investigative efforts inevitably end up involving more and more people … and eventually word gets out. Those breaches trigger all kinds of controversies and suspicions that may not be fair to the specified companies or their investors … and the resulting speculations also complicate our continued investigation."

He was all business as he continued, "Second, as soon as key people inside an organization know we're on to something, they get very busy erasing their tracks and covering their backsides. It takes many more months or years to implicate the true offenders, and in some cases, we're fairly certain that some have been able to evade us. So before we go knocking on the doors of ASC headquarters, we'd like to see if we can't fit a few more pieces into our puzzle."

"And you think I might have those pieces?"

"We doubt it, Milo, but we think you might be able to locate some of them."

"How do you know that I'm clean … that I won't start covering my own tracks?"

"There's no way to be sure, but I was able to convince my superiors that you're not the type to engage in illegal activities. I've known you my whole life, I know the family you were raised in, Milo … I told them what a good man you are."

It felt like my stomach was in a race with other vital organs to reach the top of my throat. The best friend that any person could ever want had staked his professional reputation by going to bat for my character. Great. I wanted to puke. I couldn't remember the last time I might have been willing to vouch for my character. I hoped that I didn't look as shaken as I felt.

"Luke, what are you asking me to do?"

"Milo, I can't be specific yet. The only thing I want you to do for the time being is give serious consideration to whether you'd be willing to get involved. You might be helping us prosecute close friends of yours … you very well could end up testifying at the eventual proceedings. You have to consider all the potential repercussions because we want you to be absolutely certain. If you're not, we'll forget I even raised the possibility. No harm, no foul. But if you are sure, I'll start sharing more details with you."

"So you'd be my contact?"

"At least for now."

"When do you need to know, Luke?"

"How about breakfast again next Saturday? And Milo, for the time being, let's not talk to anyone else about our friendship or the fact that we ran into each other. There will be plenty of time for that later, but until we know where this investigation might lead, we don't need the people around you connecting any dots between us."

Ten minutes later I was halfway back to my hotel, which is when it dawned on me that I was hoofing it. I must have started walking on an impulse because I sure didn't remember deciding to forgo a cab ride. The air temperature was frigid, the wind was screaming through the Loop, and I hadn't even bothered to put on my gloves or button up my overcoat. No matter, I couldn't feel a thing with my mind so preoccupied by the twisted irony. Throughout the previous week, I'd been worried that the highly principled Luke might be selling out to the almighty dollar. Instead, his intention had been to ask unprincipled me to sell-out the company that paid me outrageous sums of those dollars … a company that had been the central focus of my adult life.

Chapter Five

The next several days at the office were a touch awkward for me. I had no idea what improprieties Luke and his anonymous bosses believed might be occurring at American Service Companies, but now when I came in contact with various co-workers in the course of conducting business, I started seeing them only as hardened felons. I kept imagining how my fellow executives would look in their prison uniforms, how they'd adapt to life behind bars. Worse yet, I kept wondering which ones might be most tempted to stab, shoot, or strangle me if I turned informant. Never in my life had I tried so hard to avoid eye contact. I started retreating to the sanctuary of my sterile hotel suite much earlier in the evenings. Somehow it was easier to concentrate on becoming a traitor when I wasn't surrounded by the people and place I'd been asked to betray. Of course, there also was the minor consideration of whether one of those guilty parties might be me.

Most of that week I didn't bother turning on the TV to get my nightly fix of cable news babble. Twice I never got around to ordering dinner, making do with a few overpriced beers and snacks from the brushed steel mini-bar that also functioned as a television stand for the oversized plasma screen. I was too busy leaning against the window that spanned the entire east wall of my bedroom, blankly watching the traffic on Michigan Avenue. Or sometimes I'd wind up motionless on the wretchedly uncomfortable but still fashionable mauve couch in the anteroom, staring up at assorted faux etchings that some machine had stamped into the faux tin ceiling panels. It was like I disappeared from conscious reality for hours at a time. Occasionally there was sleep, but only brief periods. I raked through twenty-two years of memories trying to determine if I'd committed any prosecutable crimes. One by one, I anguished over decisions and directives as they came back to me. Nothing I'd done seemed to be a cut-and-dried violation of any law, but a disturbing number of past actions had breached the standards of what most would consider common decency.

Many business practices across American Service Companies were purposely targeted at those murky spaces just inside a legal boundary. Our attorneys and financial wizards had been relentless about keeping our management teams up to speed on the constantly changing restrictions and statutes that applied to our businesses. It was crucial that we understood what was black and white according to the law at any given time. Otherwise, how would we know where to find and feast on all those delectable gray areas? On occasion, lots of companies may have hidden behind a favorable interpretation of some industry regulation or legislative bill that was worded ambiguously. But at ASC, we'd turned these clever self-justifications into an art form. Such mastery could be traced directly to the meteoric rise of one Wilson Delaney—which meant, of course, that I'd been trained at the foot of said master.

I hadn't even finished my first week of bug boot camp back in 1987 before I gained my first real exposure to the culture that Delaney was fostering. It came during a presentation by the legendary Doctor Death, the seasoned PhD who oversaw Zero Bug Tolerance's proprietary research into pest extermination at a nearby lab in Georgia. Most of the company's associates didn't bother to learn his real name, because even he preferred the "Dr. Death" moniker he'd been tagged with. In our training session, he was pontificating on the efficacy of the various chemical formulas that ZBT utilized.

"With the composition of synthetic and organic pesticides we currently apply, our service technicians can rest assured that a customer's infestation issues won't recur. Our field studies have repeatedly demonstrated that with just a quarterly spray treatment, we can eliminate all forty-three species for which we guarantee total eradication."

A hand shot up from the back of the lecture hall. "Sir, then why does ZBT's standard service contract call for monthly treatments instead of quarterly?"

His ready smugness seemed to indicate that Dr. Death had encountered this question from other unenlightened newbies. "Because, young lady, by slightly diluting our pesticide compound, we can market twelve applications at sixty dollars each, versus four at ninety dollars. If my calculations are still accurate, one method generates double the revenue. Feel free to multiply that difference by our 2.1 million customers—I think you'll appreciate the grand total. Or at least Mr. Wilson Delaney, our president, prefers that math … and thus, so do I."

Many of my fellow trainees started mumbling among themselves, somewhat surprised and disturbed by the crass reality that ZBT would sell its customers a higher-priced service agreement than really was needed. I guess that disclosure may have made me a tad uncomfortable, but not enough to matter. No, I was more amazed that a pedigreed scientist would willingly display such blatant avarice. I'd always believed that PhDs took a vow to eschew capitalism. Whatever else might be important to the pathos of this company which had seen fit to hire me, I now understood greed was foremost.

During those early years with Zero Bug Tolerance, I was taught a great many tricks of the trade that one couldn't find on the pages of any official training manual. For example: the restorative properties of tap water. If profit numbers were tight toward the end of a period, we could goose them up by having our service techs dilute their pesticide applications with a higher proportion of water—at times, much higher. There were no laws that prohibited the spraying of watery mists into people's homes, and we weren't guilty of perpetrating fraud as long as we remembered to include a nominal amount of chemicals that had been registered to kill insects by a means other than drowning. Since customers already signed up for more than double the treatments they really needed, it wasn't like any household bugs were getting a reprieve because our spray guns occasionally fired blanks.

My experience with such tactics proved invaluable when Wilson Delaney started expanding my role across the corporation. As a worthy disciple, I could help inject his unique operating principles into any business division over which he gained authority.

For example, many of the managers running Evergreen Yards had been around since Norm Rosenthal launched the brand in the seventies. After picking up responsibility for this service line, Delaney was having difficulty convincing some of the holdovers that they needn't be such purists with their "customer first" philosophies. He brought me in and I eventually was able to convince those managers I didn't fire that selling customers more fertilizer treatments than they really needed made good business sense. After all, how many homeowners were going to complain because their lawns were too green?

Once we had a proper mindset in place for selling customers heftier lawn fertilization and weed killing programs, it was much easier for our local managers to accept the notion of diluted applications from time to time. Likewise, with a little persuasion, the managers of our car wash operations were able to perfect the nuances of dialing down soap or wax sprays when budget conditions became tenuous. The expense savings might have represented only a few cents with any one customer, but each of our companies served millions of customers and those pennies quickly translated to hundreds of thousands of dollars in profit. And those profit dollars quickly translated to higher bonuses for managers and higher prices for the shares of stock that officers owned. Even our janitorial and maid service companies got into the act by occasionally diluting their cleansers and polishes.

Wilson Delaney was a true pioneer in subversive business practices. His unwritten textbook could have contained an entire chapter on controlling payroll costs. Any American business running substantially over budget on payroll will look to reduce headcount or freeze salaries; that's Management 101. But at ASC, we availed subtler approaches that Delaney had taught us—like when we wanted to reduce staff costs less dramatically, so as not to draw attention from the media or investors. We simply would insist that our supervisors evaluate all their associates on a much stricter basis for a given period. Lower ratings meant handing out smaller raises. There was nothing the least bit discriminatory with this approach … for whatever amount of time required, everybody got screwed equally.

With all due respect to Dr. Death and his counterparts at the research facilities across ASC's other lines of business, I'm not sure how many actual scientific or technological breakthroughs our companies ever made within their respective service sectors. It probably wasn't a significant number, because that wasn't our strong suit. But under Wilson Delaney, ASC unquestionably became one of the most innovative institutions in the history of American commerce when it came to cutting corners, squeezing associates, and exploiting customers. I've touched on but a modest sampling of our tricks of the trade. Across the corporation, business leaders were hailed, promoted, and excessively bonused for taking actions that would have gotten them fired in most organizations.

From the opulence of my pricey hotel suite on the thirty-ninth floor, I watched human dots scurry up and down Michigan Avenue, wondering how many of them might have been shorted or gouged as customers of an ASC company. Our brands enjoyed a pretty strong presence in the Chicago area, so I figured the chances were decent that some number of victims was always within my purview. Probably even a former employee or two who had been overworked, underappreciated, and then laid off with no warning and as little severance as possible. I cringed a lot that week as I remembered the methods by which I'd advanced my career.

For weeks I'd been working my way toward manic depression. Even before Luke had blinded me with a discomforting opportunity to turn federal informer, his very presence back in my life had been enough to unleash another wave of emotional conflicts. Seeing him had awakened memories of the endless good times we'd enjoyed and the positive qualities I once possessed. Being with Luke again had reminded me of how hurtfully I'd neglected our friendship in the years since, along with so many other important relationships. Adding to the burden, I now had to process the fact that he'd gone to bat for my character. That scared me. Yet at the same time there was this hopeful surge of possibility. I yearned to live up to someone's higher expectations again.

At forty-four years of age, I wasn't naive enough to think I finally had reached the defining crossroads of my life. The selfish choices of my past were mine to live with. No matter what I did going forward, some of the damage was permanent.

How I wished I could reclaim the squandered companionship of my father. The walks we should have taken, the talks we should have had. In my youth, I'd cherished whatever time we could spend together—throwing a baseball, washing the car, or simply sitting and talking at the kitchen table. Listening intently as he extolled the virtues of family or the greatness of America. Raised in an impoverished immigrant neighborhood, those core beliefs had represented hope for him. His hopes had fueled an entire family. Good men like George Peters were destined to live long enough to become great-grandfathers; they were supposed to impart their love and wisdom to adoring generations. They didn't die from aneurisms before their seventieth birthdays. But he did. It had been audacious for me to presume the future. I'd planned his life on my schedule, certain we would have plenty of treasured moments in later years.

Ironically, George Peters wouldn't have regretted the prematurity of his passing—the anticipation of those eventual years had been my loss. My dad had been deeply grateful for the fullness of life and the blessings bestowed upon him. And no matter what choices I seemed to make, he'd blessed me with his unwavering support. Though family had remained his topmost priority no matter what, he never once said or did anything to express a single disappointment about my misplaced attentions. He must have figured I had the whole guilt thing pretty well covered on my own.

In keeping with Serbian tradition, family and friends had gathered for a repast after his burial. We drank and toasted for many hours to celebrate his life and his impact on ours. I drank also to help me forget. By the time I departed Chicago after his funeral, the aftereffects of straight whiskey may have dissipated, but the hangover of missed opportunity would linger and linger. My only solace was the recognition that George Peters, the former Djorde Petrovic, would have understood.

When I was a kid, I harbored no fantasies of grandeur. Even in college, I never envisioned that a career could become very important to me. Perhaps such a lack of expectation had been part of my undoing. I'd been blindsided by my own early successes and affirmations, not to mention the trappings that came with them. I was sucked into a vortex, addicted to the sudden rush of a new narcotic. Two wasted decades later, that ambition had driven me into the upper echelons of an organization steeped in misguided principles and unscrupulous behavior. A facade of success was my rightful reward. The smug self-importance was gone. The artificial fulfillment, the sense of superiority, it all seemed so laughable in hindsight.

By chasing false idols I'd lost out on meaningful life experiences and sacrificed relationships that couldn't be replicated. If nothing else, the world of business had taught me the meaning of accountability. The misappropriations of my past were mine to own. Moving forward, I finally could commit to altering my ways … one foot before the other, small steps first. Yet here was my closest lifelong friend, luring me to change course in a single gigantic leap. I was ready to make it.

It must have been a battle for the ages—Ashton's signature four-egg omelet versus Luke's legendary fork. Still picking over the hash brown shrapnel, he was almost gloating when I slumped into the booth on our third Saturday morning. He was raring to jump into the day ahead and I still was waiting for last night's sleep. For as long as I could remember, Luke had been the first to arrive at Ashton's—never waiting for anyone else before he ordered his breakfast. For once I was grateful. I didn't want to eat, nor did I care to watch the human garbage disposal at full throttle. The mere sight of food was stirring nauseous rumblings; however, I would have paid handsomely for a coffee IV to be inserted directly into one of my veins. The Asian waitress seemed puzzled by that request, but it may have been a language thing.

"You look like roadkill, Peters. Did our Serbian comrade tie another one on?"

"Thanks for your concern, but I didn't even get near alcohol last night."

"Must be the hour then. We can push breakfast later if these early morning wake-ups are testing your manliness."

"Hilarious, Luke … just fall-off-my-seat, roll-around-the-floor hilarious. You're positive that you didn't have a hearing problem as a kid? I'm sure your parents must have been telling you that your ancestors were geeks, not Greeks."

"Can I order you a crepe or a cup of chamomile, Milo? I hear that Ashton's now has a yogurt and granola parfait that's simply out of this world. They must have something your delicate stomach can handle."

"No, that's okay. Just order a couple dozen more eggs for yourself, maybe a side of pork, and we'll split the bill fifty-fifty like always."

We'd kicked into our relentless banter mode after only three Saturday mornings. It felt good, like we were back where we belonged. I guess I'd never pondered the unmatched pleasure of two guys verbally abusing one another. The same tired barbs had been flung and ignored dozens, if not hundreds, of times in this never-ending contest, but they still drew smiles where it counted most … on the inside. The sophomoric exchanges carried an almost mystic quality, like some primitive tribal ritual. *Heed you mortals … pay homage to the god of male adolescence. Though physical powers may wither and bodies may decay, your spirit of immaturity shall live forever.*

The place looked the same as it had for twenty-five years. The Armenian family who owned Ashton's probably had refurbished the diner multiple times, yet they'd elected to keep the decor completely intact. A worn-down hardwood floor, white stucco walls, seven or eight framed posters of Chicago landmarks hung in no particular pattern, dark wooden tables and chairs in the middle of the rectangular room, booths around the perimeter, no tablecloths, red vinyl upholstery, and fluorescent light fixtures suspended on poles that extended down from a high ceiling. Urban classic.

Besides Luke and me, two other high school buddies had stuck around Chicago for college. Gordie Hilpert enrolled at University of Chicago, in Hyde Park, south of the city. Rich Jenkins had taken classes at Roosevelt's downtown campus while living at home in Park Ridge, the first suburb on the northwest commuter line. At Northwestern, Luke was on the lakefront in Evanston. For me, DePaul was on the north side, near Lincoln Park. The four of us had settled on Ashton's as our official meeting place because of its central inconvenience to everyone. The food was good, the prices were better, and Luke had determined that the portions were the largest in the entire metropolitan area. Saturday breakfasts were mandatory; impromptu meals could be scheduled for other days and were optional. Anything before noon on a weekend was obscene by student standards, which was precisely why we'd decided on 8 AM. It was meant to be a test of wills, our weekly act of stubborn courage.

The initial intent had been to gather once a week and compare notes on whether college life was living up to all the advanced billing. I assumed the others were benefiting from their scintillating coursework, but we never got around to talking about that part of college. In fact, due to spotty attendance, I was making an assumption that my classes at DePaul were indeed scintillating. By the end of each breakfast, everyone was expected to have 'fessed up about any new experiences or social experiments that had come his way. When discussions dealt with intimate feminine contact, we upheld time-honored standards of gentlemanly discretion. We didn't want names, we simply sought assurances that progress was being made … and, yes, on occasion the details, if any unusual frontiers might have been explored. Mostly, we talked about crazy characters we were meeting, drinking games we were mastering, and methods by which we might freeze time and remain in college forever.

I don't really think any of us had contemplated that the Saturday breakfasts would last more than a month or two. By then, we each would be immersed in our various new life directions. But the stubbornness prevailed. No matter how minimal one's sleep, or how stretched one's bodily capacity, none of us wanted to be the first to drop out of the gatherings … or even be late to one of them. Granted, I often arrived ten or fifteen minutes after the designated hour, but as I reminded them, "well within the standard of deviation for punctuality." That was a little something I'd picked up by happening into one of my freshman statistics classes. Anyway, we not only sustained the weekly routine for four years, we expanded its roster of participants.

Each of us occasionally brought guests; then some of those guests started showing up regularly on their own. Hard to imagine that anyone else would have found the irreverent chaos worthy of a trip into the city at such a ridiculous hour … so I guess in our own special way we must have been irresistible. We made it a point not to lapse into any formal structures. The ground rules were simple, unspoken, and understood. Show up at eight and whether you ordered food or not, the bill got divided by the number of people at the table. No exceptions and always a spectacular deal for Luke.

The large corner booth comfortably seated nine, meaning we could crowd in up to eleven, or accommodate fourteen with three chairs wedged into the open end. When weather turned poor, only a handful of other patrons might trickle into Ashton's at that hour on a Saturday, but no one from our group would dare to opt for roomier seats in the unoccupied adjacent booths. The whole scene must have appeared rather bizarre to those few stragglers who did venture in: an otherwise empty restaurant, yet one far corner booth that looked like a human sardine can.

One of the newly adopted regulars had suggested that we vote on a name for our weekly events. The table fell silent for a rare moment. No one dared to utter a word of reaction, because that would have been tantamount to introducing due process. Instead, spontaneous body language was deployed to kill the notion of holding an actual vote of any kind and concurrently to assure that no one ever suggested the lame notion of a name again. Lack of structure was very important to us.

By spring of our freshman year, the breakfasts had gone coed. Without any advanced warning, Gordie Hilpert first brought a young lady from Seattle who lived in the dorm room next to his. He thought she might lend interesting diversity to our conversations—not because she was female, but because she was a grunger. None of us held back; if anything, the language and subject matter had been dialed up to test her. Gordie's instincts were stellar. Over subsequent months, Shelly Wasserman introduced us to lots of colorful terms from the Pacific Northwest, plus she was able to share numerous examples of romantic ineptitudes perpetrated by the male gender.

The inclusion of this initial female necessitated another unspoken understanding—Saturday morning guests shouldn't include those persons we might be dating. Inserting the dynamic of dating couples might have stifled the free-form style of breakfast dialogue and compromised some of our most fertile discussion topics. To be clear, dating meant even the loosest interpretation. If one of us paired up for any kind of one-night arrangement, we still were expected to escort said parties back to their rightful addresses before making our way into the city for our early morning breakfast. In fact, overcoming the epic obstacles associated with campus social life made our individual attendance all the more meaningful. Regardless of whatever sleeplessness, drunkenness, or morning-after companionship that might result from Friday night adventures, there were no excused absences from Saturdays at 8 AM. An unspoken code of college life valor.

After the first time Luke brought Carly Fairman to Ashton's, I didn't think we'd see her again. She stayed out of most of the broader conversations, instead trying to connect with people one-on-one. She really seemed to care about hometowns, families, personal interests, and other such tripe. I couldn't imagine why Luke had thought it a good idea to bring someone so normal and nice. Granted, she was attractive, but even that prettiness was of the wholesome variety. Smooth skin and pinned-back hair ... deep, compassionate eyes ... dimples, for God's sake. Carly Fairman was the type of girl we should take home and introduce to our mothers, not the kind I wanted to interrupt rudely, tease mercilessly, and shock intentionally. Luke convinced me to keep an open mind ... that I shouldn't allow myself to jump to mistaken conclusions because of any personal prejudices I held against decent, humble behavior. If I gave her enough time, he was confident that Carly could sink to our Saturday morning standards.

Both Luke and Carly had been pre-law at Northwestern, majoring in political science. They'd registered for many of the same classes and thus chosen to work on a few team projects together. Since Luke couldn't convince Carly of his reasons for flatly refusing to schedule team meetings on Saturday mornings, he'd finally decided to show her firsthand. After her inaugural breakfast session with us, Carly confided to Luke that she henceforth would respect the sacred status of that time slot. Further, she proved me dead wrong by returning the next week. In the weeks that followed, she rapidly proved Luke dead right. Damned if she couldn't lower both her hair and her standards of behavior.

If I'm being honest with myself, I probably fell in love with Carly Fairman the first time I laid my sleepy eyes upon her. However, opening moves with desirable members of the opposite sex were never a strong suit of mine. After I'd stumbled over my cowardly tongue for close to four months, Luke finally interceded midway through one of our breakfasts.

"Carly, can you offer this august group a single valid reason why you wouldn't go out with an asshole like Peters? I don't think I can bear to watch him ruin any more oatmeal with that pathetic drool of his."

Once Luke got me across the shaky threshold, I found my footing. Both Carly and I cancelled other plans and went out that very night. Then the next. And the three after that. By the following Saturday's breakfast, Carly and I had crossed over other memorable thresholds ...

but chose not to disclose those to the group. Privately, the two of us were of the opinion that the unspoken ground rule about not bringing dates to breakfast shouldn't apply when the two dating parties previously had been attending on their own. Technically, neither one of us was bringing the other as a guest. Of course, we knew better than to raise this issue of structural protocol, but we carefully monitored body language for several weeks before deciding unspoken consensus had ruled in our favor.

I remember thinking at the time that it might be unlikely if many joys in the years ahead could eclipse those Saturday mornings. The woman I loved, my best friend in the world, the close camaraderie of a caring group, the absence of pretense, an abundance of laughter. Everything a person should need or want. As time passed, I realized how right I'd been.

After college, we started heading out in our separate directions. We continued the Ashton's breakfasts as best we could. Some of the group stayed in Chicago for jobs or grad school; the rest of us got back to town on occasion for various reasons. When critical mass could be achieved, we'd schedule a breakfast on whatever day of the week that worked best. We moved the time up to 6:30 to accommodate the time demands of an adult world. Around holidays, we might pull in as many as a dozen. The reunions were in their own way important, but nothing was going to recapture the magic of those regular Saturday mornings.

Sitting again in that corner booth with Luke was the rightful place for me to reboot and redirect myself. The memories were so vivid, the past context so disarming. Superficiality, vanity, and self-deception didn't survive in this hallowed space. Maybe I couldn't recapture its past magic, but perhaps I could recapture some small portion of the uncomplicated goodness I'd experienced there.

Chapter Six

According to Luke, the suspicions about American Service Companies traced back to five years earlier, shortly after Wilson Delaney took over as CEO. Previously, ASC's financial performance had been more than solid, with the good quarters far outnumbering the periods when results fell short of Wall Street's expectations. But during the Delaney years, corporate earnings had met analyst forecasts for twenty consecutive quarters, neither exceeding nor falling short of forecasts on a single occasion. This type of steady predictability was exactly what the investor community sought from a publicly held company, but few could deliver results with such precision. And it was this unusual pattern of precision that had drawn the attention of whatever federal agency Luke represented.

"Milo, it could be that your corporation possesses superior skills for developing realistic business plans and combines those with tighter disciplines for executing its plans … and hence, your top executives and investor relations people are able to provide more accurate guidance to Wall Street related to earnings forecasts. But when we see this kind of impeccable performance, we naturally become a little curious."

I kept silent with my reactions. I'd experienced ASC businesses from the inside and our day-to-day performance was anything but impeccable. I'd sat through countless quarterly meetings on the senior management committee, when various company presidents would reveal huge swings in their operating results relative to the business plans they had in place—both positive and negative differences. Our types of service lines were subject to all kinds of variables that could impact profits, from weather, to fuel prices, to the dynamics of the labor pool. No amount of discipline could anticipate the effect of the dozens of uncontrollable factors that we encountered on a regular basis. In recent years I, myself, often had wondered how it could be that we were able to deliver the earnings numbers the Street was anticipating. But then I'd also recognized that Wilson Delaney would find a way to win at any game.

Luke went on to explain how once certain authorities back East had taken notice of ASC's unusually positive track record, the task of investigating for potential financial irregularities was assigned to the Midwest. Then as significant changes in ASC's financial patterns and practices were identified in the preliminary stages, the scope of the investigation and the size of the team were expanded, which was when Luke had become involved.

One pronounced change that soon became evident after the appointment of Wilson Delaney as CEO was the level of ASC's acquisition activity. Before Delaney took over, the corporation had spaced its large acquisitions by an average of fourteen to sixteen months. These were the ones through which we brought entirely new service lines into our portfolio by buying sizable companies with operations in all or most of the country. With previous CEOs, ASC also had acquired eight to twelve smaller service providers each year, and those local or regional operations were absorbed into the existing national networks to expand our footprints. But under Delaney, the number had more than doubled to an average of two major acquisitions per year and twenty-five of the smaller "fold-ins."

As corporate holding companies reached the multibillion dollar level, it wasn't uncommon to see an increase in acquisition activity to help sustain historical growth rates against a larger revenue base. Likewise, new CEOs often dramatically veered from the strategies of their predecessors. Nonetheless, a rapid progression of this magnitude was apt to raise eyebrows within the Internal Revenue Service, the Securities Exchange Commission, the Federal Trade Commission, and several other departments of the federal government. As Luke patiently walked me through this background, he was careful not to divulge which federal bird dog was paying his salary.

A second significant change at ASC that had piqued the government's interest was Wilson Delaney's decision to centralize numerous financial functions at corporate headquarters under T. Albert Guenther. These two executives had paired up during their days with Zero Bug Tolerance, when Delaney hired Guenther as his vice president of finance. As Delaney continued to move up ASC's org chart, so too did Guenther. Not surprisingly, on the same day that Delaney had become CEO, Guenther was named the corporation's new chief financial officer. Then in an immediate and rapid flurry, scores of financial responsibilities that previously had resided in the individual service lines were centralized at headquarters. Guenther staffed his own corporate departments to handle such tasks as closing out monthly financial statements for each service company, paying vendors, collecting and tracking receivables, negotiating leases, filing state and local tax returns, and distributing payroll. Other than developing and monitoring an individual company's operating budget, virtually all financial duties were consolidated and relocated to Chicago. Guenther hired a slew of high-priced professionals at headquarters, while service line presidents were forced to fire veteran financial teams in the various locations from where they managed their respective businesses.

This centralization represented a wholesale shift in operating philosophy. In the past, the corporate holding company had centralized only those activities that produced significant mutual advantage due to combined purchasing leverage—like health insurance, vehicles and fuel, or office supplies. Since every business could calculate the benefit of the lower prices that hit their P&Ls, none of the operating companies minded this type of corporate involvement. Otherwise, the field presidents had been left alone to run their own businesses as they saw fit, with the corporate CFO and a limited staff basically rolling up individual company results each quarter and reporting an aggregate to the investment community.

Luke and his associates certainly understood the facts surrounding the organizational change, but they couldn't begin to grasp the emotions it had evoked. The centralization instituted by Delaney and Guenther was gut-wrenching to the presidents of our separate service lines—a collection of headstrong mavericks who were unaccustomed to relinquishing control of any sort. They normally didn't tolerate folks from headquarters even treading onto their turf, let alone usurping major parts of it. I knew, because at the time I'd been one of those headstrong presidents. The decision to centralize these financial functions struck me as rather peculiar since I could remember how Wilson Delaney overtly had resisted any type of corporate involvement when he was out in the field running businesses. Of course, a lot of his views had changed after he completed his climb to the top and turned around to watch the rest of us struggle with the slippery slope he'd left behind him. But this announcement had come so unexpectedly … and with the number of knowledgeable, highly valued financial people we then were instructed to summarily terminate within the business units, it seemed both counterproductive and counterintuitive.

Like most of our senior operating executives, I held serious reservations about both the decision and the heavy-handed manner in which T. Albert Guenther had implemented the change. However, it was natural to assume that any such actions were being driven by our autocratic CEO. On most matters, Wilson Delaney didn't care much about how the rest of us felt; questioning a Delaney decision could mean career suicide. So along with the others, I fell complacently in line with whatever new procedures or arrangements that Guenther and his minions threw our way. But now, in light of the suspicions raised by Luke, I realized that I may have allowed myself to become too complacent.

Once a quarter, Delaney would gather all the company presidents and key corporate executives for a business review that would last a day or two. At least the first half-day was devoted to financials, with T. Albert Guenther's new breed of direct reports droning out their various updates ... the march of the Wire Rims. Each quarter I vowed to pay closer attention to all their spreadsheets and footnotes, but by midmorning my eyes would have glazed over again. I knew that as a senior officer for a public corporation I should have cared more. But it wasn't all that stimulating to hear a bunch of hotshot MBAs laud themselves for the latest application of an alternative amortization schedule or the discovery of some new offsetting tax credit. They invariably seemed to create more moving pieces, while making our business results harder and harder to decipher. I doubted that a single one of them could have killed a chinch bug.

As Luke disclosed the government's concerns, I was forced to admit to myself that I didn't properly grasp the accounting principles involved in all those acquisitions we'd been doing. I probably should have better understood the "valuation models" and "structured earn-outs" ... the "goodwill recognition" and "reserve accounts" that accompanied each transaction. But as we'd continued to add companies to our corporate portfolio, my interests had remained more basic, more selfish. As long as Delaney and Guenther could merrily report that outside investors were supporting our aggressive expansion activities, I'd been content. With thousands of personal shares of ASC stock, and sitting on option grants for thousands more, I liked watching us outperform the equity markets. I was more than happy to help Delaney court a few acquisition candidates, even close a few deals myself. How those deals got handled on the corporate books was up to the hordes of pencil pushers that Guenther kept hiring. Sure, maybe I'd had some suspicions at times, but these were questions I hadn't really wanted to ask.

I couldn't tell if Luke had expected me to be more knowledgeable about the intricacies of ASC's accounting practices and financial results. I was one of the corporation's highest-level executives. At one time or another, I'd run most of our largest service lines, so it would have been reasonable to assume that I might be familiar with all the notations on our earnings reports or balance sheet. But I'd been busy conducting business with customers, generating actual revenue, and overseeing hundreds of branches and tens of thousands of associates. As far as I was concerned, I'd understood enough about the corporation's financial realities to effectively execute my responsibilities—plus I usually knew whom to ask when I did have questions. But with Luke's revelations, it was obvious that I should have been asking a lot more of them. Just the same, I appreciated that my good friend chose not to say anything to make me feel any more derelict about my executive responsibilities than I already did.

Since Luke had been certain I would accept his offer to assist with the investigation, he wasn't the least surprised or even noticeably grateful when I informed him of my willingness to rat out the corporation with which I'd spent my career. His reaction was very matter-of-fact. "Right call, Milo ... the only call unless you know how to shave without looking at yourself in the mirror."

Having never participated in corporate espionage, I may have jumped to a few wrong conclusions about the assignments I was expecting to receive. At least initially, Luke didn't give me a single sealed envelope that I needed to burn after opening. He didn't utter a word about wearing a wire or photocopying documents with my belt buckle. His first instructions weren't likely to leap off the pages of any spy novel.

"Over the next week, just root around a little and see if you sense that any relevant corporate staff members become protective or standoffish when you probe them for more insight into why ASC centralized its financial functions so aggressively after Delaney took over ... or how they react when you ask them about the various ways in which earnings have been enhanced through acquisitions. We can talk about how people react at breakfast again next Saturday."

That was it ... "root around a little." I was surprised he didn't suggest that I "mosey on down to the water cooler and chew the fat for a bit." Besides, what was he thinking? Of course corporate staff members were going to become protective and standoffish when I asked them those kinds of questions. They'd become protective and standoffish if I simply asked them about the weather. Hell, they were corporate staff members ... they spent every waking hour building and defending their territories. There was no such thing as curiosity; any question by a senior executive equated to an imminent threat or cloaked accusation. But like it or not, I'd received my assignment. I was on my way to becoming an informant … to being branded an ingrate.

I gave a great deal of thought as to where I should start with my questions, or more importantly, with whom. After considering the possibilities from every logical angle, I kept coming back to the same obvious conclusion—Kirsten Woodrow, ASC's corporate controller. I was eager to have a private conversation with Kirsten Woodrow. But then, I'd been eager to have a private conversation with her since the day I'd arrived at corporate headquarters. In fact, I'd been hoping for a private anything with Ms. Woodrow since the first time she attended one of our quarterly review meetings three years earlier.

There were plenty of reasons why I might have taken special notice of Kirsten Woodrow. But the quality that most fascinated me was how she didn't seem to take herself too seriously, despite her obvious professional talents and a physical appearance that gave men whiplash. Her quiet, natural demeanor provided a refreshing contrast to the puffed-up grandstanding that the rest of us engaged in. She wasn't arrogant in the least, but she did exude a protective aura that suggested she didn't want to be pulled into the mainstream of ASC politics and maneuvering. Kirsten Woodrow came across as a person who simply wanted to do the job for which she'd been hired and separate herself from the rest of our poisonous behaviors.

Amid the tiresome PowerPoint marathons in our quarterly review meetings, Miss Woodrow was able to hold my undivided attention if she did nothing more than read down the line items on a budget spreadsheet. Even as she walked toward the front of a conference room, the anticipation would cause me to pull out of my customary slouch and sit upright. I wouldn't say that I was carrying a secret schoolboy crush for this exquisite woman. It was more of a secret executive crush.

As soon as Wilson Delaney became CEO, we started holding our business reviews for the winter quarter out in Scottsdale at a fancy resort. He would emphasize how our collective annual accomplishments should be rewarded with such trips to the warmer climate of Arizona. Each year, he magnanimously would host a Western style barbecue around the pool of his stately second home in a nearby gated community. Actually,

Scottsdale might have been considered Delaney's third or fourth stately home, depending on where on a map one began to count. I sort of suspected that the real reason for the yearly Scottsdale meetings had more to do with Delaney's ability to write off portions of this particular home's cost as a business expense on his tax returns. Plus, strangely, with each year's shindig I noticed more and more pool furniture, along with a rapidly expanding collection of expensive sculptures—but it wasn't up to me to approve the CEO's expense reports.

During Delaney's first two years as CEO, I'd thought that flying so many senior people across the country for no purpose other than to sit in dull meetings for a couple of days was a ridiculous waste of time and money. What did it matter if we saw a few cacti from the windows of a conference room? As far as I was concerned, the winter reviews could have been held at a Travel Lodge in Omaha. But the addition of Kirsten Woodrow to the corporate team had changed my perspective entirely. To catch a glimpse of her in cowboy boots and tight blue jeans at Delaney's annual cook-out, I'd have traveled to Arizona and back by covered wagon.

Kirsten was thirty-eight years old, but I would have guessed younger. She grew up in Casper, Wyoming, and had earned both her MBA and CPA before joining one of the Big Four accounting firms in Chicago. She'd been with American Service Companies for three years as senior vice president and controller. That was about as much as one could glean from the bio posted on our corporate Web site. It didn't say anything about her being Miss America, or at least Miss Wyoming, or having graced the pages of a swimsuit calendar. Based on her looks, some eunuch on the corporate communications staff must have deleted those facts. Nor did the bio offer a single insight about her outside interests, her favorite restaurants and movies, or her level of interest in never-been-married workaholics who suddenly were determined to find happiness. I couldn't imagine why we bothered to post such useless Web pages. Whoever was in charge of the ASC Web site clearly didn't understand the real purpose of the Internet.

One would have thought that by the time a man reached his middle forties and somehow had managed to land one fancy title after another, he might have overcome his adolescent clumsiness in initiating conversations with a female of interest. But I guess I'd been too busy mastering the ways of commerce.

During three years of quarterly meetings together, I at least had worked up the nerve to have several side conversations with Kirsten—though I would have preferred to have done nothing more than stare into those incredible dark eyes for an hour or two without saying a word. I'd even gone to the trouble of mentally rehearsing specific questions so that I might come off as worldly and interesting whenever I saw convenient opportunities to approach her. But invariably, something unexpected would occur when I got close to her. After a few pleasantries and a smooth start, we'd be interrupted. From out of nowhere, I'd hear the sound of some vapid, dull voice filling the airwaves between us with senseless drivel. Clumsy seconds would pass before I could identify my mouth as the unknown source and try to gain control of it. But once that mouth got detached from my brain, it was too late ... I'd be forced to live with the carnage.

"Kirsten, I find the typeface on your slides easier to read than what the other presenters have been using."

Or another jewel, "I bet you must have been really good in math back in high school."

And of course there was, "Since you're a CPA, do you still hire someone else to do your tax returns?"

I was hopelessly inept and I guess she felt sorry for me. Not once did she give me one of those alien stares that I routinely could elicit from the opposite gender. She even smiled at a few of my sputtering attempts at humor. At times during our quarterly interactions, I would have sworn there'd been a spark, a natural chemistry of some sort between the two of us ... but my objectivity was highly suspect.

Since moving to headquarters in Chicago, I'd been biding my time, waiting to make a more serious attempt at meaningful dialogue. Perhaps, more accurately, I guess I was trying to marshal the necessary courage and confidence. I quickly came to recognize the sound of Kirsten's steps moving through the hallway. Her office was just several down from mine, so she often passed in front of my doorway. No matter what I was doing, I'd stop and try to catch a glimpse. Even her walk was fantastic ... the tall, athletic body ... her back straight and shoulders squared ... the long black hair, flowing gracefully behind her ... round spots and flat spots in all the right places, moving in perfect harmony. Sonnets should have been written in tribute to that walk. Okay, maybe my crush was more of a fixation.

I observed that she rarely arrived early but did stay late several nights a week. I already had paused at her door during my calculated trips past her office on a few of those evenings and some of my efforts at casual conversation probably qualified as almost human. During one such exchange, the framed photos that filled the wall behind her desk caught my attention. I'd known she was divorced and raising a son as a single parent, but I hadn't been aware of his special needs. Seven-year-old Danny Woodrow looked like his mother—the same dark features, the same penetrating eyes were evident, even in photographs. Her son loved Harry Potter and was curious about almost everything. He also was confined to a wheelchair due to the complete paralysis of both legs caused by an automobile accident. A daytime nanny hadn't properly fastened the car seat before driving him to an afternoon playgroup. He was lucky to have survived the collision when another car broadsided them, but the spinal injury was irreversible. Danny Woodrow had taken his first steps a year prior to the injury but was unlikely to ever remember that sensation of walking.

As Kirsten had responded calmly to my inquiries into Danny and his accident, I became even more impressed with her overall disposition. I still hadn't completely processed the reality that this gorgeous, talented woman was incapable of arrogance or aloofness. Now, despite a tragic injury to her son, I observed the total absence of bitterness or sadness. Yet there wasn't an outward joy either. It was like she was running in neutral beneath that always pleasant exterior. I couldn't decide whether I was more intrigued by the personality traits Kirsten Woodrow did exhibit or the ones she didn't.

Following Luke's instructions at the previous Saturday's breakfast, I'd been pondering where to begin my probes into the issues he had raised about ASC's financial practices. I needed relevant perspectives on what I might be missing, or at minimum, advice on how best to gain them. My mind kept coming back to the same place as the perfect starting point, and this was no time to second-guess one's natural instincts. My first official undercover act would be to ask Kirsten Woodrow if she might join me for lunch at a decent restaurant, versus another round of deli sandwiches at our respective desks. However, I still lacked important background facts … crucial information that might significantly impact my state of readiness for the task at hand. I needed details about Kirsten's divorce and the possible presence of other men in her life away from the workplace. Fortunately I had ready access to the perfect source.

If a hundred women were lined up on a city street and the first ten pedestrians to pass by were instructed to pick out the one woman named "Edna," all ten would've selected my secretary. Edna Cutler looked exactly the way an Edna should look—like some underground genetics lab had managed to cross Margaret Thatcher with Aunt Bea. Silver hair on top of her highly held head, flower print dresses, ever-present reading glasses dangling from a chain around her neck. She was one of those timeless fixtures found in offices around the globe. Her age was anyone's guess. Somewhere north of sixty, somewhere south of the discovery of fire. No one was likely to remember when she stopped looking young, because she somehow would have slipped through those years incognito. Yet she didn't appear especially old either. She was frozen somewhere between.

With the various transitions from typewriters to word processors to desktop computers, there was no telling how many times Edna Cutler had needed to reinvent herself to remain current with the skill sets required of an executive secretary. I had no doubts that she would have been highly proficient at shorthand dictation in earlier years. Chances were good that at some point she'd ably wielded a chisel on stone tablets.

Edna had joined American Service Companies fifteen years before my arrival at headquarters. Only she knew for sure how many different Chicago corporations and executives she dutifully had served before then. Because of my lofty new title she was assigned to me on the first day I showed up, subject to my approval after a few weeks of working together. We hit it off from the beginning, but I also suspected that Edna never had met a boss who didn't experience the same instant chemistry. I was convinced she could have written one of those popular "how to" books … *The Secrets to Manipulating Corporate Executives in Three Different Centuries.*

After we'd been introduced, she set an immediate tone by closing the door of my office in order to stipulate her three "nonnegotiable" ground rules. "First, please never refer to me as your executive coordinator, administrative assistant, or any such nonsense. I am your secretary, Mr. Peters … a vital and well-understood position since its inception. Attempts to glorify this most suitable title are unnecessary, confusing, and insulting."

I made the mistake of breaking the rhythm of a preamble she obviously had delivered on numerous occasions. "Edna, my name is Milo."

"I am well aware of your full name, sir, which brings me to my second request. Please do not instruct me to call you anything other than Mr. Peters. It is important that we model standards of proper decorum through our daily interactions. Conversely, you may continue to call me by my birth name if you so prefer."

She paused, but I didn't dare say a word until she was finished. Because

I'd learned from my earlier mistake, she rewarded me with her best "*Good boy, Mr. Peters*" nod before continuing.

"Lastly, please refrain from asking me to work late on Thursdays. You're likely to observe that I arrive quite early each morning, and can be in the office even earlier if called upon. Additionally, I am available to work weekends and late into any other evenings, as you may deem. But Thursday is my poker night."

She had delivered the entirety of her message without emotion or equivocation. Edna Cutler emitted an aura of stoicism, as though whatever came her way, she'd seen it all before. She may not have realized, but on some hidden level she was daring me to test her ability to remain unflappable. I'd yet to meet anyone from whom I couldn't elicit outward reactions. I hoped I could break through that weathered surface of hers and generate visible smiles, even audible laughter ... but if that failed, I knew I still had disgust, anger, and exasperation to fall back on.

Sometime around lunch on my second day at headquarters, I notified our head of human resources that I wanted to stick with Edna on a permanent basis. I would have done it sooner but I didn't want to come across as too easy to please.

Not only was Edna Cutler sensational at every functional task, but she also possessed what many would consider to be the keys to any corporate kingdom ... knowledge. Knowledge is the currency of the modern workplace and Edna was wired into the information superhighway like no one I'd ever met. Granted, I was blown away by how she could hold her own with younger generations when it came to searching and surfing the Internet, but it was the office underground network where she ruled supreme. She somehow seemed to know every detail about ASC corporate headquarters ... from the names and ages of any employee's spouse or children, to the gist of whatever confidential memos might have been issued on a given day.

After six weeks of working together, I was fairly confident that Edna hadn't quite figured out how to read me yet—though that was only a matter of time. I figured if I was careful with how I approached the subject and phrased my questions, she could give me the lowdown on Kirsten Woodrow's failed marriage and subsequent social life without sensing anything other than a collegial interest on my part.

I waited until she brought in my morning mail.

"Edna, I've been trying to get to know more people here at headquarters by dropping into their offices for casual chats. Recently, I've had a few brief conversations with Kirsten Woodrow … you know, the controller … and we started talking about her son."

"You mean, Daniel … he turned seven last May. A darling young man."

"Yes … I'm sure. Her attachment to Danny is so evident that I was curious as to how she's able to balance her duties as a single parent with such a demanding job."

"She has live-in help during the week … Isabel, whom Daniel adores. On weekends, Miss Woodrow devotes full attention to her son."

"It must be costly. Does Danny's father provide financial support?"

"A sad situation, Mr. Peters, but he no longer does."

"How long has Kirsten—Miss Woodrow—been divorced?"

"Since about a year after Daniel's accident … so that would be four years."

Edna was an almanac.

"Was the accident the problem, Edna? Did it create stress in their marriage?"

"No, Mr. Peters, the stress was already quite present. It was work related."

I couldn't imagine how any man could allow job stress to enter into a relationship with a woman like Kirsten Woodrow.

"The difficulties of two working parents, I suppose." My reaction was more question than comment and Edna took it that way.

"Maybe a little, but I'm afraid it was more complicated than the hours and schedules."

Edna hesitated, seeking a signal from me that it was okay to delve so deeply into the personal life of one of our corporate executives. My facial expression must have sufficed and she continued.

"Mr. Woodrow was doing rather well as an investment banker … perhaps too well. From what I've heard, he placed disproportionate emphasis on his career relative to other priorities in his life and Miss Woodrow finally called him on it. A divorce was already in process when the accident occurred. They attempted to make another go of it for Daniel's sake, but the additional infringements upon Mr. Woodrow's time only strained their relationship further. Pardon my brashness, Mr. Peters, but can you imagine anyone being that self-absorbed with his career?"

Edna couldn't possibly have known that she'd just knocked the wind out of me. Yes, I could imagine someone being that self-absorbed. How else could I have allowed a woman like Carly Fairman to slip out of my life? To think that I'd naively been wondering how a guy could blow it with a woman like Kirsten Woodrow. For three years, I'd provided Kirsten ample opportunities to watch me in action with my peers in senior management, maneuvering and posturing to outshine one another. Through reputation alone she'd probably heard hundreds of unflattering stories and opinions about me. I must have epitomized the absolute worst traits of her ex-husband. I didn't know what I was expecting to hear, but this little debrief from Edna had taken a discouraging turn.

I continued to pursue a few remnant details while struggling to collect my inner composure. "Edna, I'm confused by the name references. You refer to Kirsten as Miss Woodrow, but it sounds like Woodrow was her married name."

"That is correct. She didn't revert to her maiden name because she thought it best that she and Daniel continue sharing the same last name. However, since she no longer is married, she prefers to be addressed as Miss Woodrow."

"It sounds like her ex-husband hasn't stayed very involved in Danny's life ... but if he was such a successful investment banker, why hasn't he at least helped with money?"

"Apparently, he wasn't doing as well as he believed. Soon after the divorce, one of his deals went sour and he was let go by his firm. The setback was more than he could absorb, so he took whatever savings he'd accumulated and moved to a small Caribbean island, where he has taken up with a local woman barely of legal age."

"And Kirsten doesn't pursue her rightful share of his assets to help with Danny?"

"No, Mr. Peters, the legal issues are complex and she prefers being completely done with Mr. Woodrow. Her career has continued to progress nicely and she handles all the expenses on her own."

"It sounds like we're fortunate to have a person of her character as controller. Thank you, Edna, that was most helpful ... and if you don't mind, I'm sure I'll have similar questions about others on the corporate staff in the weeks ahead."

"Yes, Mr. Peters, and may I add one more thing?"

"Absolutely ... please, Edna."

"You have very good taste, sir. I think you and Miss Woodrow would make an excellent couple."

She was out of my office before I could respond. My assessment of Edna had been premature. Already she could read me like a book ... cover to cover.

The more I was learning about Kirsten Woodrow, the more there was to admire. Her easy manner didn't begin to reflect the difficulties she'd confronted. My desire to become better acquainted was more intense than ever, but it would seem that I was precisely the sort of person she'd want to avoid at all costs.

Chapter Seven

"I can't remember the last time I went out for a decent lunch in a restaurant … it might feel good to slow down and taste what I'm eating for a change. But listen, Peters, don't think for a minute that I've fallen for your sneaky little ploy of trying to become better acquainted with your new associates here at headquarters. You can pretend, but you'll never really be one of us … you'll always be an ops guy at heart. Down deep, you'll still resent the rest of us overpaid empty suits inside this corporate ivory tower."

"Darn it. What gave me away, Woodrow? Since arriving in Chicago, I've worked so hard at fitting in. Though you may not have noticed, some of your preppy little comrades certainly must have … I've been wearing monogrammed shirts and honest-to-goodness designer socks on occasion. You know, the kind with those cute little designs that say so much about a man's breeding. I've even considered buying my very own set of suspenders with eighteen different endangered species embroidered on the front. What's a guy need to do to get accepted into your elitist cult?"

"Well, at least neither of us wants to be guilty of perpetuating any stereotypes. I'd love to join you for lunch tomorrow, Milo."

Kirsten Woodrow broke into an enormous smile that brought an instant spring to my February—at least according to the way I was melting inside. We chose a sushi place that was a brisk five-minute walk from the office. Until that day, I'd failed to recognize how erotic the act of eating Asian food could be. Kirsten's hands were hypnotic as she poured steaming tea for the both of us; her fingers seemed to caress the ornate porcelain cups. Then there was the delicate way those incredible fingers worked the chop sticks. And the way those waiting lips parted to accept each succulent bite of sushi. Thankfully our conversation lingered until well after the table was cleared. Otherwise I would have been too embarrassed to stand up until my blood had redistributed. During the entire time we were seated, not a single male walked past our table without turning back for another gaze at her. It would have been impossible not to.

The dialogue was measured at first. She'd been interested to learn that I grew up in the Chicago area. As it turned out, she was familiar with Park Ridge because she'd checked out a few real estate listings there after her divorce. I'd been curious to hear what it was like to be raised in Wyoming ... and somewhat disappointed to learn that she'd never roped a cow or shot a moose with a crossbow. In fact, her childhood in Casper didn't sound too much different from one in a middle-class suburb of Chicago. Her father hadn't even been a trail boss or a park ranger; he was a high school chemistry teacher who also taught drivers' ed in the summer.

Neither one of us appeared very eager to discuss any of the highlights from our respective careers—which was encouraging, because for me such reticence to dwell on my professional accomplishments was something new. We just sort of bumped along, feeling each other out until we got around to talking about Danny. That's when her floodgates opened.

The enthusiasm for Danny was markedly different than the blind adoration that so many parents are wont to exhibit for their genetic offspring. She talked about Danny in his own right, not simply as a son. She held tremendous regard for him as the individual he was, and that esteem had little to do with overcoming the daily hardships of his handicap. The handicap wasn't even top of mind with Kirsten Woodrow, which probably meant it wasn't with Danny either. Kirsten admired this seven-year-old boy as an unusually optimistic force and drew great strength from him. As she described his exuberance for life, his compassion for others and his faith in the future, I realized I might benefit from a hearty dose of Danny Woodrow.

I asked Kirsten if I could meet her son, if I could make arrangements to do something with Danny on an upcoming weekend. One of the museums, a Bulls game, the zoo ... the Adler Planetarium? I watched her defenses quickly go up.

"That's very sweet, Milo, but Danny does just fine. I know you mean well, but he doesn't need people trying to do special things for him because he happens to be in a wheelchair."

"Kirsten, with all due respect, I wasn't trying to do anything special for Danny. I selfishly was looking to do something special for myself. He sounds like one helluva positive influence … I could use more of those in my life right now. I've been doing a lot of self-reflection lately and I've got a great deal of work to do. But I do apologize for being so presumptuous. If you ever bring Danny around the office, I'd love to meet him."

Now the defenses came tumbling down. Her eyes welled up and she reached across the table and put her hand on mine. "I am so sorry, Milo, I didn't mean to insult you by being so protective of Danny. I know he would love to meet you … and we always love going to the zoo. But I've got to warn you, the kid knows his animals."

My head was spinning from the rapid turn of events during the previous few moments. I'd actually put my lust for Kirsten aside and become swept up in her descriptions of Danny's positive qualities. This was another encouraging sign, because in recent years I'd rarely been swept up by anything other than myself. I was so eager for change that I was looking to a seven-year-old as a potential role model. More astoundingly, I'd acknowledged to the target of my innermost desires that I was wrestling with significant self-improvements that I needed to make. Unprecedented boldness on my part. Since adulthood, I'd only unveiled myself in such candid fashion to one other person—Luke. And that crazy Greek had always known my character flaws as well as I did anyway. So with these admissions to Kirsten, perhaps a new behavior pattern was taking root. Before long I might be strolling down city streets confessing my personal shortcomings to perfect strangers.

But the miracle of miracles had been the connection I'd made with Kirsten. Me, with the clumsiest tongue in the free world. Maybe I should have dropped the funny guy routine and started expressing my true sentiments years earlier. Something had happened … a mysterious chemical reaction of some sort. Suddenly, her eyes had been watering, our hands had been holding, my face had been blushing. Next thing I knew, we had a date to go to the zoo on Saturday afternoon. Okay, maybe not a date-date, but at least a play-date with Danny and her. Perhaps I hadn't been imagining the sparks I'd sensed during our past conversations.

Over the course of our lunch I neglected to ask Kirsten a single question about the increased rate of ASC acquisitions or the inner workings of our corporate finance units. Sitting alone with her in that restaurant had been such a magnificent experience, I didn't want to tarnish it by trying to turn any awkward corners. In the days ahead, I'd have to figure out how to reconcile my next steps with Kirsten if I expected her to be of assistance with my secret investigation into corporate malfeasance. The personal connection was so encouraging that I certainly couldn't do anything that would cause her to think I was using her. On the other hand, if our relationship did blossom into something more, it would be a huge advantage to bring somebody with her knowledge and skills into my confidence.

Luke could help me—he always could when it came to women. I would talk with him about the best way to proceed at our next get-together on Saturday. *Ahh, Saturday … breakfast with Luke, followed by a joyful afternoon with Kirsten and her son.* With the right people in my life, maybe I could start looking forward to weekends again. Those two-day respites from the workplace might offer more than a reminder of how shallow my life had become.

When I returned to the office after what would rank as the best luncheon appointment in civilized history, my spirits were so lifted that I decided to call my mother and schedule a long overdue dinner. When I heard her live voice on the phone instead of her usual answering machine, a sudden impulse kicked in. I suggested that we go to her favorite Italian restaurant that very night. She was so overwhelmed by the spontaneity of my invitation that she agreed to skip "American Idol" and join me. In fact, I left work early and we stopped by the cemetery for a short visit with Dad and another with Baba Milka. Then we chatted nonstop during the half-hour drive to Del Rio in Highwood, where we enjoyed a long, leisurely meal. Winnie Peters always had lots to say, but it had been a great many years since I'd really listened to her. I couldn't remember my mom ever hugging me as tightly as she did when I dropped her off at home later that evening.

During my ride up to the executive floor early the next morning, I actually whistled out loud … some cheery, familiar tune I couldn't name. This act of whimsy was remarkable on two counts. First, there were others on the elevator who worked for me and might mistakenly perceive that my personality could turn upbeat, which was very uncorporate. Second, prior to that day, I didn't remember the last time I'd whistled and hadn't known I still could.

As I reached my office, Edna Cutler continued typing busily inside the modular workstation right outside my door, knowing not to make eye contact with me until I'd downed no less than sixteen ounces of strong coffee. Her back was perfectly erect, her arms held high above the keyboard that her hands rapidly moved across, her eyes never leaving the monitor. Everything in her cubicle was organized so that she could efficiently reach whatever she might need in the course of a day. Not a single photo or personal item anywhere in sight. Two oversized Starbucks and a bagel had been placed in their usual spot on the ledge to the side of her, so that I could snap them up on my pass-by, audibilize a guttural sound of appreciation, and retreat into solitary confinement until I was ready to face humanity. But this morning was different.

"Edna, you look radiant this morning. Would tonight be poker night?"

Her confusion over my talkativeness was evident. "Indeed it is, Mr. Peters. Is there something wrong with the coffee and bagel?"

"Not at all, you're so thoughtful to have breakfast waiting for me every morning." Rather than hurry into my office, I decided to try some friendly conversation. "So this poker group of yours ... do you play for pennies and nickels, or do you keep it to matchsticks and buttons?"

Her confusion over my good spirits was displaced by indignity. "We're partial to ten-dollar antes, twenty-dollar openers, and no limit on the number of raises. No wild cards, no silly games ... purely straight poker as the game was intended."

The way she said it, I had this funny feeling that she'd learned how to play in a saloon back in Tombstone. I decided to cut my losses on the small talk.

"Edna, when you have a chance, could you please ask Kirsten Woodrow what time works best for Saturday afternoon? I'm going to the zoo with Danny and her."

"Outstanding choice, Mr. Peters. You will find that young Daniel is extremely well informed about the animal kingdom."

This was the second such reference. I was starting to wonder if Danny Woodrow ought to have his own show on the Discovery Channel.

Later that day I happened by the office of Christopher Glickman, senior vice president of the corporate tax department. He was one of the original members of the Wire Rims. This fresh-faced trio seemed so interchangeable that it was easier to think of them as a single entity, like some rock group. Or in their case, more like a glee club on loan from an Eastern prep school. They'd been hired within sixty days of one another after T. Albert Guenther had become CFO and started consolidating

ASC's corporate finance functions. Joining Glickman had been Frederick Schumacher, who was given the dual title of treasurer and senior vice president of financial strategies—with none of us ops guys having any idea what that second part meant. No matter, because none of us cared either. Robert McCaffrey rounded out Guenther's imported triad as the senior vice president of corporate acquisitions. The three of them looked so cute together with their Hugo Boss and their razor cuts … and, of course, their designer eyewear. Close to five years earlier, they'd begun attending our quarterly business reviews and establishing their patterns of endless presentations and arrogant indifference toward everyone they met.

Since moving to Chicago, I realized I'd been remiss in not reaching out to these nifty lads sooner, so now I would make amends. I considered going for the hat trick, hosting all three for a night on the town—pounding down herbal teas and biscotti. But I decided instead to invest time with each of them individually. I'd start with Christopher, *don't call me Chris …* move on to Frederick, *don't call me Fred …* and conclude with Robert, *don't call me Bob.* Depending on what I learned, I eventually might want to have a private chat with their patron saint—T. Albert, *don't call me Al, don't even call me Albert.* They all seemed to view any casual abbreviation of their full names as an affront to their exalted status over the unenlightened masses who hadn't made it to business school.

From outside the doorway of Glickman's office, I observed that he was in the midst of some form of trance while seated at his desk. He seemed so mesmerized that I only could assume he'd discovered a method for navigating around the porn filters on our office computers. But I knew that wasn't the case when he made no attempt to shield the screen after I finally stepped in and spoke up. "Chris, do you have a couple of minutes?"

"I guess so, Milo … and, please, don't call me Chris."

The temptation had been too great. "I'm sorry, Christopher, I always forget that. You looked pretty intense, I'm sorry if I interrupted anything important."

"No problem, I was just reviewing a potential new opinion from FASB. If this one were to hold up, we could gain much greater latitude in calculating impairment on our goodwill charges, along with other intangible assets. A very exciting development."

"Yeah, I figured it was either that or the latest dancing animals on YouTube. Funny … I've been meaning to add the Financial Accounting Standards Board Web site to my favorites list."

Perhaps he hadn't known I was trying for humor, but the least he could have done was act surprised that I knew what FASB stood for. The way he was eyeing me, I feared this conversation wasn't getting off to the best of starts.

"Chris … uh, Christopher, one of the advantages of working at headquarters is that I can access our best experts with the kinds of questions I often had when I was out running companies, but never could get answered in a way that made sense. Now, with all of us here in the same building, I'd be a fool not to take advantage of so much available talent. I hope you won't mind me bugging you occasionally about our tax procedures and policies."

"Probably not … it depends on the issues. In some cases I may not be the person you need to ask. Could you give me an example, Milo?"

"Today, I was just hoping to open the door with our conversation … so I didn't come with any specifics in mind." I gave him an appreciative nod and turned to exit his office. After a step or two, I turned back. "Come to think of it, I do remember one thing I found a little curious. When we were consolidating our tax practice here in Chicago right after you arrived, it seemed like we didn't even consider transferring any of the tax specialists from our operating companies into your department. With the years of experience many of those men and women had in working through the various state and local tax codes, it just seemed like you might have wanted the benefit of some of their knowledge. But what do I know? You're the expert … and you obviously were convinced it was better to hire outside people at much higher salaries. What made you come to that conclusion so quickly, Christopher?"

He stared down at the top of his desk, coldness in his facial expression. When he looked up after a few moments, a plastic smile was in place. "You see, Milo, that's a perfect example of what I was referring to. That's exactly the type of issue you needn't bother to raise with me. You should take that one directly to T. Albert, because he made all those decisions before I accepted my position. But, please, don't ever hesitate to ask me any specific tax questions."

I returned a plastic grin and left him alone with his FASB erotica. My approach hadn't been especially tactful or subtle. I recognized that I had some style work to do as an undercover investigator, but in this case, it hadn't mattered what Luke was asking me to explore. My irritation was legitimate. For five years I'd been carrying around the very real questions that I'd just posed to Christopher Glickman. Why the hell had we chosen to fire every bleeping tax person in the organization and start over from scratch at much higher salaries?

That evening, I was foraging through a pile of paperwork when I heard the unmistakable knocks on the doorframe outside my office. No one dared to imitate that sound. Three barely audible raps, a full second or more between each. I needn't bother to lift my head; I automatically stood to greet him. As usual, he looked like he'd just stepped off a movie set. His skin was permanently tanned, his teeth permanently whitened, and his thick silver hair permanently groomed into place. His hands perfectly manicured, shirt perfectly pressed, shoes perfectly polished. Back straight, chin and chest projected forward, nothing out of place. A peacock in a tailored suit.

I extended my hand. "Wilson, don't tell me the CEO has taken to walking the halls again? Rumor has it that when you made the rounds a few years ago, we ended up with three of our best people in coronary care."

"I'm glad to see that the move to headquarters hasn't dulled any of your comedic edge, Milo."

"I'd hit you with the old standby about a man needing to keep his sense of humor when everybody around him is losing theirs, but as best I can tell, most of the folks on these floors never had one to lose. It's like the hospitals ran a special when all of them were kids: 'When we're taking out those pesky tonsils and adenoids, we'll grab that needless sense of humor while we're in there. No extra charge. Someday, when you're a corporate drone, you'll thank us.' I'm not sure I've heard a laugh since I've been here."

"Well, then it's a good thing I brought you to Chicago to rescue us from our dullness."

"I fear my arrival may be too late for some, Wilson, but we'll do the best we can. I think there's still a chance with you, but it could be close."

Wilson Delaney always had cut me a great deal of slack with my irreverence. If anything, he counted on it. I said things out loud which others dared only to think and he experienced a vicarious pleasure from watching the startled reactions I could elicit. My unfiltered brashness was but another instrument for him to manipulate … wind me up and point me at some person or subject matter that he wanted to shake up with a dose of shock value. Part of the bargain was that I had leeway to poke a certain amount of fun his way … but only a certain amount. I tried to stay keenly aware of where that line was and not cross it. Unfortunately, this line could move precipitously according to mood swings or my current standing in his secret popularity rankings.

A change in expression indicated that playtime was over. He moved into my adjoining private conference room, meaning I was to follow. Wilson Delaney took a seat in one of the high-backed leather chairs. "Milo, can I offer some fatherly advice?"

The next few minutes would be a one-way street. Whenever he resorted to an offer of fatherly advice, it meant that he believed one of his children had been misbehaving ... and there was no mistaking that he viewed everyone who worked for him as children. My turn to be taken to the woodshed.

"Of course, Wilson."

"I created your new position because this corporation needs to be bolder in developing its strategic plans. We have to challenge ourselves to rethink our fundamentals in view of an ever-changing marketplace. I remain confident that you are the best person to help ASC with these efforts."

He paused to make sure that his regal affirmation had registered. I nodded appreciation, but also knew that this gratuitous preamble was merely a stepping-stone to an admonition for whatever transgression I'd committed. He would get to that in due time and I was expected to sit quietly and listen obediently. This wasn't my first trip to the woodshed.

"Further, Milo, I've asked you to take responsibility for a host of corporate support functions. We are neither as state-of-the-art nor efficient as we need to be with human resources, technology, and the other departments that I have placed under your direction. These responsibilities go hand-in-hand with your strategic planning role, because in combination you hopefully will better prepare American Service Companies for future effectiveness."

His hands had been resting in his lap, but now he brought his right hand up and placed it on the conference table. The index finger started tapping the tabletop, which meant he was getting to the point or points he wanted to emphasize.

"So, Milo, I have to wonder ... with so much on your plate regarding our future, how and why you have time to worry about organizational decisions that have already been made? I realize you weren't here at corporate to participate in those decisions, but T. Albert and his team have moved us well ahead of where we had been with our most vital financial functions. There is no reason to revisit those actions. You need to trust that others knew what they were doing. Milo, let's worry more about your areas and trying to catch up with the progress T. Albert has made in his. Worrying about the future would seem to be a much better use of our collective time … and much more in keeping with the reasons I brought you here to further prove yourself … and for a significant jump in compensation, I might add. T. Albert's talented team is amply occupied. Milo, they don't appreciate unnecessary distractions, anymore than you ever have. So, I'd like to be able to tell T. Albert that we've reached an understanding."

This time he didn't pause to see if his message had registered. He promptly stood up and exited. End of conversation. I sat alone in my conference room, reviewing the sequence of events. Christopher Glickman obviously had gone to T. Albert Guenther after my unexpected visit; he, in turn, had paid a visit to Wilson Delaney, who consequently had felt obliged to visit me. All in the matter of a few short hours. To think that our field operators so often complained about how slowly things happened at corporate headquarters.

Perhaps I'd come on too strong with Glickman right out of the box, but I had managed to flush out a few important answers in no time at all. For one, there was a definite sensitivity about the reasons ASC might have centralized its corporate finance functions so rapidly. More importantly, whatever the skeletons were that hung in the corporate closet, Wilson Delaney wasn't comfortable with anyone sniffing around the closet door. Thus, whatever hypothetical trails we might eventually uncover, it was clear they were going to lead up to the office of the CEO. Luke and I would have a great deal to talk about.

Chapter Eight

"One of these Saturdays, I'm going to get here an hour early just so I can say that I beat you."

"Sure, Milo ... you being such a morning person. Sit down so they can start your coffee transfusion."

"I'll have you know that I already had my coffee."

"That explains why you don't look like a serial killer for a change." Luke looked legitimately pleased that I wasn't on my usual downer, but there was no way he'd say that outright. "I suppose there's nothing short of cosmetic surgery that could alter that Barney Rubble smile of yours. And please tell me you're not going to start showing up in a good mood. It would change the whole dynamic of our relationship ... you know, with your total dependence on me to cheer you up and everything."

"Nah, Luke, I wouldn't do that to you. You're a government employee ... I couldn't destroy the only sense of accomplishment you might ever enjoy. Such a pity, though—considering all the years of wastefulness you've put in. It's time we hard-working taxpayers stop forcing you proven bureaucrats to sit behind a desk and do nothing for thirty-five hours a week in order to collect your welfare checks. They should just mail them directly to your subsidized homes so you wouldn't have to miss any of your favorite game shows."

"Okay, my capitalist friend, have we learned anything this week that might shape our opinion on whether American Service Companies has been playing with its books?"

I related what had happened both during and after my visit with Christopher Glickman. The quick communication between Glickman, Guenther, and Delaney obviously reflected a strong and shared desire to keep a protective fortress around corporate finance. The challenge I now faced was how to dig further without setting off the nuclear missiles pointed at my office. The CEO had given me his friendliest warning. If a subsequent visit to my office was required, I could anticipate that he wouldn't come alone. Wilson Delaney would bring security to escort me out of the building.

Luke tried to wave me off. "Milo, you've done enough. It was probably a bad idea to involve you to begin with. This is our problem, not yours … we'll take it from here."

"Sure … get me all worked up about becoming an informer so that I finally convince myself it's the noble thing to do. At last, I have a chance to be one of the good guys; then, with the first sign of adversity, you take away my white horse and silver bullets. Not so fast, amigo."

I explained my situation with Kirsten Woodrow. First, I described her job responsibilities and the unaffected way in which she went about them. With that as a foundation I got into her many other appeals. After all, we were seated at Ashton's; we were expected to come clean on such matters.

I was certain I could ask Kirsten a few basic questions without triggering any major alarms. Even if my curiosity generated some awkward spots, she wasn't the type to go running to T. Albert Guenther's office. If that happened, I assured Luke I would back off and surrender my stallion.

Under those terms, Luke consented. He also weighed in on the social aspects. "I won't be there if you get tongue-tied, so please try to avoid saying anything outrageously stupid when you're with her this afternoon. Your normal stupid is the best we can hope for—and probably acceptable. And Milo, she sounds pretty special … just be yourself."

Easy for Luke to say … he only had one self that he needed to be. Me, I had an assortment to choose from. The uncomplicated, directionless self I'd been when he and I became friends those many years ago. The tunnel-visioned self I'd been for the past couple decades—the one with whom Luke wouldn't have bothered to associate if he'd first met that particular persona. Or finally, the self I down-deep wanted to be. Even Luke hadn't seen much of that version, but I figured it was the one he meant I should try to be with Kirsten. The problem was that self hadn't been fully road-tested yet.

⁓

Kirsten and Danny lived on the first two levels of a brownstone near Lincoln Park, on Chicago's near north side. The wheelchair ramp constructed over a portion of the front steps confirmed that I'd found the right address. I had deliberated over what to bring. Flowers seemed kind of hokey. Who knew what dietary debates that candy or any form of fun food might provoke between a mother and a son? From what Kirsten had said, Danny likely would have read all the Harry Potter books and seen the DVDs, so I didn't dare pursue that route. Wine was out because I wasn't sure whether a seven-year-old would be more partial to red or white. Ultimately, I chose to go with the theme of the day.

With February's temperatures, a person should dress appropriately for a visit to the zoo; the notion of hats had been solely practical. Following breakfast with Luke, I journeyed out to a store I remembered on the far west side. I'd seen pictures of Danny. I was convinced he would look good in a stocking hat with a big floppy lion's head sewn to the top and a mane draping down to about shoulder length. Nonetheless, I was taking a chance on how his mother might react. So for Kirsten, I'd selected something safer, more stylish and demure … the hat with a curly-horned sheep's head and soft wooly ringlets stringing down the sides. I went with the camel for myself.

The afternoon couldn't have started more perfectly. Kirsten met me at the door wearing tight blue jeans and a black turtleneck. I could have sold tickets to half the men in Chicago for a chance to see her dressed like that.

Five minutes after meeting Danny Woodrow, I knew that his mother hadn't exaggerated about what a special kid he was. Maybe he'd forgotten about his legs being paralyzed and the confinement to a wheelchair, because none of that seemed to bother him. Once we had our hats properly in place, he was the first one out the door and down to the sidewalk. The Lincoln Park Zoo was only several blocks away and I suspected that Danny could lead us there blindfolded. He slowed every few yards to allow us to keep up with him as he worked the wheels with his arms. Kirsten explained that he sometimes used a motorized wheelchair for lengthier distances, but less and less each month. He wanted to develop his upper body strength with the manual chair so that he someday might have the option of pulling himself around on crutches when he was at home or in school.

Once inside the zoo, we started with the bird exhibits. I couldn't begin to count the number of birds we saw, but Danny knew them all by name and country of origin. Fortunately, he kept it interesting for a novice like me. Kirsten had been through this routine many times, so she only was surprised on fifteen or twenty occasions by some new bird fact he'd picked up since their last visit. Most everything that came out of his mouth was a revelation to me. I must have been living in a bubble. I hadn't known that a pigeon's feathers weighed more than its bones … or that among all the native birds in North America, only swans had penises. Since Danny didn't giggle or smirk when he said the word "penis," I'd thought it best to refrain as well.

I actually had known that certain birds like the kiwi or emu couldn't fly, but it hadn't occurred to me that others might not be able to walk. Danny rattled off five birds that couldn't because they lacked the appropriate joints—the hummingbird, loon, swift, kingfisher, and grebe. I truly was fascinated to learn this fact and went out of my way to tell Danny. Then I asked him what a grebe was.

As we toured the African habitats, I was downright distraught when he told me that the hippopotamus had killed more humans than any wild animal on the continent. Hippos always seemed so peaceful in the background of Tarzan movies and so happy in all those animated cartoons. Apparently, the devious bastards were just luring us in.

I was surprised further to learn that zebras weren't black and white striped, but actually white animals with black stripes. And that tigers not only had striped fur, but the skin under their fur was likewise striped. Obviously, my teachers hadn't spent enough time on their lesson plans. Why didn't I know this stuff?

Exhibit after exhibit, continent after continent, animal species after animal species, Danny was a fountain of information. More than the facts, he conveyed a respect for nature and the evolution of life forms. I was spellbound … and not solely due to this remarkable boy. But also a remarkable woman and the obvious joy she experienced from sharing her most treasured gift.

We downed hot chocolate and corn dogs. We occasionally raced from one destination to the next … neither of us beating Danny even once. We drew stares from almost everyone we passed. Sure, it might have been the silly hats bouncing atop our heads, but I preferred to think it was because of all the fun we were having. I'd forgotten how good that fun and laughter felt. And if Kirsten's warm smile hadn't been infectious enough, seeing her laugh and frolic convinced me there indeed must be angels in heaven.

I escorted them back to the foyer of their brownstone, where Danny thrust out his hand for a farewell handshake. "Mr. Peters, I hope you had as nice a time as I did, sir. Thank you for spending the day with my mother and me … and especially for the really cool hats."

"Danny, my friend, it is I who needs to thank you. I don't know how many times I've been to a zoo in my lifetime, but you took the entire experience to another dimension. And I hope you'll call me 'Milo' in the future."

He didn't want to respond without looking at his mother. She interjected on his behalf. "If you don't mind, we'd better stay with 'Mr. Peters.' Having grown up around old-fashioned Wyoming values, I want Danny to learn how to show proper respect when he's around adults."

Between Danny and Edna, I wasn't having much success at getting people to call me by my first name. Kirsten walked me down to the sidewalk and turned to me with one of those looks that could inspire volumes of poetry.

"Milo, this afternoon meant so much to both Danny and me that saying thanks doesn't come close to expressing my deep appreciation."

"Good ... then maybe you'll agree to a different way of showing your gratitude. How about next weekend we go to the aquarium? I hate to think how much that kid of yours could teach me about sea life."

"Are you sure?"

"Kirsten, you don't understand how much today has done for me. I told you that Danny sounded like the kind of positive influence I need right now. Well, he's all that and more ... and so is his mother. In fact, after our day at the aquarium, I hope you might consider a dinner with just the two of us."

She hesitated before arching her body upward to kiss my cheek. "You're sweet, Milo."

"Should I take that as a 'no' on the dinner part?"

"Just the opposite ... but there's one condition. We come back here to my house for dinner. I'll cook and Danny will have no trouble staying occupied upstairs until his bedtime."

After we separated, I took my time walking several blocks to a busier street where I could hail a taxi. It seemed stupid to hurry even the simplest moments when life was so gloriously good ... and darned if I wasn't whistling again. Of all things, it was a Carpenters song. Who knew? I would have sworn that I hated their music.

⸙

My customary disposition for early mornings could have been described as uncivil, even worse on Mondays. Edna had to wonder if the planets were

71

out of alignment when I started the new week by arriving at the office cheerful and talkative. Meanwhile, I was becoming increasingly curious about the source of my secretary's energy. It was a few minutes past 6 AM, yet her desk looked like she'd been toiling away for hours. My two tall coffees and bagel awaited in their designated position.

"I presume you partied out of your mind over the weekend again, Miss Cutler."

She saw no reason to respond, as her fingers kept flying across her keyboard—with textbook posture, of course.

"Edna, can I interest you in a little test of knowledge this morning?"

This time I had her; I'd piqued her curiosity. She rotated her chair to face me. The upturn to the right side of her lip was barely perceptible, but I saw it. She loved a challenge. "I'm listening, Mr. Peters."

"The category is 'living things' … and answering in the form of a question is purely optional. Among all the wild animals on the African continent, which one is reported to have killed the most humans?"

"That would be the hippopotamus, Alex."

With no change in expression, she simply turned and resumed what she'd been doing. I definitely needed to step up my game if I ever hoped to evoke human emotion from this woman. Then with her back still to me, Edna added the final punctuation to our morning greetings in her usual proper tone.

"I take it your day at the zoo was most pleasant, Mr. Peters."

I swung by Kirsten's office later that morning and took a seat next to her desk. After exchanging enthusiasms about our Saturday afternoon together, I segued into the other purpose of my visit. Despite the prior week's failure with Christopher Glickman, I'd decided to stick to the same ruse.

"Kirsten, I was hoping you wouldn't mind if I bounced a few questions about corporate finance off of you. Now that I'm getting settled into my new corporate responsibilities, I think I owe it to our shareholders to become more familiar with all of our corporate departments and practices."

"Of course, Milo, like maybe why all the tax folks out in the business units were fired so we could hire new ones here in Chicago?"

I clearly wasn't off to a very solid start with undercover work. "Oh, then I guess you heard that I tried posing a few of my questions to Glickman last week."

"Sure did. Doesn't sound like that went too well for you." Kirsten's tone was sympathetic.

"How'd you hear?"

"T. Albert came by to talk to me on Friday. I think he paid the same visit to all of his direct reports. He doesn't want any of us to be distracted."

"That's all he said?"

"No, he had a few more things to say, but I wasn't listening too closely. T. Albert's a control freak and thinks the executives who run our service companies are Neanderthals. Your new position and presence on the executive committee don't exempt you from those sentiments. He doesn't want us wasting our time trying to explain what we do behind the scenes to make the corporation so successful … everyone else should just do their own jobs, generate as much revenue as possible and be grateful that the finance team knows what to do with it."

"I hate to admit it, Kirsten, but that's exactly the approach I took when I was running business units. It was just easier that way. In hindsight, that mindset was irresponsible. But now I feel an obligation to better understand the hidden genius of T. Albert Guenther and everyone else here at headquarters."

"Milo, I don't doubt that a bit. And please don't assume we all agree with T. Albert. He just happens to be our boss and the guy who signs our paychecks."

"I'm sorry. I don't want to put you in an awkward position."

"You don't owe me any apologies for being curious … for gosh sakes, you're one of the top executives in the whole corporation. As far as I'm concerned, you should have free rein to ask whatever you want. But that's not my call and it sounds like our chairman agrees with T. Albert."

"Oh, so you heard about that, too?"

"Afraid so. T. Albert was gloating about Delaney's trip to your office."

"Believe me, Kirsten, it's not the first time I've received a fatherly lecture from Wilson."

"Well, I still felt bad for you."

"So you knew all this on Saturday but never said a word?"

"Just like you chose not to ask me any of your questions about corporate finance. I didn't think Saturday had anything to do with business … did you?"

For once, I kept my mouth shut. Both of us smiled and continued our eye contact in silence. I could have stayed locked in that position for a week or two, but instead forced myself out of the chair.

Despite my promise to Luke to throw in the towel if I ran into a wall with Kirsten, I wasn't ready to give up quite yet. There had to be someplace to dig where I wouldn't stir up any attention. On paper, my title implied managerial authorities that should afford me access to confidential information on almost any subject inside the corporation. In reality, I had only as much room as Wilson Delaney wanted to give me. This had been one of my fears when I accepted the promotion that brought me to ASC headquarters—but at the time there'd been no choice. If I wanted to stay in the derby to become the next CEO, I must run the race according to his self-serving and ever-changing ground rules. Now, however, my mind was leaning toward new possibilities—emotionally preparing to make a long overdue separation. More and more each year, I'd believed I should walk away from the insidious culture that Delaney had created. Finally, I was convincing myself I could.

My motivation was more than the liberation of built-up anguish caused by years of misplaced priorities. The reasons had become much more personal. I wanted to bring Wilson Delaney down. Sure, I wanted to help Luke with his investigation on behalf of shareholders and a free market economy. Of course, I wanted to help preserve truth, justice, and the American way. But underneath all those higher callings, I wanted to see Wilson Delaney pay for exploiting the thousands upon thousands of ASC employees who trusted him, as CEO, to look out for their best interests. I wanted to see him exposed for the deplorable ways in which he encouraged our companies to abuse customer relationships. Mostly, I wanted to see him punished for all the times he'd preyed upon my weaknesses, my dark sides, and made me such an eager accomplice.

It was nice to have clarity for a change … to at last draw a line in the dirt. For far too long I'd hidden in the gray areas, but this was black and white. This time people needed to be prosecuted and sent to jail. I couldn't erase the excesses of my past ambition, but I definitely could start anew by salvaging some self-respect.

I'd returned to the roots of Chicago at a crossroads. Now I knew for certain that I wanted to become that adult I'd always meant to be when I was growing up in Park Ridge. I still had time to be the son that a father like George Peters deserved … to be the friend that a guy like Luke Papadakis deserved. To be the kind of man that a woman like Kirsten Woodrow deserved.

Chapter Nine

"Top of the morning, Edna. I heard on the news that the Chicago cops are clamping down hard on underage drinking. Please be careful with those fake IDs of yours ... I know how embarrassed you'd be if I had to come down and bail you out in the middle of one of your pub crawls."

"Good morning to you, too, Mr. Peters."

She didn't bother to look up from the stacks of envelopes she was stuffing. But getting even the slightest of smiles from her merited a second attempt.

"Sorry I'm late, Miss Cutler ... it won't happen again, I promise." I'd slept in. It was nearly 6:20, a full fifteen or twenty minutes past my normal arrival time.

"Your coffee should be sufficiently warm, Mr. Peters."

Okay, if not a smile, maybe a grimace of disgust or irritation. But nothing. The envelopes continued to warrant her full visual attention. Zero for two. There would be other days.

"Edna, when Cynthia Richards gets in, please let her know that I'd like to meet with her."

"Of course, sir. Miss Richards typically arrives sometime between eight-twenty and eight-thirty." Despite its high-tech equipment, the air traffic control tower at O'Hare had nothing on Edna Cutler.

As head of corporate human resources, Cynthia Richards reported directly to me. Last time I'd checked, T. Albert Guenther couldn't stop me from talking with one of my own people. In keeping with my new corporate position, I had an obligation to become more familiar with the entire headquarters staff. At least that's what I told the always perky and cheerful Miss Richards. I didn't know where Delaney or Guenther might have moles, but I was certain they had them and I couldn't disclose to her that my only real interest was in the corporate finance team.

"Cynthia, let's start by getting me the complete personnel files of everyone in Chicago above the director level. I realize I'm asking for a lot of extra work here, so whoever pulls the copies can start sending them up to me piecemeal. But it would help to know when I might expect to receive the first batch."

I was eager to get my hands on those files, but I also was empathetic to the fact that some hapless HR assistant probably would be required to spend days standing at a Xerox machine churning out copies on my behalf. I must have sounded sheepish because she gave me one of those *"Oh, how cute!"* looks.

"Milo, give me about ten minutes and you can have the personnel files on every associate at every level here at headquarters. We went totally electronic several years ago. Why don't I simply issue you a protected password that allows you access to the restricted personnel sections at our corporate intranet site?"

"I guess that would be fine … that is, as long as you think that's easier." When coming off as clueless, it often paid to go that extra mile … then one's subordinates could better appreciate how vital and irreplaceable they were.

"Certainly, Milo, we're always glad to be of help … and have a terrific morning." In a flash, Cynthia Richards was scampering out of my office to spread her relentless sunshine elsewhere. What was it about HR people? For a good minute or two afterwards, an aura of sweetness and happiness hovered around the chair where she'd been sitting. I felt momentary sadness for her. People afflicted with such permanent enthusiasm would never experience the suspense of daily mood swings.

Upon receiving my own protected password, I dove immediately into the classified file on each of the Wire Rims. After rummaging around for thirty minutes, I decided to print out hard copies so I could place them side by side by side. The parallels were astounding. They each had started five years previously, within weeks of each other, and each at the exact same salary. In every year since, their salaries had increased by exactly the same amounts. They'd received top-box ratings on every attribute in every one of their annual performance reviews. Each year, they'd maxed out on their bonuses.

As much as I found it humorous that T. Albert Guenther's three minions dressed and acted alike, the discovery of these other similarities suggested a different kind of funny business. No matter how outstanding three individuals might be at their jobs, it was illogical that three separate officers, responsible for three separate functions, all could be evaluated and compensated at the uppermost levels for five consecutive years. Unless, of course, their boss had cut a deal to make sure that was the case.

I dug into their pre-employment backgrounds, where the remarkable parallels continued. Each of the three had been in his early to mid-thirties when he was hired by Guenther—young ages for such senior positions. Each had been a vice president with his previous employer for a relatively short period of time before joining ASC as a senior vice president. Each had been offered dramatically more in compensation—which wasn't especially unusual when changing jobs. However, in less than two years, each of the Wire Rims was earning well more than double what he'd made previously. That seemed highly unusual.

I reviewed the documentation of how they'd been recruited. Each was interviewed by only a smattering of corporate officers. According to corporate policy, Wilson Delaney had signed off on all three before final job offers were extended. Perhaps most noteworthy was the fact that Guenther had hired Glickman, Schumacher, and McCaffrey without the assistance of an outside executive recruiter. Completely on his own, he'd managed to find them, negotiate terms, and slot them into newly created positions within just his first two months as CFO. Either T. Albert Guenther was a modern-day corporate magician, or he'd somehow started with an inside track on the Wire Rims. I needed to find out what their prior connection had been.

Though all three Wire Rims had earned MBAs, none had attended the same business schools or undergraduate colleges. They'd grown up in three different parts of the country and likewise worked in different cities. Before joining ASC, Christopher Glickman had been in the tax group of a sizable manufacturing company in Pittsburgh. Frederick Schumacher was with one of the big banks in Charlotte before taking over our treasury function. Robert McCaffrey had done acquisitions with a holding company in Texas that owned restaurant chains. Going further back, none of their individual career paths had intersected at earlier jobs. I pulled up Guenther's file and reviewed his bio. Once again, nothing. No evident ties to a single Wire Rim.

Maybe the connection had been made indirectly, through their spouses or families? The files revealed that T. Albert Guenther was married to his high school sweetheart from a small town in Michigan; McCaffrey, to a gal he'd met in Texas. Glickman had been married and divorced twice. I Googled my way to the available background facts on each of these women, but nothing matched up.

Schumacher hadn't been married, but it widely was rumored that away from the office he experimented with alternative lifestyles. For obvious legal reasons, there were no related details in his personnel file. I didn't even contemplate searching down that trail on the Internet, for fear of what Web sites might pop onto my computer screen.

I was coming up empty. Whatever prior connection the Wire Rims might have had to one another or to T. Albert Guenther, the answer wasn't in the corporate personnel files. I would have to explore elsewhere and pull that off without tripping any of Guenther's three human alarms.

As another direct report to Guenther, Kirsten Woodrow would have spent hundreds of hours in meetings with her boss and the Wire Rims. Maybe she would have gleaned some outside connection between these four men. I debated on whether to impose on her, but figured I'd merely be asking an innocent question.

She was traveling, so I shot off a quick e-mail: "How might Guenther have known Glickman, Schumacher, or McCaffrey before hiring them?"

Like almost anyone else traveling on business these days, she was in constant contact with her e-mail while out of the office. Within an hour, she responded from her BlackBerry: "Milo, this subject remains off-limits." Clearly, she feared crossing Guenther's edicts in even the slightest fashion.

For twenty years I hadn't considered T. Albert Guenther worth the bother of disliking. Now I was changing my mind. This irritant had descended into my life back when I'd been put in charge of my own branch with Zero Bug Tolerance. He'd been easy to dismiss. As Wilson Delaney's financial officer and right-hand man, he was the one who pestered us when costs ran high or expense reports were submitted late. We were the anointed field warriors, yet a week rarely went by without the nit-picking Guenther calling some misstep to our attention. He was Delaney's hired annoyance ... a world-class nagger. The man's personality was so perfectly suited to those duties. In every way possible, he looked the part of a prototypical bookkeeper, plucked from the pages of Dickens. Adding to his persnickety image, he insisted upon being called by his full name at all times, including that god-awful first initial. No one knew for sure what the "T" stood for, but it was hard to imagine anything other than "Tedious."

All Guenther had to do was step up to the podium at ZBT's annual conventions and he would evoke an outbreak of yawning throughout an auditorium. He inevitably would beseech us to "hold firm to your budgets" and "manage those headcounts." He attempted to inspire us with profit optimization models and pro forma calculations. On those rare occasions when his subject matter was more substantive, Guenther's mouth might have been moving but the words clearly were Delaney's. T. Albert Guenther was a puppet. A vassal, a henchman. Lacking in imagination. Completely devoid of charisma.

Physically, Guenther appeared much the same now as he did then. A slight man with pale, doughy skin. He was small boned, narrow framed, and definitely on the short side. His hips and backside were borderline petite, but he carried a small paunch up front. He'd been progressively balding for as long as anyone could remember. In recent years, T. Albert had taken to shaving his head completely, which had been the first and only evidence that he might notice or care how he looked. Regardless of changing fashion or the migration to "business casual," he stuck to his dark suits, white shirts, and dull ties. The wire-rimmed glasses were a permanent fixture on his crooked nose. He still didn't make eye contact when he spoke; his voice was forever a monotone. The way he looked, the way he acted, T. Albert Guenther must have been the target of much ridicule throughout his life. But odds were high that he would have been oblivious.

It was preposterous to think this milquetoast, this nebbish, could have conceived a sophisticated and undetectable financial scheme that required a structure of highly placed corporate accomplices. Guenther had been riding a very specific set of coattails since the 1980s, when Wilson Delaney hired him. He'd carved a lucrative career out of doing Delaney's bidding during every stage of their ascent through the ranks of American Service Companies. I was certain nothing had changed. T. Albert Guenther was a plodder, not a plotter. The moment he'd gotten wind that I was poking around the fringes of their charade, he'd gone running to the one man who always called the shots. The one place Guenther always would run.

For the first time in years, my outlook on life was improving steadily. But in this particular area, momentum had stalled. I was straining with where to go next regarding Guenther and the Wire Rims. Like I said, it had become personal for me ... I wanted to see Wilson Delaney and the whole lot of them go down. But those frustrations weren't the only cause for my dampened spirits.

I was trying to cope with the physical absence of Kirsten in the office. Seeing her on Monday had been the high point of my work week. Since then, she'd been traveling to various cities, reviewing the financials of a number of our service lines. As corporate controller, Kirsten Woodrow not only was responsible for ASC's overall financial statements and audit, but also was required to sign off on each operating company's fiscal results. With twenty-nine different service lines, that meant twenty-nine sets of books and multiple trips each quarter. Four days in a row without a casual chat or seeing that smile of hers was taking a toll. The executive floor seemed empty without the sound of her voice and the echo of her footsteps. Proximity to Kirsten was the only part of my vaunted promotion to headquarters that held much meaning to me. The rest was becoming more extraneous by the day.

It was Edna's custom to poke her head into my office on Friday afternoons before departing for the weekend. As another week drew to a close, I didn't even bother to caution her about safe sex or fling a single inappropriate comment her way. My uncharacteristic behavior must have concerned her, because she stepped in and closed the door.

"Mr. Peters, is something wrong?"

"I think I just need a weekend, Edna."

"The Shedd Aquarium should do you some good then."

The woman was uncanny. I hadn't made reference to my plans all week. "You must have spoken to Miss Woodrow."

"No, sir."

She wanted to make me work for it. "Okay, how did you learn about tomorrow's plans for the aquarium?"

"Daniel and I text each other on occasion. You've made quite the favorable impression. Early in the week, his school friends teased him about a rather unusual hat … but he continued wearing it because 'Mr. Peters had given it to him.' He is most excited about another Saturday afternoon with you and his mother."

I was dying to know how this stoic, ageless woman had ended up in a text-pal relationship with a seven-year-old. Inwardly, she must have been dying to tell me, but I wasn't going to give her the satisfaction of asking. I'd decided to reverse roles … make her come to me for a change. She didn't and I was left wondering.

Finally, she broke the silence by shifting topics. "Mr. Peters, several days ago I noticed some personnel files spread across your desk. You had left your office for a meeting and I saw them when I brought in your mail."

"I figured you were the one who turned them upside down. It was careless of me to leave confidential information like that out in the open. Thank you, Edna."

"I wasn't fishing for compliments ... it is my job to look out for you."

"So why did you mention those files?"

"As I said, Mr. Peters, my job is to look out for you. I don't know what might be going on with the gentlemen whose files you were reviewing, but they seem to have developed a sudden interest in you."

"Meaning?"

"This morning, while you were holding your staff meeting downstairs, I found Mr. McCaffrey in your office looking around the desk. I asked if I could help him, but he said he was searching for something he'd misplaced earlier in the week and hurried out. I may be wrong, Mr. Peters, but I don't believe you had any meetings with Mr. McCaffrey ... so I can't imagine why he would have cause to look in your office."

"That is odd. I can't remember Don't-Call-Me-Bob McCaffrey being in my office this week or any week."

"Plus, Mr. Peters, yesterday I received a call from IT. A friend, who shall remain nameless, informed me that Mr. Glickman had requested the password for your office computer from Mr. Quinton."

The Wire Rims had failed to recognize that I was armed with the ultimate secret weapon—Edna Cutler and her underground network. Wes Quinton, head of information technology, was another of my direct reports. If needed, Wes could go into the system and pull up anyone's computer password. With my password, Christopher Glickman easily could access my e-mail files or anything else that I stored on my desktop computer.

"That's a pretty naive request by Glickman ... Wes Quinton can't release that information to him."

"He could if the CEO authorized it. My friend said Mr. Glickman made the request on behalf of Mr. Delaney."

"So Wes gave it to him?"

"Actually Mr. Quinton instructed someone else to look up your password and provide it to Mr. Glickman ... which is how I found out."

"Well, now that I know my computer's under surveillance, I'll need to drop out of a few online dating services ... at least the kinky ones." I tried to make light, but I was seething.

"I'm sorry, Mr. Peters, I thought you should know."

"I'm glad you told me. Thanks for watching my back, Edna ... it means a great deal."

She'd worked at ASC headquarters for a decade before Delaney had become CEO. Knowing Edna, she would have been watching closely as he and Guenther instituted their wholesale changes to the organization. But up until now I hadn't wanted to probe her about their past activities and arouse her curiosity. With her keen sixth sense, it wouldn't have taken long before she suspected I was exploring possible financial irregularities. As yet, no specific improprieties had been alleged by anyone. I'd been upholding my fiduciary responsibility as a senior officer by not saying or doing anything that might prompt unfounded speculations. But now he was out of bounds. Too many times in the past I'd allowed Delaney to violate my integrity; this time he'd violated my privacy with the snap of his fingers. The whole situation was becoming more personal by the minute.

"Edna, you don't have to answer the questions I'm about to ask you ... but I assume you remember the period of time when T. Albert Guenther was building out his new corporate departments after Mr. Delaney named him CFO."

"Vividly, Mr. Peters ... and I have no objection to answering your questions."

"Thank you. When Mr. Guenther hired Christopher Glickman, Frederick Schumacher, and Robert McCaffrey, do you recall if he interviewed a lot of other candidates for their positions?"

"I can tell you for a fact that he did not. I have a certain knack for keeping up with things on the executive floor. My memory could be wrong, but I don't remember any other individuals being considered for those positions."

Edna Cutler admitting to a certain knack for keeping up with things on the executive floor was like Henry Wadsworth Longfellow acknowledging that he had a quirky ability for rhyming words. Plus, the inevitability of death and taxes would be tested before her memory might be proven wrong.

"Were you aware of how Guenther was able to find these three gentlemen, or whether he'd known any of them previously?" I asked.

"No, Mr. Peters, I have no specific knowledge about that. But I can tell you that he displayed an immediate chemistry with each of them ... and as you must have observed, Mr. Guenther doesn't generally exhibit much personal chemistry with anyone."

"And how about among themselves ... did Glickman, Schumacher, and McCaffrey already seem to know each other or hit it off quickly?"

"That would be difficult to say. When they were around Mr. Guenther, they all seemed to get along famously. But when they were on their own, their moods changed. It's still that way. They behave differently when Mr. Guenther isn't around."

"How so?"

"Sir, those young men appear to be quite troubled about something ... and they have since the day they started here. I almost feel sorry for them."

"Almost? Why the hesitation?"

"Mr. Peters, I've seen a lot of business professionals come and go during my lifetime. Some are great at their jobs, some not. Some are genuinely good people, some not. Some can be trusted, some not. Over time, I've developed my own set of instincts. These young men, these boys, are too arrogant for their own good."

"And you say they're troubled ... what do you mean by that?"

"Sir, sometimes it appears as though most individuals who have managed to work their way up to an executive floor are troubled in one way or another. Everyone seems to be wrestling with their own personal demons ... the trade-offs that at some point must have been deemed necessary for one's success. It's unfortunate, but those decisions often go with the territory. Well, whatever demons these three are fighting just seem to be a great deal deeper and darker than any I've seen."

All these weeks I'd been under the impression that human resources had assigned me a secretary as a standard operating procedure. Now I realized what really must have happened. Some council of deities must have noticed the mess I was making of my life and they'd sent down this corporate incarnation of Merlin to help bail me out. There was a vast difference between conveying knowledge and offering wisdom. Rare were the persons who could do both as effortlessly as Edna just had done. I stood up from my desk and escorted her all the way to the elevator.

"Edna, you are one in a million. Have a wonderful weekend."

"Give my best to Daniel and Miss Woodrow tomorrow. And, Mr. Peters, what I said in your office about those demons ... I think you're going to win your own battle. Good night, sir."

Chapter Ten

A February dawn was breaking as I took my seat across from Luke. Due to the surrounding buildings and elevated train tracks, direct sunlight wouldn't hit Ashton's until late morning, but at least it wasn't pitch dark outside. These early breakfast meetings didn't feel nearly as surreptitious or sinister when the sun was out—or maybe I'd totally worked through the guilt of ratting out my very own corporation.

Luke informed me that his teams were increasingly sure that ASC's books were dirty and it would be only a matter of weeks before they were ready to bring forth formal charges. I debriefed him on what I'd learned about the Wire Rims. He concurred on the suspicious nature of their swift recruitment, as well as the fact that they'd been hired at levels of responsibility and compensation so far above their previous positions. When I got to the part about Delaney requesting my computer password, Luke interjected.

"Milo, you remember how I wanted to pull you off this investigation last week … and with what you've just told me, your situation seems even more precarious. Clearly, Delaney is worried you may be on to something. The problem is that I think you are … so we really need you to keep digging into how Guenther managed to lure those three birds of his. I'll get our folks working on it, too. But, obviously, you need to be extra careful … especially with anything you do on your computer. Based on what you've said, they already must know that you've been examining their personnel files. Is there anyone else you can trust other than this secretary of yours?"

"I know I can trust Kirsten Woodrow … you remember, the controller who happens to make me light-headed in her presence. But like I told you, she's already been warned by Guenther to steer clear of me. I don't want to mess anything up for her."

"But she and her son are still going to see you again this afternoon?"

"That's different … it has nothing to do with business. We've agreed to keep those interactions separate."

"Well, that's up to you … do what you think best. But if this whole thing blows up on you or your lady friend, we eventually can square things for the two of you with ASC's board of directors. You won't have to worry about Delaney or Guenther messing with anyone's careers … they won't be around."

"Luke, if Kirsten were to get mixed up in this investigation, you and your high-powered associates definitely have to protect her. As for me, if you need to square my reputation with the board … fine, but that's all. I don't care about the career part. As soon as we're done with this whole mess, I'm hanging it up. I'm done with corporate life."

"Milo, there are other companies out there … other CEOs that aren't like Wilson Delaney."

"I may want to stick it to Delaney, but he's not the reason I'm fed up with the whole corporate game. I'm the reason … I don't like what I was willing to become to win at it."

"What will you do?"

"Not a clue, Luke, but I'll have plenty of time to figure something out. My dad had the right idea when he started his second career … you know, 'make your living out of what you love to do.' My problem is that I've been so busy making a living for all these years, I don't have anything else that I love to do."

"Well, well … wouldn't your father have some fun with you now? The prodigal son in search of his own windmill."

"Okay, so I'm a slow learner."

⟡

Outside of family, my father's grandest passion was reading. His appetite for books had been voracious—history and science, but especially fiction, the classics. Sitting in his favorite chair by the living room window for hours on end, he would escape into the works of the world's greatest authors. The room could be filled with giggling kids or blaring music, it wouldn't matter. His thoughts were elsewhere, a joyful smile on his face. If ever there was a man destined for higher education and lively exchanges with professorial types, it had been my father. His family's situation may have forced him to forgo college, but he never stopped pursing that higher education through his books.

By 1985, when the venerable Goldblatt's Department Store chain finally filed for bankruptcy, my father had put in thirty-eight years and was able to secure most of a modest pension. He was fifty-six and too energetic for full retirement. Apparently he and my mother had talked often about someday running their own antiquarian bookshop. They must have worried that such a romantic notion would have been unsettling to my brother and me, because we'd never heard a word while we were growing up. Their announcement came as a complete surprise. Among all the classics, *Don Quixote* struck the deepest chord with my dad. To George Peters, there could be no worthier pursuit than chasing dreams with noble intentions and jousting with the attendant windmills. The shop would be called Noble Windmills.

They leased space in downtown Park Ridge within walking distance of home. Their bookshop opened less than four months after my father's last day with Goldblatt's—Tuesdays through Saturdays, 10 AM to 6 PM. My parents mostly worked the store themselves, together. My older brother was already out of college, engaged to be married, and working in St. Louis. I was a junior at DePaul, so I occasionally could help out during their first few years. As needed, they employed hourlies, who usually were cousins or family friends.

Despite the bankruptcy, my dad remained steadfast in his gratitude toward Goldblatt's for having given him a chance when he was a mere eighteen years old. I never once heard him speak an ill word about his job or the many bosses he must have had over the years. He forever would carry an Old World loyalty for this company that had provided him a career. Through words and example, he tried to encourage his entire family to feel the same loyalty toward Goldblatt's. Whatever setbacks or inequities my dad might have experienced, I never knew ... he kept them all in proportionate context, as well as to himself. Another measure of his character, another stark contrast to his youngest son and the unseemly windmills I'd chosen to chase.

Operating Noble Windmills represented much more to my father than a second career, it was the culmination of his two lifetime passions. "To think that I actually make money by spending the day with the world's greatest woman amid the greatest literature of all time." Legions of customers heard him express those sentiments in exactly that way.

He restricted another of his favorite observations to just my brother and me. "Boys, life is preciously short … if you're able, find a way to make your living by doing what you love." His face would glow when he talked like that.

The first five or six years the bookstore was open, my parents struggled to make money. Those, of course, were years when I was gaining traction in my own career and getting pretty full of myself. Though I was pleased to see my parents so happy chasing a dream, my snowballing ego compelled me to share my vast worldly opinions concerning their business acumen. I couldn't imagine why my mom and dad were risking their money and wasting their time on something as fanciful as an antique bookstore. I constantly would tease my dad about trying to make money out of a fetish for leather bindings—a joke my mom never did appreciate.

Ultimately, they got the last laugh. In time, they developed an extensive clientele of collectors who paid handsome sums for rare volumes that my parents would track down for them. People of all ages and academic standing loved coming into the bookshop for coffee with my mother and scholarly discussions about the classics with my father—this son of illiterate immigrants, this man who never made it to college.

Like I said, my dad was too energetic to retire. My parents' intent was to operate Noble Windmills for as long as both remained healthy. For thirteen years, they did just that. My father was humming a Sinatra song and getting dressed for another day in his beloved Noble Windmills when my mother heard him collapse in 1999. He died instantly and, I'm positive, without regrets.

My mother chose to keep the shop open because it had meant so much to the two of them, but she rarely spent much time there. My oldest cousin started managing the place and most months turned a profit, which he split with her. I hadn't stepped foot inside Noble Windmills for at least a dozen years.

⌒✐⌒

Following breakfast with Luke, I had an important errand to run, where a lively debate ensued and lasted for close to twenty minutes before I finally stepped up and made an executive decision. Hat selection for our trip to the Shedd Aquarium was not as easy as I'd anticipated and the sales clerk hadn't helped with her constant giggling at all my suggestions. In the end, I went with the pirate's hat for Danny. Since I also purchased a skull and crossbones flag to attach to the back of his wheelchair, the giggler threw in an eye patch.

For Kirsten I selected a ship officer's hat—dress white, black brim, and anchor insignia. This choice probably had something to do with the fact that I'd grown up watching "The Love Boat." As a teenage boy, the only scenes I really cared about were the ones that featured the pretty social director in her all-white uniform. Some fantasies had more staying power than others. I decided it might be too early in my relationship with Kirsten to buy her the shorts and knee socks … so for now I'd stick with the hat. Maybe the rest could be added later.

For myself, I opted for a plain white sailor's cap. And since I was in for an ounce, why not a pound? A long-sleeved red shirt with a white collar and bellbottom jeans completed my ensemble. I showed up at their brownstone doing a full Gilligan.

I'd been to the aquarium numerous times as a kid, but couldn't remember ever spending more than a couple of hours there. After all, we're talking about a few big tanks of water with a bunch of fish in them. On this particular Saturday we arrived before noon and I wouldn't have thought it possible that a 6 PM closing time would pose a challenge. As with land animals, Danny was tireless and his enthusiasm contagious. Plus, it didn't hurt that I could be perfectly content staring at a blank wall for six hours as long as I was in the company of his mother.

Once again, we didn't miss an exhibit and rarely missed a food stand. We laughed often, getting downright goofy a few times. Like the previous Saturday, we mostly enjoyed each other's company. And once again, I felt like I should have been earning college credits in zoology. I hadn't known that sharks were the only animals that never got sick. Why had Mother Nature chosen to make them immune to every known illness and disease? My initial reaction to this startling revelation caught Danny off-guard.

"Thank you, thank you! For nearly thirty-five years I've been wondering about Mrs. Teagarten."

"What do you mean, Mr. Peters?"

"Danny, don't you and your classmates privately celebrate when you arrive at school and learn that your teacher is sick and you're going to have a substitute?"

"Sure … who doesn't? It usually means we'll get to watch a video or something, and we won't have any homework."

"Exactly. Well, Mrs. Teagarten was my fifth-grade teacher. We didn't have a single substitute teacher that whole stinking year … and when I talked to older kids who'd had her as a teacher, they said the same thing. No one understood why she never got ill. But at last you've solved the mystery. Mrs. Teagarten was a member of the shark family."

"Mr. Peters, I think you're being silly again."

"Maybe so, Danny, but I'm sticking with my theory ... and, believe me, I'm going to be pretty busy for the next few days. I've got a lot of former classmates to track down and tell."

Among the amazing animal facts pouring out of Danny, I learned that the much maligned catfish was equipped with over a hundred thousand taste buds, ten times more than humans. I pledged never again to refer to them as bottom-feeders.

I also learned that giant squids were the largest creatures without a backbone, growing to more than fifty feet in length and two-and-a-half tons in weight. And blue whales emitted the loudest sound, with a whistle that could be heard underwater for hundreds of miles. Not unexpectedly, the kid was an encyclopedia of sea life, from angel fish to zebra fish. But this time I'd come prepared.

I had dug through my files to locate a discolored twenty-two-year-old binder—the one that preserved my handwritten notes from ZBT's bug boot camp. I normally wasn't much of a saver, so subconsciously I must have known that someday I'd come face-to-face with a miniature Dr. Doolittle. I waited until we were driving back to their brownstone before I tossed out my first teaser.

"So, Danny, who in this car do you think is least likely to be bitten by a mosquito? And, Kirsten, please feel free to chime in."

"Gee, Mr. Peters, I don't know. I haven't studied much about insects yet."

Music to my ears. "Just as I suspected ... God's forgotten creatures. Well, you'll be happy to know that a mosquito prefers kids to adults and blonds to brunettes. So with your youth and my light hair, we both look more appetizing to a typical mosquito than your mom does ... which goes to show you how really stupid mosquitoes are."

I had him. My challenge would be pacing myself so that I didn't fire all my insect factoids too quickly. For a limited number of days or weeks, I might be able to hold my own with a seven-year-old.

"And, of course, you know why citronella repels those pesky little mosquitoes, don't you, Danny?"

"No ... why? Please tell us."

"The smell of citronella irritates their itty-bitty feet ... and like the rest of us, mosquitoes hate when their feet are bothering them. Just a little something I picked up during basic training back in '87."

"You were in the army, Mr. Peters?"

I summoned my best John Wayne voice—not that Danny would have known who John Wayne was … let alone a good rendition from a bad one. "Nah, not the army, kid. I don't like to talk much about it, but I was recruited by an even more elite killing team that went by the code name, Zero Bug Tolerance."

Kirsten had been listening with amusement from the driver's seat of her SUV. She now felt compelled to comment. "Danny, if you're really good, maybe Mr. Peters also can tell you about the special training he received in cleaning office buildings and fertilizing lawns. We can sleep more soundly knowing he's protecting our nation from empty toilet paper dispensers and crabgrass."

I gave her a fake frown from the passenger seat and then turned to her son in the backseat. "Danny, I took a solemn oath of silence. You realize what would happen if I revealed all my company secrets to you …"

Recognizing that we'd slipped into the goofy zone again, he played along by responding with a mechanical, drawn-out, "I know, I know … I get it … you'd have to kill me."

"I guess that's one alternative … but I was thinking I'd probably have to take you out for ice cream."

When we got back to their house, Danny showed me around while his mom began preparing dinner. Each room was decorated tastefully but also reflected a natural warmth and easiness. No single element pushed too hard to make a statement, yet the entirety of the home exuded the comfort of a country inn. Every antique, painting, and area rug looked like it carried some significant personal meaning. There were countless cozy spots where I could envision Kirsten curled up with a book or a magazine or, better yet, me.

Danny selectively pointed out his grandparents and other relatives among the many framed photographs throughout the house. In some of the pictures it had been obvious that his dad was included, but Danny chose not to call attention to him. That, of course, didn't stop me from sizing him up and wondering if I could take him in a fight. The guy was large and looked like he was in fantastic shape, so I decided to refocus my musings on what a lousy husband he must have been.

Furniture was carefully arranged to allow easy passage for Danny's wheelchair. The stairway to the second floor had been widened to accommodate a ramp. Danny could handle descents on his own, but he still needed help going upstairs. Once I'd pushed him to the top, he practically flew to his room, which really was more of a suite. In the first room, there was a television with electronic games sprouting from every available portal, plus a small refrigerator. Clearly, Kirsten wanted to make it easy for Danny to be self-sufficient once he was on the second floor. His bedroom included a bed equipped with handles and rails that allowed Danny to get in and out without assistance.

He made a beeline to the desk and his computer. I had no idea there could be that many software packages devoted to animals. For close to a half-hour he toured me through his favorite interactive modules and video clips. Finally, I told him I needed to go downstairs and help his mom with dinner. As I left his room, he already was online searching out the best programs about insects. My advantage would be short-lived.

In the kitchen, Kirsten had opened one of the bottles of Chianti Classico I'd brought. A Billie Holiday CD was playing, eggplant parmesan was in the oven, and she was standing at the island counter slicing vegetables for a salad. The whole setting was so intoxicating that I did something completely out of character. On impulse, I walked up behind her, put my arms around her waist, and kissed her on the side of her neck.

"I have a confession to make. This is the first time I've ever come down from playing in one of my buddies' rooms and thought about kissing his mother."

She turned to face me, keeping my arms in place around her. "Am I mistaken, or wasn't that more than just thinking about it? And, by the way, Danny would be thrilled that you referred to him as one of your buddies."

"I was sort of hoping you might react to the other part of what I said."

Then in one of the most magical moments of my life, Kirsten put her hands behind my neck and pulled my face to hers and kissed me on the lips. Not just some gratuitous peck, but a long, lingering movie kiss. In fact, Hollywood couldn't do justice to that kiss. Shakespeare, Browning, and Byron together couldn't capture the splendor of that single kiss.

When she pulled her head back, her face was red, but I don't think she was blushing. I, too, was flushed.

"There now, Peters, we've gotten that out of the way. I've been thinking about it all day."

"Hell, Woodrow, I've been thinking about it for weeks. Let's not wait so long next time."

I leaned down and we kissed again. Then we laughed like school kids … me, looking like Gilligan, and her, more desirable than Mary Ann and Ginger combined. I grabbed a knife and started chopping carrots with her.

We didn't finish dinner until three hours later. We had several glasses of wine during the leisurely meal preparations. Good food shouldn't be hurried. After I burned the first loaf of garlic bread, we fired up a second. By the time we sat down, I'd opened the second bottle of Chianti. There were the logistical interruptions along the way. I took a tray of food up to Danny and later retrieved it. Kirsten snuck up at one point to tuck him in for the night. Plus, we periodically needed to stop and rest our palates, but we made efficient use of those down times by practicing our kissing. Once the dishes were washed and put away, we moved right to the main event—a good old-fashioned make-out session by the fireplace in a small den off the living room. I somehow managed to keep my hands where they belonged, but it wasn't easy.

We stayed by the fire until two in the morning. I think we each dozed off a few times, but neither of us seemed eager to draw the evening to a close. The conversations and admissions became bolder as the night had progressed.

I asked Kirsten how difficult it was for her to travel on business as much as she did and leave Danny at home. She acknowledged her angst but hoped and believed such absences were helping him develop more self-dependence. On most days the regular babysitter, Isabel, picked up Danny at school and stayed with him until Kirsten could get home from work. If Kirsten was out of town during the week, Isabel stayed overnight. When business travel occasionally spilled over into weekends, Kirsten counted on Edna, whom she said Danny adored.

I corrected her. "You mean Daniel."

This connection explained the text messaging and why Edna showed such unusual interest in anything related to Kirsten and Danny. My secretary was a fraud … beneath that stoic, unflappable exterior beat the heart of a softy. But I couldn't dare reveal to her that the secret was out.

To Kirsten, however, I did reveal that the office hadn't been nearly as enjoyable when she'd been traveling for most of the previous week.

To which she replied, "You mean you missed me?"

"Me and every other guy in the building. You can't imagine the glorious experience of walking behind you." The wine was having a playful effect.

"Mr. Peters, if talking business wasn't off-limits tonight, I think I could bring harassment charges against you."

"Miss Woodrow, I like the idea of you bringing anything against me."

"In due time, mister ... in due time."

I went on to confess that I'd taken special notice of her the very first time she attended a quarterly review meeting and that the controller's report instantly had become my favorite agenda item. "Maybe I would have enjoyed the presentations of your predecessor, too, if I'd bothered to stay awake. Howard Mosner was a nice enough man ... he was just such an accountant."

She pretended to be indignant. "Excuse me, but I also happen to be an accountant by training ... that's what corporate controllers are."

Since I'd already dived into the pool, I decided that I might as well swim to the deep end. "You've hit on a very important subtlety. You are a fun, highly interesting, and incredibly attractive human being who 'happens' to be an accountant. On the other hand, Howard Mosner, like most controllers, was first and foremost a gloomy, anal retentive accountant who 'happened' to be a human being, or something almost equivalent."

"Thanks ... if nothing else, I'm grateful I could disabuse you of any unfair stereotyping."

"Oh, you haven't altered my opinion one iota. Controllers, and accountants in general, remain the dull, irritating subspecies they've always been ... you can't change that. You're simply a freak of nature, an aberration that's bound to occur every thousand years or so."

"You certainly have a smooth way with words, Milo. Am I blushing? I can't remember a man ever trying to win me over by calling me a freak of nature."

I poured on the false modesty. "It's something a man either has or he hasn't ... that ability to come on to a woman."

"Like complimenting her on the typeface of her PowerPoint slides?"

"Oops, my cover's blown. I was hoping you might not remember how lame I was every time I got around you."

"Lame? I can't imagine anything more flattering to a woman than seeing a big, important executive get all awkward and clumsy when he's trying to strike up a conversation and impress her. I was touched ... you were adorable."

No one had referred to me as adorable since Baba Milka after a second-grade music pageant, when I lost my balance and fell backwards off the top riser during *Puff the Magic Dragon* . Who possibly could have known there were advantages to being tongue-tied?

"For three years I assumed you saw me as superficial, political, and overly ambitious," I said.

"I did and you were … and so was everyone else in those meetings. But underneath your less endearing qualities, there always was this genuine streak of goodness that came out through your sense of humor. I kept hoping you might ask me to join you for a drink, or at least a cup of coffee … and now I'm quite glad you finally did. Since your arrival at headquarters, I've been learning there's a whole different side of you that I didn't know existed."

"You didn't know about it, because it wasn't there. Since moving back to Chicago I've been working hard to undo a lot of bad mistakes. I'm hoping there's still time to start liking myself again."

"Milo, I think one of your mistakes has been that you're too hard on yourself. The strong character and positive traits I've observed didn't appear out of thin air because you made a bunch of new resolutions a few weeks back. Besides, it's not like the rest of us don't wish we could undo some pretty ugly things in our past. When I'm with you I can forget the bad stuff and just be happy for a change."

She took one of my hands and leaned her cheek against it as we sat together in an oversized leather chair. The conversation unexpectedly had transitioned into serious, philosophical territory. Nothing more needed to be said, but it was nice to know we were comfortable expressing substantive thoughts and exposing our vulnerabilities to each other. Clearly, there was more to this budding relationship than laughter and passionate kisses—but those were the parts we chose to delve back into for the balance of that particular Saturday evening.

⌣≫

"Okay Edna, let's see if you're on your game to start the new week."

She patiently waited. I was sure I had her this time.

"Which organism can live for a full week after its head has been cut off?"

"That would be the cockroach, Mr. Peters. Anything else this morning?"

Her expression never changed, but in her own way she was taunting me … smugly sitting in that cubicle, begging me to ask her another question. I chose to cut my losses and walk away. I'd thought my Saturday trip to the aquarium would have thrown her off. She should have been anticipating a question about sea life, not insects. Foiled again. Her vast knowledge was more than impressive, it was intimidating.

"Can I presume you had a satisfactory weekend, Edna?"

"Most satisfactory. Thank you."

"So we shouldn't expect to see any more unflattering pictures of you in the tabloids, Miss Cutler?"

No response. She pretended to direct her full attention back to what she'd been doing before I arrived at the office. But she no doubt had more to say. I was catching on to her tricks. As soon as I turned to enter my office, she would utter some snappy barb about my weekend activities with Kirsten and Danny. I took several steps into my office before stopping to hear whatever clever comment she'd had locked and loaded.

Silence.

I waited several moments before returning to her workstation.

"Alright, Edna, you must have something you're dying to say about our trip to the Shedd Aquarium or my evening at the Woodrow home."

"No, sir. I must have forgotten that you were spending time with the two of them again."

Her response surprised me. In fact, it disappointed me. I thought the three of us had enjoyed such a great time on Saturday. Danny should have provided Edna some sort of rundown. I was well into my office for the second time when she finally spoke up.

"Daniel had a wonderful afternoon, Mr. Peters ... and he was surprised how late it was when he heard you depart."

Formalities completed and faith restored, I now could start another workweek.

Chapter Eleven

I read the e-mail and then reread it. I couldn't help but smile. Whichever Wire Rim had been assigned the duty of monitoring my computer on Monday morning must have gagged on his latte after he'd logged into my mailbox. A message was sent to me on Sunday night by "FriendInHighPlace."

"Looking into past connections between Three Little Pigs and Big Bad Wolf. We should have something soon."

I decided not to respond immediately, thinking it might be more fun to toy with Guenther and the Wire Rims by waiting. Though it was reasonable to assume that Wilson Delaney would be made aware of the late night e-mail, I was confident he wouldn't be stopping by for a follow-up chat anytime soon. No doubt, he would be concerned that an outside party had somehow become involved and that the criminal acts he and Guenther were perpetrating might soon be exposed. But such worries would be superseded by his pure, undiluted outrage. He would want to stomp all over me for disregarding his direct command to cease my inquiries. This not-so-cryptic e-mail made it clear I was persisting and that others were involved.

I knew how Delaney's mind worked. The prospects of arrest and conviction weren't nearly as horrific as being forced to tolerate a direct report's insubordination … especially a direct report who had fetched every bone thrown his way for more than two decades. Nonetheless, Wilson Delaney couldn't divulge that my computer was under surveillance—it would demonstrate fear and weakness on his part. He had no choice but to avoid me completely. If he merely saw me in passing, he wouldn't be able to contain his anger. He knew it and I knew it … he just didn't know that I knew it. I experienced more than a little satisfaction from being the one manipulating him into a corner for a change.

Just before noon, Kirsten popped her head in my office. I'd phoned her on Sunday afternoon simply to tell her how much I enjoyed our previous evening together. The call should have taken five minutes max; I'd always hated talking on the telephone. We hung up an hour and a half later. What's more, I hardly could wait to pick up our conversation from where we'd left off. Standing in my doorway, she beat me to the punch.

"Does Gilligan have any lunch plans?"

"No, I've given Edna explicit instructions to keep my middays open for the balance of the year, on the off-chance that Miss Woodrow might be available to grab a sandwich from time to time."

"Can we go somewhere private? There's something I need to tell you."

As soon as those dreaded words left her sensuous lips, my heart sank. It figured. Things had been going too well, the new positive energy in my life had been flowing too easily. After selfishly chasing false idols for so many years, fate, of course, must cast an ugly shadow across my sunny horizon. I didn't deserve to start rediscovering my long-lost principles and at the same time hit it off with the woman of my dreams. Kirsten Woodrow would be the woman of any man's dreams ... why should good fortune smile so brightly on me of all people?

Kirsten must have slowed herself down and come to her senses; she must have realized that she had no business hooking up with a clueless clown like me. *"There's something I need to tell you."* All the dark thoughts I harbored about myself came rushing out of their hiding places. In her own pleasant way, she was going to tell me to take a hike. By the time we were seated and ordering food from the lunch menu, what I really wanted was a stiff drink.

Once the waiter was out of earshot, I couldn't hold off any longer. "Okay, mysterious lady, what is it you needed to tell me?"

"Milo, this is really hard to say ... " She paused and fumbled with her salad fork. I knew it. The kill-shot was coming. "Milo, I think you should leave ASC."

What did she say? Under normal circumstances, one corporate officer encouraging another to resign his position might be taken as an insult, or at a minimum be unnerving. In this case, I had to restrain from signaling the waiter and ordering champagne. I felt like the governor just called with an eleventh-hour pardon. Since she had no idea that I already was leaning toward quitting in the near future, my immediate verbal response may have surprised her.

"Oh, is that all?"

Seeing her reaction, I didn't want to come off as too flippant—so I started vamping. "Kirsten, I hope you don't feel uncomfortable because we're dating. I'm sure we can keep things discreet when we're at the office."

"I'm not worried about that one bit … and if I was, I certainly wouldn't expect you to leave the company. You're higher in the pecking order and have many more years with ASC … I'd be the one who should find another job. But my suggestion has nothing to do with us, other than the fact that I care what happens to you."

"What are you worried might happen?"

"Milo, I have no idea what you're up to with all your questions, but in the short time you've been at headquarters, you've managed to make your removal the number one priority of T. Albert Guenther. He'll do everything possible to get you fired. He was ranting like a madman at our senior staff meeting this morning."

"About little old me?"

"You and some mysterious e-mail you received … he's monitoring your computer."

I needed to protect Edna's source, so I couldn't divulge that I already knew. "Kirsten, you mean that Guenther not only has the audacity to invade my privacy, but he actually acknowledges it in front of his entire staff?"

"No, Milo, just his senior staff … the four senior VP's … McCaffrey, Schumacher, Glickman, and me. He shares everything with us. He was flaunting how he and Glickman got your password –'Not2Late.' I had to smile over the irony when he threw it out to us this morning. You must have set up that password as soon as you arrived at headquarters … and it's obvious what was on your mind. Here you are trying to get your life headed in a more positive direction, and there's Guenther trying to find a reason to bring you down. Apparently, he didn't hesitate to instruct Christopher to get your password. He knows that companies have a legal right to access whatever content they choose on any employee's computer. If challenged, T. Albert will maintain that he somehow was looking out for the corporation's best interest. He has a way of covering himself so that nothing ever sticks to him."

"From your concern, it sounds like Guenther might be trying to do more to me than read my e-mails."

"He hasn't admitted that yet … but I know what he did when he wanted to get rid of my predecessor."

"Mosner … how would you know if you weren't even here?"

"Like I said, Guenther shares everything with his senior staff. He and Howard Mosner didn't see eye-to-eye on some key issues, so after Guenther had been CFO for a couple years he finally told Mosner that he wanted to hire a controller that would fit better on his team. He asked for Mosner's resignation, but the poor fool refused to give it to him. So Guenther instructed some of his people to dig up whatever dirt they could. A few weeks later, Mosner resigned to pursue other opportunities and forfeited the substantial severance package he would have received if he'd simply cooperated in the first place."

"Kirsten, it's not like Guenther has private investigators working in his department of number crunchers. What could they possibly have found … did the evil accountant, Howard Mosner, round one of our profit dollars down when he could have rounded it up?"

"Okay, funny guy, they didn't even bother digging into his work product. Guenther had people review all of Mosner's expense reports. Not only did they find dozens of infractions to corporate policy, but they noticed how he regularly scheduled out-of-town meetings late in the workweek and returned to Chicago on Saturdays. Most people will do everything possible to schedule their meetings so they can get back home by Friday evening, in time for a full weekend. Guenther became suspicious, and when the travel records of a certain woman who worked for Mosner were pulled up, the exact same travel pattern emerged. It turned out that Howard Mosner may not have been the dull accountant you thought him to be."

She continued, "Guenther confronted the woman and promised not to fire her if she confessed … which she did. Then he confronted Mosner about carrying on a prolonged extramarital affair with a subordinate, threatening him that the matter would become quite public if he still refused to resign. Mosner was married with seven kids … so he opted to leave quietly."

I let the details sink in before reacting. "In my wildest contemplations of Howard Mosner, I wouldn't have imagined anything so outrageous. I guess you never really know some people. Seven kids … that's amazing."

She ignored the attempt at humor. "Milo, T. Albert probably has people rooting around in your past right now."

"Well, they're likely to die from boredom. The most they might find is an occasional meal where I exceeded our per diem limits … and if they do, I'll write them a check for the difference. It's a little embarrassing, but my life has been monotonously dull. You'd think as an unmarried hotshot executive, I could have done better. But alas, dear maiden, I've never done anything untoward on company time or expense … unless you count some of the thoughts I've had about you."

At first she pretended to be insulted, but she couldn't contain her coy smile. "You do have an odd way of injecting compliments, Peters … but I wasn't really thinking about whether you cheated on your expense reports. I'm more worried about some of the questionable business practices that have been rumored to occur out in ASC's field operations. Are you comfortable that all of your decisions and actions over the years would stand up under closer scrutiny?"

"I'm not proud of how we've often chosen to run our businesses, Kirsten, so it's not surprising that you would wonder. But I've given that whole subject a lot of thought in recent weeks … and though plenty of our practices wouldn't compare very well to accepted standards of decency, I'm fairly certain that I haven't done anything illegal. Besides, since it was Wilson Delaney who taught me all of his tricks, anything that he and Guenther might uncover in my past won't come as a surprise. ASC's unwritten philosophies about conducting business would prove far more embarrassing to Delaney than to me … and believe me, I get no satisfaction from admitting that. I wrestled with my conscience a great deal through the years, but my conscience always seemed to lose."

"Milo, a lot of senior people have been forced to wrestle with their personal values if they wanted to do well at ASC. But in this case, you're wrong to assume that Wilson Delaney might be involved with a witch hunt into your past. It's strictly Guenther who has it out for you."

"I think you might be a bit naive on this one, Kirsten. Where did Guenther go running after I asked Glickman a few harmless questions … and who promptly paid me a visit? I realize you work for the man, but from where I sit, T. Albert Guenther hasn't had an original thought since he joined ASC. He has made a very lucrative career out of letting Delaney pull all the strings."

"Milo, you're underestimating T. Albert. One of his greatest strengths is effectively orchestrating actions so that it looks like Delaney is completely in charge. He fuels Delaney's ego to better serve his own purposes. The man is ruthless and quite capable of satisfying his personal agenda with or without Wilson Delaney."

"Then why was it Wilson Delaney who authorized Glickman to get my computer password from IT?"

Kirsten's confusion showed. "First off, are you sure Delaney was really involved? I happen to know it was Guenther who told Glickman to find a way to get your password ... so maybe Christopher took some liberties. But second, are you saying that you already knew your computer and e-mails were being monitored?"

"I'm sorry I didn't tell you a few minutes ago, but I was trying to protect my sources."

"I'm not worried about whom your source might be ... just seeing how much Edna has taken to you, I wouldn't have to be Sherlock Holmes to figure that one out. She knows everything. But Milo, if you were aware your computer was being monitored, I'm more concerned that you went ahead and sent me that e-mail last week when I was in Baltimore."

"The one asking you how Guenther might have known the Wire Rims before they started at ASC?"

"Yeah, that one ... and what are the Wire Rims?"

"Oh, I'm sorry ... that's my pet name for those adorable lads who follow Guenther around like ducklings. I sent you the e-mail before I knew I was being electronically stalked. Since then, I've been quite careful about what e-mails I send ... but I'll admit to being a little reckless with some of my Internet searches. If those boys are closely tracking my computer activities, they must be wondering how I have time for so many varied interests ... soap carving, square dancing, taxidermy, famous dentists in history, to name just a few."

She chuckled in a way that made me wish we were sitting by her fireplace again. "Why do you insist on making me laugh during serious conversations? I promise I won't tell them what you're doing."

Then something dawned on me. "So when you promptly responded to my e-mail, you knew your message would be passed along to Guenther?"

"Not for sure ... I only found that out this morning. But knowing Guenther, I had a sneaking suspicion."

"So your response that the subject was off-limits ... that was just you being careful?"

She nodded her affirmation, but tentatively.

"Kirsten, did Guenther know any of the Wire Rims before he hired them?"

She stared at me. Her solemn expression made it obvious that she didn't want to have this conversation. Until now, business matters hadn't really interfered with our relationship and I was placing her in a difficult position. But she was the one who had initiated the whole dialogue by telling me I should quit.

She must have reached the same conclusion, because she chose to answer. "Yes, Milo, he knew them all."

It was completely insensitive to push further, but I couldn't help myself. "Just one more question, I promise. How did he know them?"

Her look became more anguished and I wished I could withdraw the question. "You remember back when Sarbanes-Oxley was passed after the problems at Enron, Tyco, WorldCom, and elsewhere?"

I nodded that I did. Sarbanes-Oxley was the act adopted by Congress in July 2002 that broadly reformed the standards by which public corporations both implemented business controls and reported financial results.

Kirsten continued. "Well, it seemed like most financial people in corporate America were being shipped off to seminars so that they could better understand those new regulations and the added demands on their companies. ASC sent most of its senior financial team to an intensive ten-day work session hosted by its outside auditing firm. It was early 2003 and Albert Guenther wasn't CFO yet, but he certainly was senior enough that his attendance was required."

Kirsten was taking her time with the back story, as though she knew I didn't want to hear what was still to come.

"As it so happened, Milo, the three companies where Glickman, McCaffrey, and Schumacher were employed at the time, all used the same auditing firm as ASC. So coincidentally, the three of them attended the same lengthy seminar in New Jersey as Guenther."

I mentally was kicking myself for not having thought to check for mutual ties that these characters might have had through relationships with accounting firms, law firms, or other shared business partners. But Kirsten wasn't finished.

"During the ten days of meetings, there were lots of meal breaks and open time blocks when attendees could get to know each other better. It wasn't unusual that Guenther and your Wire Rims would have become well acquainted."

There was more and she was waiting for me to ask. I didn't want to hear the obvious answer to an obvious question, but I had no choice. "How come you're so familiar with the details of this seminar?"

"I'm sure you've already guessed that I was there, too. I worked for the accounting firm that hosted that seminar in New Jersey ... and I spent a great deal of time with everyone in attendance."

I was done asking questions … maybe forever. We both picked at our meals, but eating was the last thing either of us felt like doing. I eyed the chandelier that hung high above our table, hoping it might fall and land on my head … not hard enough to kill me, but enough to cause a memory loss. We tried making small talk about Danny, the weather, and Chicago politics. The attempts were futile. The subject now being avoided had taken total possession of our thoughts. We each privately were playing out the weighty ramifications from what Kirsten had revealed to me.

Walking back to the office, I put my arm around her shoulder and pulled her tightly against me while we waited for the light to change at an intersection. Nothing needed to be said. We were alone on the elevator as we rode up to the thirty-fourth floor. Just before we arrived, Kirsten stretched up onto her toes and kissed my cheek. Then she broke our silence. "You can't possibly know how sorry I am, Milo. Go ahead with whatever you have to do." The doors opened and she went hurrying toward the women's restroom.

Back in my office, I pretended to be busy for close to an hour. I riffled through a stack of phone messages but wasn't in the mood to talk to anyone. The best I could do was toss out the ones from people whose calls I never returned. Strewn atop my desk were files related to issues that needed my attention, so I did some tidying up. I placed them into orderly piles according to priority, in case I felt like doing real work again on some future date.

All I wanted to do was think about Kirsten. Edna could sense something was wrong and didn't question me when I packed up my briefcase and left in the middle of the afternoon. At the hotel I hurriedly threw on an old pair of corduroys and stuffed my coat pockets with an assortment of conveniently sized liquor bottles from the mini-bar, not sure how long I might be gone.

I walked north to where Michigan Avenue ended at Oak Street Beach and climbed onto some big rocks near a breaker wall. I sat down and stared out over Lake Michigan. The winter ice around the shoreline was breaking up, with big slabs banging into one another amid the choppy currents. The sky was completely overcast, which made the water appear dark gray. The temperature was hovering around the freezing mark and a light rain was mixed with sleet. Not another soul to be seen. The bleak, desolate canvas perfectly captured what I was feeling. I reached into a pocket and grabbed what turned out to be a bottle of scotch and then changed my mind and shoved it back among the others. Drinking wasn't going to change anything. My fears from earlier in the day may have been misdirected, but they'd been justified. The recent turnaround in my life had come too easily and now fate wanted to even the score.

Not once had I contemplated the possibility that Kirsten Woodrow might be part of the financial improprieties that Wilson Delaney and T. Albert Guenther were committing. Maybe at first I was blinded by a three-year infatuation that I'd carried from a distance. But now, knowing her more intimately, seeing her with Danny, and experiencing her uncomplicated goodness, the notion of her involvement seemed even more preposterous. I racked my brain trying to come up with some other reasonable explanation, some other meaning to what she had revealed at the restaurant and her words upon exiting the elevator. *"You can't possibly know how sorry I am ... go ahead with whatever you have to do."*

Upon returning to my office after our lunch, I hadn't bothered to pull up her personnel file. I could do that later for final confirmation if I wanted, but I knew what I'd find. It would show that like the others Guenther had hired, Kirsten would have received a sizable jump in compensation and responsibilities when she joined ASC. In the years since, she would have received superior performance reviews, significant pay increases, and maximum bonuses. Guenther's methods and motives were obvious. He and Delaney had been willing to pay top dollar for continued complicity. Easy enough for them, it wasn't their money.

After his anointment as the next CEO, Wilson Delaney had convinced the board of directors that ASC should centralize a multitude of core functions, including most every area of finance. Previously, corporate finance had consisted only of the CFO, the controller, and a relatively small staff of accountants. For everything else, the CFO would have relied upon senior financial officers that were integrated among the various service lines out in the field. Under the restructuring, the only senior position T. Albert Guenther didn't need to fill immediately would have been Howard Mosner's.

With acquisitions, tax, and treasury, he'd been handed a blank slate. Guenther hadn't even considered the transfer of experienced professionals from inside ASC's operating companies, nor apparently did he attempt to recruit outside candidates with more proven track records. Instead he promptly lavished huge sums of money on three individuals he'd met a few years earlier. Each was an up-and-comer with appropriate expertise in their respective subject areas. But each also would have been too junior to challenge Guenther, and too grateful for the huge jump in title and compensation to feel any such compulsion. Together, Guenther and his Wire Rims proceeded to hire dozens and dozens of more junior associates to build out their staffs—again, not bothering to consider anyone from inside the organization, individuals who might carry the institutional knowledge to raise unwanted questions.

After biding time for two years, presumably for outward appearances, Guenther finally had gotten around to dealing with Howard Mosner. Guenther was so terminally unimaginative that he went back to the same well—the connections he'd made at that New Jersey seminar in 2003. With the recruitment of Kirsten Woodrow to become his controller, the last piece of a master plan had fallen into place. Through her awkward reluctance to answer my questions, and the sullen expression when she finally did, she as much as admitted the entire arrangement. Then the pained exhortation … *"go ahead with whatever you have to do."* Why would she have been that forthcoming? Why hadn't she obeyed her boss and simply stonewalled me?

Each question exploded into dozens more. Why would a person of Kirsten's character and talent have affiliated with someone like T. Albert Guenther? Could she possibly have known she would be expected to perpetrate felonies … that she'd be risking jail time? If she were to be caught and prosecuted, what did she think would happen to Danny? He meant everything to her … how could she take such a horrific chance?

She'd known for weeks that I was nosing into places that Delaney and Guenther didn't want me to go, yet she chose not to avoid me. She even had confided what Guenther was saying and doing behind closed doors as it related to my efforts. Why had she been willing to share these details with me? With so much at stake, why would she have allowed me into her personal life at all? Into Danny's? How could she have allowed me to fall so deeply in love with her?

As I tried to grasp the complexities, only one thing remained certain— my feelings for Kirsten. I knew there would be an explanation for her actions. There had to be. My sole concern was her well-being.

Chapter Twelve

I hadn't anticipated that the phone call might wake her up. I looked at the digital clock over on the desk in my hotel room—1:48. I'd lost track of the time. I wasn't sure how many hours I'd sat staring into the darkness of Lake Michigan, or how long I'd walked the sidewalk that traced the shoreline. It was like I'd blanked out the world around me.

After emptying my pockets of the unopened liquor bottles, I'd taken a lengthy shower to warm up before sprawling onto the couch with my eyes riveted to the ceiling. Staring into nothingness seemed to have become a routine in recent weeks. Then suddenly, I'd sat bolt upright, feeling this urgent need to hear her voice. With the events of the day, I realized it was more critical than ever that I get something hugely important off my chest. Even after being awakened in the middle of the night, Kirsten Woodrow sounded warm and caring when she heard my voice.

"It's late … but I'm glad you called, Milo. I stopped by to see you this afternoon, but you'd already left the office. I wanted to call your hotel, but thought maybe you wouldn't want to talk to me."

"Hardly. The only thing I've done since lunchtime is think about you. Kirsten, this may not be what you want to hear right now, but I have to tell you that I've fallen in love with you."

There was a slight pause before she responded. "I must say, Milo, that wasn't exactly the reaction I would have expected following our conversation at the restaurant today."

"My timing kind of stinks, doesn't it?"

"Just the opposite. I can't think of a time in my life when I so desperately needed to hear those very words. I know we've only been dating, or whatever it is we've been doing, for a few short weeks … but I feel the same way. But I'm so ashamed of past decisions I've made and how I must look to you."

"Kirsten, you still look like the most extraordinary person I've ever known."

"You're going to make me cry if you're not careful."

"No way. I'm that guy who makes you laugh … remember?"

"Good luck on that, mister. What are we going to do, Milo?"

"Let's not get into any of that tonight … we can worry about those things later. This call is for two purposes only. First, I wanted to sweep you off your feet by professing my undying love … which is what I just did, I hope. Second, I wanted to ask you to relay a message to Danny."

"What could you possibly want me to tell Danny?"

"Tell him that he'd better clear out some room on the shelf of his closet, because the silly guy who keeps bringing him all those hats is going to be stopping by a lot more often."

"Okay, I'm not all the way to laughing … but you've made me smile. I love you, Milo Peters."

Next thing I knew, I was listening to screechy tone blasts that signaled my phone was off the hook. I think she ended the call, but maybe I simply had passed out from shock with the receiver still in my hand. I'm not sure. I just kept hearing those words over and over. *"I love you, Milo Peters."*

I darted into the bedroom and grabbed my watch. I needed a second hand. Then I did my best to replicate the way she'd said them. As close as I could measure, Kirsten had uttered those remarkable words in slightly more than two seconds. In slightly more than two seconds, Kirsten Woodrow had replaced gray skies and crashing blocks of ice with singing birds and kids running through sprinklers. *"I love you, Milo Peters."* In slightly more than two seconds, she had taken this dire and dreadful day and turned it into the best one of an entire lifetime.

"Thanks for update. Rumors abound that one of the little pigs likes to eat from both sides of trough. You may want to check out. Maybe Big Bad Wolf prowls in unusual places."

I typed in the e-mail address for FriendInHighPlace and hit the send button. I figured that little missive might stir some interesting dialogue between Delaney, Guenther, and the Wire Rims. Okay, maybe the rumors weren't abounding, but over the years I'd heard plenty of people speculate on Frederick Schumacher's alternative lifestyles. In truth, I couldn't care less about his sexual preferences—whatever floated Schumacher's boat away from the office, or anyone else's, was of no concern to me. Besides, I now knew Guenther's original connection to the Wire Rims. My electrically charged e-mail was both inaccurate and insensitive. Nonetheless, my privacy was being invaded and I couldn't resist having some fun with these boys.

Though Luke had enjoyed playful pranks for as long as I'd known him, he wasn't likely to engage in any such guy games while performing his official government duties. I wouldn't have dared suggest it to him. In all likelihood he would have instructed me not to take such a frivolous risk. No, the e-mail ruse had been mine and mine alone. However, I'd conceived the electronic exchanges for more than their amusement value; I hoped they might provoke a misstep or two from one of my secret stalkers. Creating an outside e-mail address was simple enough. Sure, some techie might have been able to trace back through the Internet and uncover that I'd become my own "friend in a high place," but I figured Delaney, Guenther, or the Wire Rims wouldn't want to involve another person to check it out.

The preceding Sunday night, I'd gone to an Internet café and sent that first message to my office e-mail address. "Looking into past connections between Three Little Pigs and Big Bad Wolf. We should have something soon." By late Tuesday afternoon, I figured I shouldn't let any more time pass before responding. Hence, the cryptic and suggestive message about young Mr. Schumacher's private life. I felt rather clever.

Of course, by late Tuesday afternoon, I was feeling downright terrific about everything.

⌒⁂⌒

Following our landmark phone conversation in the middle of the night, I'd been eager to pay a visit to Kirsten's office on Tuesday morning. Despite the seriousness of other looming issues, we couldn't contain our giddiness. There would be ample time to deal with more complicated realities later … right now, there were other pressing considerations. I asked Kirsten if she was free for lunch, and she asked if I had a place in mind. We both smiled. I told her that I'd become partial to the room service menu at my hotel and then we smiled some more.

During the early morning hours, we'd expressed our love to one another for the first time; the appropriate next step was obvious. We needed some shared activity that might consummate those declarations. Conveniently enough, the two of us had reached the same conclusion on what that activity might be.

I have to be honest … we never got around to looking at the room service menu. All I wanted to look at was her. I hadn't known that a woman could be so uninhibited and giving. I was even more amazed that I could be. I'd previously had no reason to give much thought to the distinctions between lust and romance … between sensual pleasure and emotional fulfillment. But now I knew what happened when all those experiential forces were unleashed at the same time and got all wrapped up together. For me, it was like someone had finally taken off the training wheels. When we were done the first time, I wanted to applaud. After the second, I wanted to ask Kirsten to stand up and take a bow. Ultimately I decided neither reaction was the most suitable punctuation to our passionate lovemaking. But as we walked back to the office, I couldn't resist a final temptation. After all, I was still a male … irreverence won out.

"Best nooner I've ever had. Can you tell me your name again?"

I think the look of anger was faked, but the slug to my arm was most definitely real.

"Okay, bad joke … I'm sorry … and actually, Kirsten, I have a confession to make. I may be forty-four years old, but you're my first official nooner. Leave it to me to finally sneak away to a hotel room in the middle of a workday for the sole purpose of making love, and do so with the woman I actually do love."

Continuing to walk with her eyes straight ahead, she seized the opportunity. "I can't tell you how glad I am to hear that, Milo … believe me." She let that hang for a moment before adding her own special punctuation. "Maybe with some experience, you'll get better."

I assumed she was kidding. Paybacks are hell.

⁓⁓⁓

The other subject on our minds only could be avoided for so long. Before leaving work on Tuesday, we made a date for dinner on Wednesday. No restaurant, no hotel room … her house. With Danny around we wouldn't be tempted to pursue more preferable diversions. Whatever wrongful acts to which Kirsten had been a party since joining ASC, we needed to get them out in the open and deal with them together.

The dinner menu was my responsibility, so I loaded up on Thai food from a nearby restaurant. Upon arriving I told Kirsten to busy herself elsewhere because Danny and I would handle the preparations. Hearing my pronouncement, his face lit up and he took off toward the kitchen. After I emptied the various cartons of food onto serving plates, Danny was in charge of nuking them to perfection. I'd made sure he was properly attired by bringing him an enormous chef's hat. He looked like the Pillsbury Doughboy as he wheeled around the kitchen.

When we finally called for his mother to join us in the dining room, she was measurably impressed … at least that's how I interpreted her reaction. It was hard to say for sure because she was sort of speechless. The room was candlelit and the table was set for six. We had taken the liberty of pulling out her formal china. There were three seats for us, of course. The other chairs were occupied by life-size cardboard cutouts of Barack Obama, the Queen of England, and Bart Simpson. I'd snuck around and placed our celebrity guests and other props by the backdoor when I arrived.

We met her at the entryway from the kitchen, both Danny and I clad in blue blazers with crimson ascots. "Kirsten, I hope you don't mind that we invited a few friends to join us for dinner. Danny prefers a guest list with eclectic interests and personalities, and I concur … it makes conversation so much more stimulating. Don't you agree?"

She was touched but tried to pretend otherwise. "I couldn't understand how you guys could make such a racket by merely heating up a dinner, but I think I get the picture now. In the future, I see that I'll need to be more careful about leaving the two of you alone for very long."

Her eyes went back and forth between Danny and me, as though unable to decide which of us was the most mischievous. If forced to declare, I had a pretty good idea how she'd lean. As we escorted her to her place at the head of the table, she allowed a smile to escape, and finally a laugh.

Based on the amount of laughter during the rest of dinner, it was hard to imagine that the crystal goblets were filled only with ginger ale. I hadn't brought wine or even beer, thinking ahead to the serious discussions that needed to follow. Plus, in recent weeks my drinking had slowed dramatically. I was focusing a great deal more on people and times I wanted to remember, rather than behaviors I wanted to forget.

With the reflection of flickering candles in her eyes, Kirsten became even more irresistible when she laughed. When I looked over at Danny, I saw the same gleam. In fact I saw the same dark hair, the same dark eyes, the same smile, and the same inherent goodness. For the duration of that meal we were the only three people on earth. Nothing else mattered but the contentment of each other's company. It was the way an evening at home should feel. It was the way life should feel.

Following dinner, Kirsten took Danny upstairs to help him get ready for bed. Once I'd handled the dishes and returned the kitchen to relative normalcy, I joined them in his room. He hardly could wait to show me a downloaded video on South American ants and another on brown recluse spiders. I had a funny feeling that my advantage with insect trivia was history. There were at least a dozen more downloads he wanted to play for me, but his mom reminded him that it was bedtime. She kissed him goodnight and disappeared … I think because she wanted Danny and me to have some guy time alone. I watched as he pulled himself out of his wheelchair and slid into bed. Danny then asked me to tuck him in.

"Mr. Peters, I have something I want to say to you."

"Go ahead … I'm interested in hearing anything you have to say."

"I think you're a really nice man and I like it when you come to visit us."

My voice went a little shaky. "Danny, I think you're a terrific kid and I love coming to see you and your mother. Good night, sport."

"I wasn't done, Mr. Peters."

"What else did you want to say to me?"

"Thank you … thank you for making my mom so happy. She needs that. Sometimes she gets sad and it's hard for me to keep her happy all by myself."

Now I couldn't talk at all. The best I could do was bend down and kiss Danny on the forehead. When I joined Kirsten in the living room my eyes were still watery, which she couldn't help but notice.

"Is anything wrong, Milo?"

"Not a thing in the world … at least when I'm with that kid of yours."

Now her eyes welled up. Which, of course, meant I had to wrap my arms around her in a tender, comforting hug. Which, of course, meant we could feel each other's warmth. Which, of course, meant we wanted to kiss. Which, of course, we did. Which, of course, kindled even stronger desires. But then I remembered there were other things we needed to talk about.

Breaking from that embrace may have been the most difficult physical act I'd ever performed.

We lit a fire in the den and took our position in the big leather chair, waiting for flames to light up the room. I sat silently. It was Kirsten's story to tell and it wasn't one she could jump right into. After a few minutes she folded the fingers from one of her hands between the fingers of one of mine. Then she began.

"Milo, you remember I told you about the seminar in 2003, where I first met T. Albert, plus Glickman, Schumacher, and McCaffrey? I think I should start there."

I nodded, hoping my expression conveyed that no matter what she might tell me, I would be there for her. She began what would be a long, difficult admission.

"Close to a hundred of our firm's clients attended. All of our U.S. offices had been required to send midlevel associates to help with the hosting duties and I was one of the representatives from Chicago. We each were given a list of guests to shepherd during the ten days we spent in New Jersey. We were supposed to see to it that our assigned guests were scheduled for sessions most relevant to their areas of expertise and that they received the required reading materials. Plus, we made sure all their questions were answered and that any meal or accommodation arrangements were tended to properly. T. Albert Guenther was one of the guests on my list ... as was Robert McCaffrey. Glickman and Schumacher were assigned to other associates.

"From the very beginning, Guenther stuck out as an oddball. We put together dinners and evening activities for different combinations of people so that our clients could get to know one another ... and simply to make their time away from home more enjoyable. T. Albert never showed any interest in joining the events we organized. He preferred to stay off on his own. Even in the meeting sessions, he would sit at the back of the presentation rooms by himself. For the sessions he attended, he would be one of the first to arrive and the last to leave. He'd remain in his seat and watch as other people paraded in and out in front of him. During the actual presentations, he spent as much time studying others in the audience as he did listening to the speakers.

"But by the time we were into the second week of the seminar, he somehow had connected with McCaffrey, Glickman, and Schumacher. The four of them were doing their own thing each night for dinner ... and most of the time, sitting off by themselves at the general breakfasts and lunches held in the conference center. During that second week, T. Albert kept inviting me to join them. Since he and McCaffrey were assigned to me, I finally felt obliged … so I took the four of them out to a nice restaurant on the very last night. I tried my best to make the dinner pleasant, but to be honest, the whole evening was strange. There were these horribly awkward moments when the four of them would stare at me and then look back and forth at each other. I felt like a piece of meat. I can't tell you how glad I was when the check finally came. Fortunately, none of them worked at client companies in my work group back in Chicago, so by the time I returned to the office, I'd pushed them out of my mind."

Kirsten stopped and watched the fire in silence, as if to mark the end of the first chapter of her story. I had no idea how many chapters were still to come, but I was certain she wanted them all told. Our hands were still interlocked, so when she was ready to begin again, she gave my hand a light squeeze and continued.

"Every month or two after that, T. Albert would find a reason to contact me. Sometimes it was a phone call with an accounting question … even though I wasn't on the team assigned to American Service Companies. Sometimes he would send me a copy of an article he found interesting and write a short note on it. Sometimes he simply e-mailed me to ask how I was doing. He obviously wanted to remain connected, but I had no idea why. As much as I wanted to ignore his various attempts, I couldn't. He was an important client of the firm, so I tried to find ways of responding that were polite and respectful without being encouraging. My biggest fear was that he was looking for some sort of social or extramarital relationship.

"When I first met T. Albert at the seminar, my marriage may not have been healthy, but Sean and I hadn't reached the officially troubled stage. We still were pretending that nothing was wrong. Danny was less than a year old and we were able to mask our growing problems behind the excitement of becoming new parents."

For the first time I felt an irrepressible impulse to interrupt her. "Darn it … my bad, Kirsten. I'd been meaning to ask you to keep your ex-husband's name a secret from me. It was so much easier to picture the guy as an ax-murderer when you only referred to him as your 'ex-husband.' But now that I know he had an actual name, I also have to accept the probability that he possessed some honest-to-goodness positive qualities … that he didn't hypnotize or ransom you into marriage. Worse yet, I've always liked the name Sean. Tell me, at least, that his middle name was Attila or Rasputin."

She gave me one of those looks that only women can give, because only men can evoke them. "His middle name is Griffin. Can I go on, funny guy?"

I shrugged an apology. "Sure … but I can't promise I won't misbehave again." Then a follow-up urge kicked in. "Sean Griffin Woodrow … sounds kind of affected to me. I bet he was a bed-wetter as a kid."

I got another of those looks before she picked up from where she'd left off. "Anyway, Milo, about four months after the seminar, Sean and I decided on a trial separation. I didn't try to keep it a secret at the office and one of my associates assigned to the ASC account must have told 'I'. Albert, because in one of his e-mails he referenced my marital problems. He wanted me to know that I could count on him to be there for me in the future if I needed his help. And I have to tell you, that really spooked me … I didn't even consider him a friend, let alone someone I might turn to.

"Two months later came Danny's accident. For the next year, my whole world felt like it was imploding. At first the doctors weren't sure Danny would live; then he was in traction for those many, many months. Sean and I tried to patch our marriage back together, but the stress made things even worse. We argued all the time over every little issue. He wanted to sue the babysitter, the driver of the car that hit them, and the company that manufactured the car seat. He spent all of his time pursuing lawsuits and I spent all of mine with Danny and the doctors, believing there would be some miracle and he'd be able to walk again.

"Almost a year after the accident, Sean had come up empty on the legal side and I'd come up empty on medical miracles. Our insurance covered the hospital bills, but the attorneys had told Sean to forget about other restitution. The babysitter had run a four-way stop when our car was broadsided. It was her fault. She'd been in a hurry and not fastened the car seat properly, so the manufacturer was in the clear. And the babysitter herself had no assets or liability insurance to go after. She was driving our car, covered by our insurance. We couldn't sue ourselves. There was no other recourse, which made Sean incredibly bitter. He was short with everyone and lost his focus for most things. He became careless at work and some of his deals started going poorly. First, the big bonuses disappeared … while we still were married. After we were divorced, he lost his job.

"Thankfully, the accounting firm provided me a great deal of latitude to tend to Danny's medical situation after the accident, then his special care needs, and eventually the details of my divorce. I had a secure position and income, but I certainly had lost any career momentum. I think I was able to give them firm fair return on my salary, but I definitely moved to the back of the line when it came to advancement opportunities. At the time I didn't care … my number one priority was Danny.

"Over the course of the next two or three years, I ran out of money. What little I'd received from Sean was gone, and he'd moved on to a carefree lifestyle in the islands. My attorneys said I would run up an enormous legal bill by going after whatever resources he still might have … and even if successful, we couldn't be sure there'd be enough to cover the legal costs. So I decided to close the door completely on Sean … the same way he'd closed the door on Danny and me. I accepted the fact that Danny and I were on our own from that point forward. It would be up to me to cover the mounting costs."

I interjected a question. "Didn't insurance continue to help with Danny?"

"Only when it was medically related … therapy, doctor appointments, special back and leg braces, new wheelchairs as he progressed in size. But the cost for childcare was up to me … not to mention the sizable mortgage for this townhouse that I now was handling alone. When Sean and I had purchased it, we were two aspiring professionals … we couldn't fathom that money would ever be an issue. But now I didn't even have the money to handle the ramps and other renovations we needed for Danny … I had to take out a home equity loan.

"I was living from paycheck to paycheck and running up my credit cards. I was starting to put more time against my job, but I couldn't imagine how I'd be able to catch back up with my peers in the race to become partners. Finally, I made a decision to downsize our lifestyle and was in the process of putting this place up for sale.

"While all that was going on with me, T. Albert had become CFO of ASC and quickly hired your three friends … your Wire Rims. Meanwhile, he'd continued to reach out to me more persistently. He seemed to be following my personal situation through his sources inside the accounting firm. At one point he even was bold enough to ask if he could help defray some of the costs for Danny's day care. I just kept putting him off as politely as possible. I certainly hadn't realized it, but he was setting me up. Three years after becoming CFO, he finally found the means to get rid of Howard Mosner. He phoned me the day that Mosner resigned and asked if I'd be interested in talking about the position of controller. How could I refuse? I was feeling desperate. I can't tell you how many times since that day I've regretted how eager and willing I was to listen to a man who made my skin crawl."

What Kirsten already had covered was difficult enough, but now she was working her way into the harder parts of her story. I leaned down and kissed her cheek. "Regardless of whatever else you're going to reveal, I'll still be glad you were eager to take his call. Somehow, curling up by a fire like this with Glickman, McCaffrey, or Schumacher doesn't hold much appeal."

"You're insufferable, Milo Peters … lucky for you I was the one girl back in Wyoming who always laughed at the class clowns."

"Lucky for me that none of those witty young cowboys was able to charm you into staying in Wyoming."

"What a sweet thing to say." She pulled my head down and gave me a quick kiss on the lips. "Now don't blow it with one of your wisecracks."

I moved my fingers across my lips in a zipping motion and settled back in the chair so she could resume.

"The whole interview process with ASC was a blur. I came in and talked to T. Albert for a couple of hours; then we went to lunch with Christopher, Frederick, and Robert. That was it. The next day he invited me back to meet with Delaney and a few people from human resources. I left with a firm written offer in hand. When I read it, I was blown away. The base salary alone represented a 60 percent increase over what I'd been making, plus there was a significant sign-on bonus. In one fell swoop all my financial worries were gone if I accepted his offer. It seemed too good to be true, which should have served as fair warning … but I couldn't resist the temptation.

"I let pride overtake me. I would be proving I could do just fine as a single parent. With the bonus opportunities and stock options that went with the job at ASC, Danny and I wouldn't have to worry about money. But I also admit that part of my decision was based on pure bitterness toward Sean and the desire to show him up. I was so caught up on all the upsides, I didn't bother to contemplate the inevitable downsides. If someone with my level of experience was being offered such excessive compensation, there had to be a catch … plus, I'd be working for a man I really couldn't stand. But with the money involved, I convinced myself that I'd probably been too tough on T. Albert … so what if he had a quirky personality? Just like I was able to convince myself that ASC's senior management really thought I was worth that ridiculous amount of money. Talk about greed blinding you from reality. I bought it all … hook, line, and sinker. I couldn't dial the phone fast enough to accept."

"Kirsten, the guy was monitoring your personal situation so that he knew exactly when to approach you. You're only human ... most people would have jumped at the chance you were given, whether they had your financial burdens or not."

"That's part of what makes me feel so horribly guilty, Milo. My financial burdens may have been stressful, but they weren't overwhelming. I was making decent money at the accounting firm. If I'd continued to work hard, I eventually would have made partner there or somewhere else. So what if I had to sell this place and move to an apartment for a few years? But I wanted everything to come instantly and easily ... too easily, as things turned out. Plenty of people run up against tougher challenges than I was facing, yet they work through them without losing their perspective or compromising their character. But I succumbed to all those immediate gratifications and unknowingly prostituted myself to T. Albert Guenther."

"What was he asking you to do?"

"When he made the offer and I accepted it ... nothing appeared unusual. I naively thought he was hiring me to execute the duties of a controller, pure and simple. I felt like I had the background and conviction to ensure that ASC accounted for and reported its results in complete compliance with applicable laws and regulations. That was the controller's job ... and for the first few months, that's exactly what I thought I was doing."

"Then what happened?"

"Well, I joined ASC during the last few weeks of a fiscal year. As you know, after the corporation closes its books and posts the final results for a year, three of us are required to sign off on those results in accordance with the law ... basically attesting to their accuracy and total compliance. After so many irregularities were exposed inside various companies during the years surrounding Enron, the CEO, CFO, and controller of any public corporation now must assume personal liability when they sign year-end statements ... meaning heavy penalties or possibly prison time if they knowingly or even carelessly sign off on numbers that misrepresent a company's actual performance.

"Our fiscal ends on December 31, but it typically takes us until mid-February to pull all our numbers together for the year we've just completed. I'd started in late November and was working with my team to collect and calculate the final operating results from our different business units. At the same time, my team was working with treasury, tax, acquisitions, and the other groups in corporate finance to determine what adjustments needed to be made to operating results based on activities in those respective areas. The folks working for me indicated that some of those groups were behind schedule, but that hadn't been unusual in recent years.

"I tried lighting a fire under Frederick, Christopher, and Robert, but they seemed to ignore me. So I expressed some concerns to T. Albert and he told me not to worry … that everything was well under control. And to be honest, that was my first moment of truth and I failed it. I knew that ultimately I needed to be comfortable with every number and decimal point in the annual results that we were going to post … I should have demanded more transparency into what those other groups were preparing to submit. But I was new and still overwhelmed by the lucrative pay package T. Albert had thrown at me, so I deferred to him without the slightest challenge.

"More weeks passed and still my team wasn't getting the information we needed from the other groups. I was growing more nervous by the day, but T. Albert continued to tell me not to worry … and like a good little lamb, I listened to him. Then literally two days before the deadline for submitting our annual results to the SEC, the adjustments to earnings came pouring in from treasury, tax, and acquisitions. I barely had time to review the top-lines of those submissions, let alone the reams of unexpected assumptions and calculations beneath them.

"I went to T. Albert once more and tried to protest. How could I comfortably sign-off on numbers that I didn't have time to fully comprehend? With so many different service lines and the quantity of acquisitions ASC had done that year, the financials were complicated … and I was too new to fully understand every nuance and complexity without more time. Since day one, I'd trusted others to some degree … but this was pushing well beyond any reasonable limit. Yet once again, T. Albert told me to calm down … not to worry. But then he threw a real curve ball. He informed me that he and Frederick Schumacher had been reviewing all the final submissions in great detail over the prior few weeks and that everything was in good order. I couldn't believe what I was hearing.

"If he and Frederick had received the necessary input, why hadn't they been sharing it with me? I was the controller. Before I could even react, he assured me that they'd been acting in my best interest. Being so new in my position, he didn't want to put undue pressure on me to fully weigh into the close-out of a year that was virtually over when I'd started, so he'd asked Frederick to step in and help. He went on to explain that I should accept the special nature of Frederick Schumacher's role as head of both treasury and financial strategy ... that on occasion Frederick might handle duties that typically would be performed by a controller's office.

"Nothing about Frederick's 'special' role had been mentioned before I accepted the job ... and now I was expected to sign-off on the year's final results based on assurances from him and T. Albert. Questioning their efforts would be tantamount to challenging either the competency or the integrity of my boss ... the man who'd hired me. I was speechless ... and I was trapped ... but T. Albert cleverly offered me an out. He said that if I insisted on adequate time to thoroughly immerse myself in the details submitted by the other corporate finance units, we could apply for an extension with the SEC— which also meant we would have to inform the investment community that ASC would be late in posting its annual results. He was quick to remind me how Wall Street analysts usually viewed such unexpected announcements as a red flag and our stock price was likely to take a hit. He also cautioned me that such a move was hardly the way for me, as the new controller, to earn the confidence of senior management, shareholders, or anyone else concerned with the company.

"I swiftly caved. After only a cursory review of the many critical factors that impacted our final results, I signed the forms. Sure, I can tell you I was misled and misinformed ... nonetheless, I did knowingly prostitute myself. With my most important responsibility as controller, T. Albert Guenther had purchased the complicity he needed."

The conversation had reached a painful stage. I got up to toss a log on the fire, but when I sat back down I pulled another chair close to her. I thought it important that Kirsten and I look directly at each other, eye to eye, as we confronted the realities ahead. I knew we weren't going to be discussing petty mistakes that could be smoothed over with heartfelt admissions and apologies. In the next few minutes, Kirsten would be revealing the role she'd played in punishable felonies. Seeing the anguish in her face was gut-wrenching enough for me. I couldn't imagine what it had been like for her to carry such a burden inside for three years.

"Kirsten, I know you don't want to hear this ... but you can't be too hard on yourself for what you did. The man was your boss ... you were brand-new in the job. He and the CEO were signing the same forms as you ... and doing so willingly. I'm sure you're going to tell me that those first results you signed off on were improper ... but I have to ask, where was our accounting firm? What about Wilson Delaney ... what was he saying and doing? When did you even realize what they'd pulled on you ... why were you unable to blow the whistle then?"

"All good questions, Milo ... questions for which I have embarrassingly poor answers. I'll fill in the pieces as best I can. First off, I didn't learn about the fiscal improprieties at any one point ... but over the course of weeks I came to the conclusion that they'd definitely occurred. As you can imagine, with the way Guenther had handled the whole end-of-the-year reporting, I became very suspicious. On my own, I started digging into every detail behind the various adjustments in our earnings statement, which caused me to go back and look deeper into prior years. A consistent pattern emerged.

"You need to know that T. Albert and the others are very good at what they've been pulling off. They've carefully calibrated their actions and don't take outrageously large chances that might draw attention. As you know, after Wilson Delaney became CEO, ASC ramped up its acquisition activities to double or triple what they'd been previously. I have to believe this increased transaction rate was driven greatly by Guenther. As I told you once before, T. Albert has been very effective at getting Delaney to do what he wants. And first and foremost, T. Albert was looking for more room to play games with purchase accounting.

"At the time of each transaction, ASC creates a number of reserve accounts on its balance sheet. Most corporations will reserve for potential eventualities that tie directly to a new entity that they've purchased, but ASC has been more aggressive than normal. Due to the accelerated pace of acquisitions and related reserves, we rapidly built a war chest of available funds on our books ... and we continue to add to it with every new deal. With each new company purchased, ASC takes current dollars and sets them aside ... reserving them for future expenses that might result from pending lawsuits, uncollected receivables, workers' comp claims, or a whole host of other items tied to the acquired entity. Each item, in its own right, provides a viable reason to reserve funds against future expenses, so future earnings won't be penalized unfairly by the costs left over from doing a deal in prior years. The expense of setting aside this cash to establish the reserves is treated as part of the transaction cost for that specific acquisition. I'm sure you know this, but the investment community looks at these total transaction costs as separate from regular operating costs in a company's earnings statement in that given year. So, in essence, ASC gets a pass from Wall Street on the current expense of setting up reserve accounts.

"When I was with the accounting firm, I counseled clients to take these same actions at the time of an acquisition so future earnings wouldn't be adversely affected by the anticipated one-time costs that resulted from past deals. It's a very standard accounting treatment. But ASC has been taking an unusually aggressive approach ... both in the number of future cost items for which we reserve and the amounts being reserved against each. Then down the road, when it safely can be determined that a previously anticipated expense is unlikely to occur, or that the final costs will be less than originally estimated, the dollars set aside for that specific cost can be reversed or released. And as you know further, when those funds are reversed, they're recognized as an immediate gain in income ... having a positive impact on that current period's earnings.

"ASC has enjoyed an incredible track record of meeting Wall Street's expectations related to earnings ... in fact, a frighteningly good record. One of the key reasons has been our ability to pull funds from these 'cookie jar' reserves in order to meet the forecasts of the investment analysts who follow us. They love us ... as they do any company who consistently meets its earnings forecasts. We just happen to have more of an advantage than most when we go into each period. We may pull only enough out of reserves to affect quarterly earnings by a cent or two per share ... sometimes even a fraction of a cent. But to the investor community, those small differences relative to forecasts are huge. When T. Albert took over as CFO, he knew exactly what it would take to become a hero with Wall Street and immediately went about building a team, an organizational structure, and an earnings strategy that would assure his success."

I was scratching my head. "Kirsten, what you describe sounds brilliant, not illegal."

"It is brilliant. Pushing the limit on reserves and then subsequently reversing them is done all the time. What might be considered as crossing the line is often a pretty gray area, even for government regulators. But intentionally setting aside excessive reserve funds so that ongoing quarterly profits can be systematically managed is not a gray area. It's brazenly illegal ... it's just very difficult to prove. But I happen to know for a fact that T. Albert has been giving very explicit instructions to McCaffrey to push every envelope when it comes to finding reserve opportunities in the acquisitions that he pursues.

"In subsequent years, I learned about other abnormalities ... nothing blatant ... no one tactic used too often. For example, T. Albert enlists Schumacher and Glickman to occasionally go into the computer system and change the dates on customer contracts so that they can move amortized revenues from one period to another in order to smooth out any unusual dips or peaks in sales. Our branches continue to work off of original hard copies of their customer contracts—the electronic versions are kept at corporate, used only for accounting purposes—so local personnel and customers never know the difference.

"To attempt tactics like that, the only hurdle T. Albert might have run up against was Howard Mosner … so he needed a controller whom he could count on to play along, and I fell right in line for him."

"What about our outside auditors, your old accounting firm … where have they been while all this has been going on? Aren't they required to review all of these reserve accounts and independently decide if a client has crossed the line? And shouldn't they have picked up on the shifting revenues?"

"When this situation eventually blows up, I'm sure they'll share some of the culpability because they haven't been as diligent as they should be. But, here again, T. Albert has been very clever in how he played them. When he first took over as CFO, he raised concerns about the partner who headed up the accounting firm's audit team. This guy had worked on the ASC account for many years and T. Albert suggested that a new set of eyes would keep everyone more alert. A smart maneuver … what accounting firm isn't going to respect a client CFO who seems insistent on stronger vigilance? A new partner was assigned shortly thereafter, but several months later T. Albert began expressing concerns about this woman's tenacity. Once the next fiscal year closed out, another partner was put in charge of the client relationship.

"It took three partners, but Guenther finally got the person he wanted in place. This partner, Janine Scott, was a peer of mine at the firm. She's young for a partner and, on the surface at least, very assertive about maintaining her audit team's independence with clients. But privately, she's even more assertive about her own career aspirations and I know she someday hopes to become a CFO for a major public company. Her true loyalty will go to the person or persons most willing to help her. T. Albert figured that out and has played to it, and in return she and her team have been lenient in many of their interpretations.

"But here's another example of Guenther's shrewdness. A number of times he has pushed blatantly beyond current accounting standards in depreciating assets, applying amortization schedules, or other accounting treatments … so far beyond that even Janine Scott has been forced to cry foul and contradict her favorite client's judgment. But in each of these instances, Guenther has insisted that she take the issues in question back to the accounting firm and obtain independent rulings from one of the senior oversight committees that any public accounting firm keeps in place. Each time, the rulings have gone against ASC. The fact that the accounting firm regularly has opposed ASC allows the firm's senior leadership to feel diligent independence has been maintained. A terrific trade-off for Guenther … a couple of times a year he pushes for rulings that he doesn't expect to win, but in so doing, skirts by with less rigid interpretations on all the reserves that ASC sets up when it does acquisitions. Only a financial executive who has had the opportunity to watch and work closely with accounting firms over a sustained period of time would be savvy enough to conceive and pull this scheme off. Playing loose with reserve accounts tied to transactions was one of the big things that blew up on Tyco executives, but Guenther has been much more subtle, more incremental with the adjustments that get reflected in our earnings statements.

"As to the revenues that were moved across periods, it normally wouldn't be up to the outside accounting firm to go into the computer system and check the dating on customer contracts. Within ASC, that responsibility lies within internal audit—and not surprisingly, that group reports to Frederick Schumacher. Internal audit couldn't possibly review the millions of contracts in the system; they only do spot checks. And since Frederick would approve the instructions on which businesses to spot check during which periods, he and Christopher are easily able to maneuver around them. T. Albert thought through everything."

For more than twenty years I'd underestimated the ambitions, skill levels, and malevolence of this strange little man. If Guenther's actions were exposed, the value of ASC stock would experience a major setback and punish the many associates across our companies who had put significant amounts of their savings and retirements into the corporate stock plan. Then there was my more immediate concern—the tenuous situation facing Kirsten and Danny. If all this became public, charges most definitely would be brought against her. By repeatedly signing off on financial results that reflected intentional earnings manipulation, she was as guilty of a felony as the slimeball who had taken advantage of her. Complicating matters, my fiduciary responsibility as a corporate officer had now been irrefutably triggered. Knowing that financial improprieties absolutely had occurred inside ASC, I was required to report them to the appropriate authorities. My own ticking clock had just started. I was legally liable if I didn't disclose such information in a timely manner. As I sorted through the complications, I felt a building anger. My natural tendency was to point my anger in one direction.

"Kirsten, what role did Wilson Delaney play in this whole mess?"

"None, other than his willingness to trust T. Albert to do the right things as CFO. Guenther has been masterful with Delaney and the board of directors. He covers them off very matter-of-factly regarding the purchase accounting treatments we use, as well as the times that he has tried to be aggressive with the accounting firm and lost. To them he looks like a guy who pushes hard for results, but is kept in check by the outside auditors ... exactly what a board should want out of their CFO."

"So Delaney is blameless?"

"In reality, I would have to say that's the case. However in today's political climate, the SEC and other officials might rule otherwise. They're clamping down pretty hard on CEOs and boards for not asking enough of the right questions."

"I guess I carry too much baggage with Wilson. Ever since I started having suspicions about ASC's financials, I've wanted to believe that he was the mastermind behind some devious plan."

"Sorry to disappoint you, Milo ... it wasn't him. When did you first become suspicious?"

"It's hard to say exactly. But in recent years, I've often been surprised by how we keep hitting our earnings forecasts. I sit through one business review after another where we dwell on unanticipated revenue shortfalls or windfalls in some of our service lines ... or unexpected expenses or savings that hit our P&Ls ... but then quarter after quarter, we miraculously nail the exact earnings number that analysts have forecasted. Since I've long believed that Wilson Delaney had some kind of monopoly on unscrupulous behavior, I began to suspect that funny games were being played up here at headquarters."

"So I guess you were paying more attention in all those meetings than you let on, mister?"

All I could do was shrug. I didn't want to tell Kirsten about Luke. I wasn't even sure myself how I was going to deal with the commitments I'd made to him. Obviously, the authorities didn't have the hard evidence they needed to come down on ASC. That's why they'd needed me in the first place. To the outside authorities, the lines crossed by T. Albert Guenther and his minions would appear hazy. Unless it could be proven that ASC's earnings were intentionally manipulated, a case might be difficult to prosecute. What if I simply kept my mouth shut?

"Kirsten, believe me, I don't want to make you uncomfortable ... but once it became clear to you what Guenther was up to, why didn't you go to Delaney or the authorities?"

Through most of the conversation her mood and countenance had been somber, now there was sorrow.

"How I wish I could offer some explanation that justified my actions. I can't. After those first few months ... after I'd dug into the accounting treatments and recognized our excessive dependence on reserve accounts, I went to Guenther with my concerns. He told me I was wrong ... that in his and the judgment of the other senior VPs, everything was completely kosher ... that I needed to remember I wasn't part of an independent accounting firm any longer ... I should be less rigid in interpreting regulations that aren't as black and white as 'the outside purists' liked to pretend.

"Again, like a cowering lamb, still enthralled with my new position and salary, I backed down and went away. But it kept eating at me. Halfway through the next fiscal year, I went to Guenther again and raised the same issues, but this time, I told him I wanted to challenge the accounting firm to take a harder look and provide an independent reading on the whole body of reserves. He hit the roof. He laid into me about the chance he'd taken by putting me into such a senior position. He warned me that if I wanted to raise questions about my own corporate team through an independent auditor, I would be undermining my credibility and reputation. He reminded me of the many eager, young financial people who had ruined their careers by being so reckless. So once again I caved.

"As months passed, the signs became more evident. Eventually, Guenther and the others started talking openly in front of me about what they were doing ... and that's when I became aware of the other manipulations like the changed dates on contracts ... things to which I didn't have exposure because I hadn't been given the full latitude that's normally afforded a corporate controller. I was caught in between. If I went forward now, I'd be admitting that I'd signed off on that initial earnings statement without doing my due diligence ... and further, I'd been privy to continued irregularities for many months without being more proactive or exercising my sworn duty to take formal action ... and finally that I'd been irresponsible from the beginning by accepting a controller's position in which many of the expected responsibilities were delegated to Frederick Schumacher and others. The truth was I still should have done what was right ... it might have been embarrassing, but I probably would have gotten off with a slap on the wrist. But that would have been enough to derail my career for some period of time.

"So I succumbed to pride and ego. I was making enough money so that Danny and I didn't need to worry. I was proving I could go it alone … I was thumbing my nose at Sean. I didn't want to give any of that up. I didn't want to admit that I'd been manipulated into taking a job that was over my head … that I'd made so many rookie mistakes … that I'd yielded to the repeated bullying of my boss. The whole situation just snowballed … and three years later, I've managed to completely disgrace myself. For three years I've worried about what will happen to Danny if all this is discovered. Meanwhile I've continued to play along by keeping my mouth shut. Last year, I threatened Guenther that I was going to inform Delaney and the board, that I planned to submit my resignation. He told me to go ahead. Then he laughed at me … he knew my weaknesses better than I did."

I got up from my chair and slid back into the leather one with Kirsten. She nestled into my arms, resting her head against my chest. I'd managed to live my entire adult life without feeling truly responsible for anyone other than myself. Until that night.

Chapter Thirteen

Life moved in slow motion over the next two days. I tried tending to my actual job responsibilities, but focus was impossible and I fell further and further behind on matters that no doubt required my attention. I figured they all could wait. Chances were fifty-fifty I might be throwing the whole lousy corporation into a tailspin anyway. On Saturday morning I needed to tell Luke something, but I must have misplaced my ethical compass. Whatever that right answer might be, it kept eluding me.

I was completely aware of the legal obligation involved. The choice was black and white, no gray whatsoever. As a corporate officer, I was duty-bound to come forward. Kirsten had as much as urged me that day on the elevator ... *"Go ahead with whatever you have to do."* If I chose to sit on the knowledge that ASC senior officers were colluding to manage corporate earnings, I'd be complicit. I could end up standing in front of a judge alongside Guenther and the Wire Rims. What a grand thought.

The moral obligations were more complicated. On one hand, there was the issue of my integrity, the character I'd hoped to rebuild brick by brick. Here was my biggest test. Once and for all, I could distance myself from a corporation where I'd willfully wallowed in political games and underhanded business practices for more than twenty years, and from a CEO who had fostered such a corrosive culture. Plus, there was Luke, the most loyal of friends. For reasons I couldn't conceive, he'd always stood by me. Maybe, for once, I might live up to his expectations.

Then on the other hand, there was Kirsten—the damage to her reputation ... possible jail time ... Danny's dependence on her ... my desire to be with her.

If I wasn't forthcoming with the information I now had about Guenther and his cronies, Luke and his anonymous government agency might have difficulty bringing charges against American Service Companies. Thinking back, I realized that Luke had been coy. He'd wanted me to believe that his team had accumulated significant evidence of wrongdoing within ASC, yet he had shared nothing more than vagaries. The government wanted names and specific individuals they could prosecute. Understanding what Guenther and his senior VPs had been pulling off, I recognized how hard it might be to prove they'd acted criminally. As for changing the dates on customer contracts … they would deny having had anything to do with it. ASC might be fined, but Guenther and the Wire Rims could evade individual prosecution.

The bigger case would be the accounting reserves and that would come down to demonstrating intent. Had the senior financial officers of ASC purposely set out to manage or manipulate earnings, or had they merely taken an unusually aggressive approach with purchase accounting? The first was a felony; the latter fell into a hazy category that might cause the government to impose sanctions, but wouldn't be prosecutable. Intent wasn't going to be uncovered by a bunch of federal agents crawling all over spreadsheets and financial statements. Intent only could be established through some type of informant, an inside source.

My lifelong best friend had been playing me … in his own way, guilting me into donning a white hat so that I might finally feel good about myself. But if I gave him what he needed, I'd be incriminating the woman I loved … the woman who was giving me new hopes for the future. And amazingly, I cared more about that woman than I did myself. To say the least, my life wasn't short on ironies of late.

I'd traveled the lower trails for more than two decades. During the months that preceded my move to Chicago, I had convinced myself I could find the high road once I got back onto home turf. Subconsciously, I doubt I'd really believed it. Those positive changes I'd sought to make in my life forever had been around one corner or another. Yet somehow, I never got around to making them. Sure, back in Chicago I might try a little harder because of some positive memories and associations, but my overall pattern was deeply engrained. Year after misspent year, I'd focused on putting one thing above all else. Me.

It had been convenient for me to pretend that I could become more invested in others, but really trying meant dropping the veil of smugness. Really caring about others would open me up to unwanted vulnerability. Caring about people meant putting my genuine feelings out there in the middle of the action, where weaknesses were exposed and wounds potentially hurt more. Now, finally I understood that taking that chance was an enormous part of the emotional fulfillment. With Kirsten I'd learned that such wide open exposure was what made a personal relationship more meaningful, more exhilarating. No wonder the real stars in a circus prefer working without a net.

Not since college days had I been able to let down my guard with people in my life. Even with family and longtime friends I'd erected barriers. Lord knows, I'd put plenty of walls into what once had been an uncomplicated relationship with Carly. With any woman since, I hadn't come close to achieving intimacy. But something about Kirsten had made things different. I was able to take that leap of faith with her. When I was around Kirsten and Danny, I felt like I could unfurl my true self from its lengthy confinement. I could be exactly who I was without worrying about the consequences.

Granted, Kirsten was sexy and gorgeous in every sense of the words. But I'd known and dated other attractive women. Physical desirability wasn't the reason I now was willing to drop all my carefully crafted facades. No, there was a genuineness about Kirsten Woodrow that had pierced through the inertia and the uncertainties. She wasn't perfect and didn't pretend to be. And now she had bared her soul to me ... her innermost regrets, her precarious legal situation. There could be no deeper covenant to our intimacy. How could I possibly do anything that would negatively impact her or Danny?

Returning to Chicago, I'd hoped to find the resolve to start living up to the moral standards of the people I most revered—my father, my uncles, Luke, the icons of my youth. At the same time, I had hoped to find a balance to my self-centeredness, to learn what it might be like to put the interests of others ahead of my own. In a few short months, events had converged to offer me this defining opportunity to do both. Unfortunately, I was forced to choose one or the other. O. Henry himself would have been hard-pressed to conceive such perfect irony.

⌒⁊⌒

Edna must have sensed that Kirsten and I were struggling with some sort of complexity, because on Friday morning she showed an overt interest in our activities for the coming weekend—very uncharacteristic for the Queen of Stoicism. I think she wanted to make sure that we remembered to allot proper attention to Danny.

"Mr. Peters, have you made plans for this weekend? Daniel so looks forward to the time the three of you spend together."

"No, Edna, we haven't. Do you have any ideas?"

"I should think that one of the museums might prove appropriate. Both of the Woodrows also enjoy taking in an action film from time to time. Or, of course, if you thought that Daniel could benefit from an opportunity to experience more traditional male interaction, a hockey game is a potential consideration. The Blackhawks have an afternoon game tomorrow and I believe I might be able to locate three tickets if you're interested."

She wasn't offering up possibilities. The answer to her question had been in the back of the book. I would have bet even money that she already had the tickets locked in her desk drawer ... and they couldn't have been easy to get. The regular season was winding down and the Blackhawks were making a run for home ice advantage in the play-offs.

"Edna, the hockey game sounds perfect ... but why don't you come with us?"

She didn't even hesitate with her response. "Thank you, but no."

"You don't like hockey?"

"Love hockey, abhor the United Center. I haven't attended a game since they tore down the old Chicago Stadium. The crowds used to make the rafters shake ... but with all those fancy skyboxes and club levels, the fans aren't the same. Everyone's too worried about mussing up their hair or spilling beer on their expensive shoes."

End of conversation. I'd wait for a demolition derby or monster truck show to hit town and see if she might care to join us on a future outing. Leave it to Edna. I'd been so preoccupied wrestling with my conscience that I'd lost sight of Danny's expectations. A seven-year-old boy had no idea about the complications caused by adult greed and pride. He simply knew that his mother and the new man in her life were making each other happy, and that he was an integral part of this happiness. Nothing should be more important than preserving the joy and security he was experiencing from our three-way interaction. Especially now, with so many unsettling possibilities looming. There was no reason his well-being should suffer ... in fact, there was every reason it mustn't. Yeah, leave it to Edna.

Friday evening, Kirsten and I left the office together. We weren't broadcasting our relationship, but we no longer were trying to hide it either. Our snuggly little blip would have hit Guenther's radar screen, and I assumed that he was none too pleased by this new development. Kirsten was being excluded from some of the closed-door sessions he called with his senior staff, and frankly, she was relieved not to be part of them. Like me, she was ready to move on from American Service Companies. The only question was whether the next stops in our journeys might involve uniforms and bars on the windows.

We headed straight to her house. Early March had coughed up one of those teasers. The temperature had shot into the sixties, suggesting that Chicago might have an actual spring for a change, instead of the two-month drabness that usually connects winter survival and summer street festivals. Our plans for Friday evening consisted of burgers on the grill and a walk to get ice cream. Danny came barreling toward the door as soon as we arrived. He stopped briefly next to Kirsten so she could bend down and kiss his cheek.

"Hi, Mom."

Then he quickly wheeled over to me.

"Mr. Peters, is it true? Is it true? Are we really going to see the Blackhawks tomorrow?"

Edna obviously had been texting again.

"Yes, Danny, we are. Assuming, of course, that you want to go."

"You bet I want to go. I've been hoping all week that you'd choose the hockey game."

I guess I should have been grateful that Edna had allowed me to participate in the decision at all. I was curious as to how many weeks in advance she and Danny might now be working.

"Well, Danny, it came down to either the hockey game or a special demonstration at one of the department stores … tips to more memorable gift wrapping, I think it was."

His face momentarily registered a combination of disgust and uncertainty, but then he broke into a smile. "You're teasing me again, aren't you, Mr. Peters?"

"Maybe … but I need to remember to return all that ribbon I bought."

The collective laughter was much heartier than this inane little banter should have evoked. Clearly, Kirsten and I needed an outlet from the stressful realities that had moved to center stage in our lives. Time with Danny was exactly what we needed.

On the way back from the ice cream shop, he surprised me with a question. "Hey, Mr. Peters, do you know why bees make a buzzing noise?"

I didn't have a clue. As feared, my singular intellectual advantage was already toast. In another two weeks, the kid would be able to teach college-level entomology. I took a stab at an answer. "Because they don't know how to whistle or sing?"

"No … the buzz is actually the sound of their wings moving up and down more than eleven thousand times per minute. And you know what else? Bees kill more people every year than all the poisonous snakes combined."

I kept my immediate reaction to myself. *Sure, Boy Wonder, go ahead and rub it in … nobody likes a show-off.*

Later that evening, when we were putting Danny to bed, he surprised me with a whole different line of questioning. "Mr. Peters, are you going to marry my mom?"

But I think Kirsten was even more surprised than I was. "Danny!"

I directed my first comment her way. "It's okay … in fact, it's only appropriate that a responsible son should inquire about the intentions of a new man in his mother's life."

Then I looked at Danny. "Your mom and I have been dating for only a short time, so I don't think either of us is ready for that question. But I can tell you that any man would be most fortunate to have the two of you permanently in his life."

The answer seemed to satisfy him. It seemed to satisfy all of us. Downstairs, Kirsten and I opened a bottle of wine and planted ourselves by the fireplace. We'd only seen each other for brief moments since our lengthy discussion in this same spot on Wednesday night, so it seemed natural to pick right up on that conversation.

I'd had a few days to live with the various facets of T. Albert Guenther's illicit scheme. Strangely, I found myself marveling over what the guy had conceived and orchestrated. He'd demonstrated a remarkable aptitude for deception and misdirection—in fact, his often-ridiculed image throughout the corporation had provided a brilliant cover. I, among many, wouldn't have thought that Guenther's vision stretched beyond next month's budget forecast. His introverted personality and fastidious personal habits suggested a strong aversion to risks of any kind. Yet, here he was, living on a thin line between prestige and prison. For how many years had he been plotting and laying the groundwork?

Guenther had convinced Wilson Delaney of the business advantages to completely centralizing ASC's financial functions, which in turn had created great latitude for him to operate with no one watching too closely. He'd eliminated the positions of any persons inside the organization who would have known the right questions to ask.

He likewise had prevailed upon Delaney and the board to grow revenues much more aggressively through acquisitions and in so doing, established the steady flow of transactions he needed to shelter reserves and manage corporate earnings. Prior to being named CFO, he'd already begun identifying the individuals who would become his high-level accomplices—people who on the surface seemed just as unlikely as Guenther to participate in sustained and sophisticated securities fraud. And somehow he had lured each of them to crawl out onto that lonely limb beside him.

No wonder T. Albert had gotten along so famously with Wilson Delaney for all these years—at their core, they were the same. Both wanted success at the highest levels and neither worried about who or what principles needed to be trampled upon to ascend there. But who was I to judge? I'd played by those same rules and been fortunate not to break any laws. If pushed, I might have been willing ... I could never know for sure. In earlier years when my ambition and ego were soaring to new altitudes, the thin air might have made it difficult for me to recognize the boundaries.

I shared these perspectives on Guenther with Kirsten, as well as the doubts about my personal character. She misread my intent.

"Milo, it's nice of you to try and make me feel less corrupted by what I've done, but not very credible. Regardless of how you portray yourself, I can't imagine that you ever were as bad as you're inclined to believe."

"I'm sorry, Kirsten, I wasn't looking to make this about me ... I'm not looking for affirmation. Despite whatever mistakes I might have made in the past, I couldn't be happier than where I am right now."

As soon as those words left my mouth, I couldn't believe that I'd said them. My look must have registered the surprise.

"What's wrong, Milo?"

"That's the second time I've expressed feelings to you that I wasn't sure I was capable of. First, I've told you that I love you ... repeatedly, I might add. Now, I've gone on to acknowledge that I'm content with life. I've spent so many years being discontented that I guess I assumed that disappointment was a permanent state. I hadn't even thought about the fact that I'm actually happy until I blurted it out just now ... and I was right ... I am. You and Danny are a pretty potent combination."

"Emotions go both ways, you know. You've jumped into our lives in a mighty powerful fashion yourself. This house has never felt as full or happy as when you're here with us. You've filled spaces that have been empty for a long time, Milo. Everything's almost perfect … except for this one small matter."

"Yeah, how about we flee the country? I don't care that much about baseball and apple pie … we'd still be able to call our mothers."

"Milo, we can't keep putting it off … I need to turn myself in and admit what's been going on with ASC earnings. If I don't, you're going to get caught up in a whole legal mess of your own."

"Please, don't do anything until I've had a chance to check in with a friend of mine. He might be able to help us."

I'd maintained my confidence with Luke, having referenced neither him nor the government investigation to Kirsten or anyone else. But perhaps he could somehow protect her in exchange for her coming forward. That is, if I chose to disclose what I knew about ASC's manipulated earnings. Part of me was becoming increasingly convinced that we still could skate by due to the subtleties of Guenther's scheme—otherwise, the government would have launched a formal and public investigation by now. Conceivably the government teams had been prodding around for years, looking for an entry point to gather the inside information they needed on ASC. My latest promotion and ties to Luke had dropped one on their doorstep. But now I wondered how much Luke really had been counting on me to do the right thing. My proven pattern had always been to do what was right for me … he more than anyone knew that. But for once I wasn't thinking about me; the issue was Kirsten and Danny. I deplored the very notion of abetting Guenther and his lapdogs through my silence, but the alternative was even more unsettling. I had until the next morning to decide how much I was ready to reveal with Luke.

A few other things had been bugging me. "Kirsten, I understand how T. Albert exploited your personal vulnerabilities to recruit you and get you entangled in this whole mess. How do you think he was he able to convince McCaffrey, Glickman, and Schumacher to participate?"

"Good question. They all had joined ASC well before me, so I can't be sure of the exact way he went about it, but I've been around them long enough to know that those three have their own vulnerabilities. Some time ago, I checked with friends back at the accounting firm, and as it turned out, Guenther asked a lot of questions in advance about the various financial people from other client companies who would be attending the seminar in New Jersey. He obviously was planning to establish connections with individuals he would need and could exploit in the future."

"Let me guess … once upon a time, there were three darling lads secretly separated at birth and put up for adoption. Guenther somehow discovered that the Wire Rims' real parents had bad haircuts and a horrible sense of fashion and he threatened to go public."

She looked at me, waiting for the sophomoric urges to subside. I smiled and shrugged to let her know I'd do my best to control them ... no promises though, considering whom we were discussing. She continued.

"It turns out that Christopher Glickman has had a few marital problems. When he joined ASC, Christopher already was divorced once and his second wife had caught him playing around with a girlfriend. That second divorce proceeding was underway in Pittsburgh. He'd had a child with each wife ... so not only would he be dividing his assets a second time, but he also faced mounting child support payments. As you've probably noticed, Christopher likes to live a little large and he was digging himself quite a hole. He would have been ripe for the lucrative comp package that Guenther was offering.

I held up one finger. "Okay, that's one down."

"Robert McCaffrey had another type of marital issue. His wife comes from big money in Texas and he was doing deals for one of his father-in-law's companies. After eight years, Robert was falling well short of both his wife's and her daddy's expectations. He would have jumped at an opportunity to wave a lofty job offer in front of them ... and to get out of Texas."

I held up a second finger. "That leaves Freddie boy."

"The situation with Frederick Schumacher is a lot more sensitive and, to be honest, sordid. The rumors about his lifestyle are true ... his preferences skew to the kinky end of the spectrum and wherever he has worked, the word inevitably has gotten out. Actually the guy is quite good at treasury and broader financial functions, but regardless of any legal protection against discrimination in the workplace that he's supposed to have, people around him have found it difficult to view his contributions objectively. As a result, he has needed to keep changing jobs to advance his career. You can imagine how he might have been accepted inside the culture of a large conservative bank, which is where he was before joining ASC. With the way that T. Albert openly teases Frederick about his sex partners and fetishes during our meetings, I have to presume the guy was given every assurance that none of his unusual tastes would interfere with the significant monetary success he could enjoy at ASC."

I raised a third and fourth finger. "So, including you, Guenther identified four individuals whose personal situations might render them receptive to his highly attractive job offers and the less attractive strings that ultimately went with them … I've got that. In your case, the expectation that you'd be complicit with Guenther's fraud was revealed over time. Was it the same with the others, or did they know what they were getting into?"

"Milo, I don't really know … the subject is too uncomfortable for me, so I've never talked to any of the others about it. I think Glickman, McCaffrey, and Schumacher will talk more privately among themselves, but I'm not even sure of that. I do remember how the three of them and Guenther kept looking at each other during our dinner together on that last night in New Jersey … like they were part of some secret fraternity. And regardless of what they knew or didn't know, I can tell you that each of them seems extremely stressed out and unhappy about the whole situation now."

"Edna describes them as being very troubled."

"As usual, she doesn't miss much. If I had to guess, I'd say they didn't know exactly what they were stepping into until they'd already become part of Guenther's team. And like me, once they'd savored and strutted the benefits of their new positions, the trade-offs associated with preserving their integrity became too severe. We each had our prices."

"Okay, Kirsten, maybe I can understand what Guenther's hand-selected lieutenants had to gain, or what you feared losing once he had you entrapped. But what did T. Albert hope to gain for himself when he was planning all this? He had to know Wilson Delaney was going to become the next CEO and that he would be named CFO … so there was no other title to shoot for. He'd already accumulated significant wealth as Delaney's right-hand man over the years, and the compensation package he would receive as CFO, even if he only lasted a few years, would guarantee that he walked away with more money than he could ever spend. If he hadn't set up all those reserves to manipulate earnings, ASC's fiscal performance still would have been decent enough … a little more erratic, perhaps, but solid relative to most companies. Why take the risk? For what reason would Guenther have planned this effort for so long, and then patiently execute the details quarter after quarter, putting him further and further at risk?"

"Milo, for one thing, people like T. Albert Guenther never think they've made enough money. Money is how the score is kept. With his plan properly in place, he has maxed out on every aspect of his compensation … salary increases, annual and deferred bonus pay-outs, profit sharing, and the number of stock options he receives each year. Then with the confidence he has helped instill with investors, the value of every share he owns continues to increase dramatically. The same has been true for all of us, but at much lower levels. The difference to T. Albert would be in the tens of millions.

"And, Milo, you've seen how he gets ridiculed by the business presidents and other senior officers because of his appearance and personality. Being the butt of jokes is hardly new to him … it's been the mainstay of his life. The nerdiest boy in town who married the nerdiest girl in high school to live nerdily ever after. For T. Albert, success equates to revenge. Every dollar next to his name in the proxy, every quarterly acclaim from a Wall Street analyst further validates his victory over the countless people who refused to take him seriously."

"So you think it all goes back to some kid who made fun of his toy truck in a sandbox?"

"Something like that. As you've heard me say before, you can't underestimate what Guenther is capable of. Milo, the guy is seriously spooky."

End of questions, the ball was in my court. I could hardly wait to see what I did with it when I met Luke at Ashton's the next morning. In the meantime, we had an open bottle of wine we'd barely touched … not to mention a few other things that required attention. We lost track and the flames in the fireplace died out, but we generated plenty of heat on our own. Sometime after 1 AM, I told Kirsten I needed to leave because of my early morning breakfast.

She thought I was pulling her leg. "Milo, no one schedules a six-thirty meeting on a Saturday … and even if you did, why not skip it?"

"Trust me, Kirsten, these breakfasts go back to my college days. Missing one isn't an option."

"Perhaps I've got a better option. Let's go upstairs and you can spend the night here. I'll even set the alarm for six if you're dead-set about making it to some mysterious breakfast."

There was no place in God's universe that I'd rather be than upstairs with Kirsten's warm body sleeping against mine, but I knew she was speaking through too many glasses of wine. "Kirsten, we don't want Danny waking up and wondering why good ol' Mr. Peters is sleeping in his mother's bedroom."

She knew I was right. We pried ourselves from the chair and made our way to the front door, where I leaned down for one last lengthy kiss. "Good night, lady."

She reached up and lightly placed one hand on my cheek. "You never want to hear this, but you are an especially good man … and Danny is extremely fortunate to have someone like you looking out for his best interests."

Chapter Fourteen

Luke had known me since first grade. At breakfast the next morning, he quickly recognized the evasive way I was answering his questions.

"Who are you protecting, Milo?"

I responded by staring out the window at the empty street. Though I hadn't acknowledged anything, he knew I was holding out on him.

A combination of frustration and anger caused him to lash out. "I guess the answer is pretty obvious. I hope she's worth it; more importantly, I hope you're sure about how she feels about you—or whatever stories she has told you about her involvement. You're my oldest, closest friend … I can't stand by and just watch you take on this kind of personal risk. You're required to come forward. You'll be tying my hands with how much I can help you if all this blows up. You'd better have thought long and hard about what you're doing."

That's all I'd been doing for the past several days … and on Saturday I'd awakened from a short night's sleep with my mind finally made up. I wasn't ready to give Luke what he needed … now or probably anytime in the future. Let him and his secret government pals make their case without me, and I didn't think they could. Guenther would never know, but by maintaining my silence I was signing up to become another of his entrapped accomplices. In time I would think of some appropriate, less public means for dealing with him. I simply wasn't willing to chance that Kirsten could end up in jail.

For once my motives weren't selfish. Granted, the thought of being separated from Kirsten during whatever prison sentence a conviction might entail was dispiriting. But I had no doubts that our feelings for one another would continue to strengthen and we'd be able to set out in new directions together once she was released. My bigger concern was Danny. His life would be thrown into turmoil if his mother was sent away. I had no idea who would end up caring for him. More importantly, I feared the impact from seeing his mother arrested ... seeing her in handcuffs ... in a prison uniform ... the emotional damage of being separated, wondering and worrying about her day after day. The anger, the bitterness, the fear and hurt he would experience.

Kirsten may have made choices she regretted, but she'd been duped and exploited. Guenther was the only sure culprit. Kirsten Woodrow possessed as many strong qualities as anyone I'd ever known. Her reputation, her character shouldn't be slurred because some malicious coward with a wounded psyche wormed his way into her life during a period of weakness. I wasn't sure how, but I'd find a way to make him pay. Luke was counting on me to do the right thing, and I'd decided to do exactly that. In this instance, we just happened to have opposite views on what the right thing would be.

I'd been to Ashton's hundreds of times with Luke. Illnesses, tragedies, hangovers, it didn't matter—always there'd been the camaraderie, the naturalness, the laughter. But this Saturday morning was different. We were like two strangers. The gaps grew wider and wider between the limited words that were spoken. By the end, neither of us was making much effort at eye contact. For what I think was the first time in my life, I'd pushed through the limits of Luke's temperament. Finally, I decided to cut the misery short.

"Sorry, Luke, gotta run. Full day ... going to the hockey game and the puck drops early because of the TV network."

"Sure ... I understand. You guys enjoy."

"See ya next Saturday."

"Yeah ... I hope so, Milo ... I really hope so."

His last comment jarred me. He probably was making a veiled plea for me to change my mind before next week's breakfast and come forward with the information he needed. But he seemed concerned that I might not be there at all. How could he have known that I already was wrestling with whether to show up the next Saturday, or the ones after that? If I wasn't going to live up to a commitment, where was the use in pretending?

⌇

Since it was Danny's first Blackhawks game, he may have concluded that the team personally welcomed every new fan to the arena. We sat behind one of the nets in an area that accommodated wheel chairs. During warm-ups the players made it a point to circle around to us, perhaps because they'd noticed a young kid sitting in the special section. But I'd like to think it was the three enormous foam rubber "puck heads" we were wearing. Danny and I looked ridiculous, of course. Somehow Kirsten managed to look sexy as hell, which may have been the real reason we drew so much attention from a bunch of red-blooded male athletes. Either way, Danny stared in awe as one-by-one the Blackhawks skated behind the net to high-five the hand he held pressed up against the glass. During second intermission, the equipment manager brought over a hockey stick signed by the team … probably to express their appreciation for Danny's uninterrupted cheering. Fortunately, the Hawks won easily, because by game's end his voice was gone. An overtime might have caused permanent damage to his larynx.

The weather was unusually mild for a second day in a row, so we checked out the action in Millennium Park and then grabbed early dinner at a sports bar. The choice of eateries was Kirsten's. As it turned out, she was big-time into college basketball and wanted to catch the early rounds of the NCAA tournament. Who knew? She and Edna had a ten-dollar bet on their brackets. No wonder I'd fallen so head-over-heels in love … she was the perfect woman.

We watched the late games back at her house. Danny went to bed utterly exhausted, which allowed us to be more uninhibited than usual in our downstairs activities. As a gentleman, I shouldn't comment on details; but then, I'm only a borderline gentleman. So let me simply observe that monuments should be dedicated and ships christened to honor Kirsten Woodrow's carnal abilities. My natural skills weren't nearly as impressive, but I was improving as fast as I could. And I was more than willing to step up our practice sessions … two-a-days, if necessary.

I spent most of Sunday at home, as in Park Ridge. During our dinner a few weeks earlier, my mother had several times made reference to a lengthening list of "manly" chores that she no longer could handle. I'm sure she figured that I'd purposely ignored her blatant hints. I shocked us both by waking up early on Sunday morning and calling her with a sudden desire to tackle her list. More shocking, I still remembered how to wield a hammer, a shovel, a pipe wrench, and assorted other devices that self-respecting senior executives paid others to wield on their behalf. I had forgotten what sweat and dirt looked like when they ran together. During my business career I'd generated plenty of each, but not the kind that showed.

The hard work felt good ... in fact, better than good: cathartic. This type of hard work produced instant feelings of accomplishment. No committee meetings to gather input, no required approvals in advance, no overinflated CEO yammering about what should have been done differently. Most importantly, the results were tangible. They weren't subject to the whims or interpretations of petty minds who sought to make their reputations by ripping apart the efforts of those who dared to produce. By day's end, I'd vowed to go out and buy myself a toolbox.

While I worked down her list, my mom was preparing my favorite meal—a hot Serbian stew that Baba Milka had taught her to make. She wanted it to be a surprise, but for hours I'd been anticipating what would be waiting for me in the kitchen. The unmistakable aroma of banana peppers and onions simmering around chunks of beef sirloin had filled the house, the yard, and much of northern Illinois. I didn't let on, but as with most things, the anticipation added measurably to the ultimate satisfaction. I sopped up every last drop on my plate with thick slices of fresh bread from the local bakery ... my mom beaming from across the table. On this day, I truly was home.

Later that Sunday evening, I paid a visit to an Internet café. I was feeling particularly feisty toward one individual and wanted to jumpstart his Monday. I'd had a lot of time to let my mind wander while toiling away on projects all afternoon. I would have preferred to dwell on happier thoughts about Kirsten and Danny, or even erotic thoughts about Kirsten alone. Instead, my brain had kept churning in one direction ... toward T. Albert Guenther. The audacity of this despicable man. So what if he harbored a few memories of being teased and harassed ... who didn't? Doctors could label him with any number of complexes, psychoses, or syndromes and I still wouldn't feel the least bit sorry for him. The guy had played recklessly with the lives of other people ... and not just Kirsten and Danny, or his beloved Wire Rims and their families. Guenther had taken it upon himself to dabble in the livelihoods of tens of thousands of ASC associates, not to mention the hundreds of thousands of ASC shareholders. No different than the growing parade of disgraced executives who'd made national headlines.

ASC employed more than ninety thousand people. Surely, there were many who approached their jobs as nothing more than a paycheck. There were others who put forth only enough effort to get by, and some who didn't even do that. But there were many, many more who had bought into something bigger. They wanted to be part of a company they could count on, be proud of ... a company into which they could pour their hard work and faith. They committed their careers to a place where they could build and secure a future for themselves and their families. I knew, because I personally had interacted with thousands of them and, yes, abused that trust in my own way.

Most longtime associates would have recognized certain realities about the ASC culture. They must have known that their interests rarely, if ever, would be placed ahead of the almighty profit dollar. In one fashion or another, they would have come to grips with that hard truth. But at least they should have been able to presume that their employer, a publicly held corporation, was operating legitimately ... that the senior execs who earned millions of dollars each, could steer the mother ship between the clear, bright lines of the law. Many of those ninety thousand had staked nest eggs and retirements accordingly.

I felt lousy enough about my numerous contributions to a corporate culture which devalued their loyalty, but T. Albert Guenther had pushed through an envelope that was light years beyond. He had taken actions that put every employee and investor at serious risk. One man had placed his own urgencies above the well-being of any and all other persons affiliated with an entire corporation. If his manipulations of earnings were to become public, the stock price would plummet and the whole future of American Service Companies might come into question. One vengeful man who couldn't leave past scars behind. Maybe the teasing had started in grade school or his teen years ... skinny legs, acne, some such nonsense. A lifetime since to move beyond, to pursue his dreams ... yet he'd remained mired in nightmares. He had chosen to take on his demons ... and whether Guenther knew it or not, they'd already won. Their trophy, a worthless piece of garbage.

I reread the e-mail message one final time, smiling. Maybe I would talk to Luke about doing undercover work in my next career. I carefully gazed around the room and didn't see anyone who might recognize me. Not a soul was behaving suspiciously ... except maybe the one young lady who sported an array of goth tattoos on her arms and neck. Every few moments she would shout, "Rot in hell, you mutant freak." I assumed she was playing a computer game, but she could have been online with a boyfriend.

I hit SEND, logged off, and left. My computer at the office would receive another confidential communication from FriendInHighPlace.

Come Monday morning, Guenther and the Wire Rims would have plenty to chew on behind their closed doors.

"Rumors pursued. Appetite of one little pig, definitely voracious … eats from all sides of trough, plus prefers very unusual attire at mealtime. Sorry, but must confirm your own Miss Goldilocks is part of story. **Regarding Big Bad Wolf, be careful!** Freuds conclude he's a textbook whack job. In way over his head and probably feeling it. Likely to come unglued … danger to those near."

With the "Goldilocks" reference, I'd wanted to acknowledge Kirsten's suspected involvement in the still-unspecified activities that the e-mails hinted at. I didn't want the others to think her complicit involvement was being ignored because she was cooperating in an investigation of some sort.

Frederick Schumacher would grow increasingly concerned that the intimate details of his private life were being investigated by some unknown entity and might soon be made public. I hoped his discomfort would start mounting. I wanted pressures to build from every conceivable direction. If I wasn't prepared to blow the whistle on what Schumacher and the other Wire Rims had been doing as part of Guenther's scheme, I at a minimum needed to find a way to scare them into stopping … and ultimately into leaving the corporation.

Hopefully, Guenther would seethe over the "Big Bad Wolf" references. If his underlying motivation for committing securities fraud had stemmed from self-esteem issues, then I wanted to open up those old wounds as wide as possible and start shoveling salt. Here was a man who coveted the respect and acclaim of the financial community. Reading that some unnamed authorities had concluded that he was in over his head should spark all kinds of psychological fireworks … not to mention, seeing himself reduced to a "whack job."

For the Wire Rims, the suggestion that their leader and protector might be on the verge of a breakdown should add an interesting dynamic to all those private discussions they liked to hold. No matter how much Guenther protested or what he said, his three highly paid accomplices would be eyeing him with new reservations, wondering about the danger he might pose "to those near." After four decades of abusing my singular natural talent, at last I'd uncovered a meaningful application for a warped sense of humor.

As soon as my alarm went off on Monday morning, I recognized something was horribly wrong. I couldn't tell if I'd lost total feeling in my left arm, but I definitely wasn't able to move it. I tried the other arm with much the same result. Then it hit me that Kirsten had been right. I'd been naive about T. Albert Guenther and the lengths to which he might go to protect his precious scheme. Though this conniving lowlife had proven he was capable of screwing with the welfare of many thousands of people, I still hadn't thought he would resort to physical harm. But somehow he'd managed to slip a debilitating substance into my system.

Not knowing how long I might have to live, all I could do was lie in bed and wonder how he'd pulled it off. A hypodermic needle while I was sleeping? Maybe the toothpaste or mouthwash I'd used before going to bed. Had he done the dirty deed himself or directed one of his obedient Wire Rims ... or more boldly, contracted a professional?

I figured the drugs would soon work their way up to my throat and mouth, if they hadn't already. I needed to call out for help before full paralysis set in. I slowly lifted my head off the pillow to yell.

"Oh shit!"

It wasn't exactly what I'd intended to shout, but the pain in my neck had been excruciating. My head dropped back on the pillow. I laid there assessing the situation. My neck throbbed, but that at least meant I still could feel something. In fact, sensations were surging through my arms. My legs, too. And my back. Not mere sensations ... horrible aches. I didn't have much tolerance for pain and never had.

"Shit!" I winced. Attempting to roll over onto my right side had been a bad idea.

"Shit!" Same for the left.

Apparently no one could hear me. I'd shut the door between the two sizable rooms of my hotel suite. There were two solid doors and over thirty feet between me and the hallway outside my room. I was immobilized in the bed ... no choice but to stay on my back and reflect on the tragic ironies of an abbreviated life. The unbridled happiness I'd experienced during my final earthly weekend had surpassed any I could remember. The simple pleasures of a cook-out, an ice cream cone, a hockey game ... the easy laughter with Kirsten and Danny ... the amorous passions of the woman I adored ... tightened bonds with a loving mother ... the uncomplicated joy of rolling up my sleeves ... "SHIT!" Suddenly, it hit me.

T. Albert Guenther hadn't done a thing to me. I'd done it all myself. The pruning, the wood-splitting, the stump removal. The broken storm windows, the rusted-out light fixture, and so much more. Lying on the bed of my hotel room, I sequentially assigned the assorted body aches to their respective tasks from the previous day. My muscles and joints were hurting intensely from the effects of age. With the relief of that recognition plus the reminiscences of a joyous weekend, I hardly could wait to hobble and limp into the new week ahead … that is, once I mustered the courage to try getting out of bed again. And as a sidebar, all those reported accounts had been accurate. A near-death experience does change one's perspective.

I eventually made it into the office, but close to an hour later than usual. Hoping to go unnoticed, I tried shuffling past Edna's workstation as quietly as possible.

"Rough weekend, Mr. Peters? Will we be reading about your exploits in the tabloids?"

Of all things, she sounded chipper.

"Good morning, Miss Cutler."

I continued moving forward. Two could play her game. I'd leave her wondering.

"I just reheated your coffee, Mr. Peters. Since you were running late, I called Anthony, the security guard in the first floor lobby, and asked him to notify me when you entered the building. When I finally heard from him, he indicated you wouldn't be arriving anytime soon. I guess he was right … I would have had time to brew a whole new pot."

Her voice was out-and-out jubilant.

"That was nice of him, Edna."

My right hand cramped as it wrapped around the first coffee cup waiting on the ledge next to her, but I sooner would have cut off that hand than slow down long enough to shift the cup to my left. I steadily progressed toward the sanctum of my office.

"Daniel said you were downstairs rather late again on Saturday night … and also on Friday. Perhaps you dozed off in an awkward position or something. I read somewhere that certain wines can sneak up on you."

"Thanks for your concern, Edna … I'll have to remember that."

The chair behind my desk beckoned to me like an oasis in the desert. Head straight, eyes focused, I traversed the final feet and finally reached my target.

"Shit!" Even sitting down hurt.

Edna didn't miss a beat. "Coffee too hot, Mr. Peters? You might want to take things a little slower this morning. Sometimes our bodies have a way of reminding us that we're not as young as we think we are."

146

There was an eight-inch wall between my office and Edna's workstation, but I still could see her turned toward her computer, head held high. I could envision the gleeful expression on her face as plainly as if she were sitting right in front of me. I could hear it in her voice. She was smiling from ear to ear. This was no tiny crack in her early morning stoicism; it was a mile-wide crevice. At last I had prevailed. Ridicule may not have been the method by which I'd intended to evoke a detectable human emotion from Edna Cutler, but I would take my victory anyway I could get it.

Later that morning, once my body had rested long enough to handle a trek down the hall, I set out for Kirsten's office. I prayed she would be there. Otherwise she might be startled to return and see me writhing on the floor while I waited for her.

As it turned out, she was startled by the mere sight of me in the doorway. "My God, Milo, what happened to you?"

I closed the door and dragged myself to one of the guest chairs in front of her desk, gingerly sliding into it. "Good deeds do not go unpunished. Yesterday I took on seventeen different projects at my mother's house. In hindsight, I should have bought her a new home instead."

Once Kirsten knew the source of my physical maladies, her amusement paralleled Edna's. "Maybe both you and your mother need to remember that little Milo isn't a teenager anymore."

"Yeah, and it's a good thing, too. When I was crawling around in the attic, I found my old stash of dirty magazines. If we'd had the Internet back then, I don't think I ever would've seen the sunlight."

I'd earned another bad-boy look. I tried giving her one my patented shrugs, but the pain made it impossible.

Our conversation quickly turned more serious. My purpose for coming to her office was to inform her that I'd decided against seeking any assistance from my government friend and, further, to plead with her about not going forward to the authorities. I related my concerns about Danny and my belief that authorities wouldn't be able to prove ASC earnings had been manipulated.

"Milo, how can you be so certain?"

"Because if any of those government agencies could make their case, they wouldn't have been counting on me, of all people, to come through for them." I no longer could keep my promise to Luke. Kirsten needed to know the whole story.

She looked completely puzzled. "Whatever are you talking about?"

I started with the seemingly trivial decision, two months earlier, to nurse my latest hangover at Ashton's. Over the course of the next two hours, she learned about Luke and a lifelong friendship; she heard the history of Ashton's as a gathering spot; and she listened nervously as I described the thick folders that the government had been amassing on ASC activities. I came clean on every detail ... even the convenient choice I'd made to start my official investigation by getting to know her better. I described how I'd dug through the personnel files of Guenther and the Wire Rims. The built-up disdain for Wilson Delaney. My late night visits to the Internet cafes and the cheesy trail of e-mails.

Her reactions and emotions ran the gamut. Her anxiety was obvious when I discussed Luke's investigation, but I kept assuring her that the agency or bureau for which he worked didn't have the smoking gun it needed. In an odd sort of way, she was charmed that I had wanted to reach out to her first. She was amused by some of my antics with the Wire Rims. But she was particularly concerned about my relationship with Luke ... our loyalty to one another ... the importance of demonstrating to him and myself that I possessed the depth of character that would make both of us proud.

"Milo, you are so very, very hard on yourself. I'm sure that since you were kids, Luke has known exactly what I do now ... that you have more strength and values than you'll ever be willing to recognize. Your standards are so high that you always feel like you're falling short."

I knew how many people I'd let down ... how I'd frittered away the opportunities, one relationship after another. Responding to Kirsten's comments would have further convinced her of my inability to see myself in a positive light. But my body language must have spoken volumes.

"Look at you ... you can't even stand to listen to my compliments. I wish you'd try to like yourself even a little ... but I guess you're forcing me to love Milo Peters enough for the both of us. Lucky for you, I'm up to the task."

By the time we were done with all her questions, it was well past noon. We'd beaten the subject to oblivion. For the sheer sake of our mental well-being, it was time we moved onto something completely different. I hesitated sheepishly, before deciding to roll the dice. "How's your appetite?"

She responded by putting a finger to her chin, pondering what to say. A playful grin followed.

Miraculously, my pain seemed to vanish. I rose from the chair and grabbed her coat from the back of the door. "I'm not hungry either ... how about we go out for a long, late lunch?"

As we hurried past the security desk in the building's lobby, I noticed a puzzled look on the face of Tony Scarpaletti, who was stationed behind it.

"Good afternoon, Tony, or should I say, Anthony?"

He nodded his head. "Afternoon, Mr. Peters."

Halfway out the revolving door, I looked back and saw that he still was watching me with odd fascination. I circled all the way around and stopped long enough to address his curiosity. "I remembered an old Italian cure for sore muscles."

At first he looked even more dumbfounded, but by the time I'd caught up with Kirsten outside on the sidewalk, he'd put the pieces together. When Kirsten wasn't looking, he gave me an enthusiastic thumbs-up through the window.

Chapter Fifteen

I started adjusting to the whole idea of life on the lam … to the romanticized notion of deep, dark secrets following me to my grave. The more I pondered the situation, the more confident I became that the government didn't have the necessary goods to bring charges against American Service Companies.

From the morning Luke had recruited me to become his inside informer, I'd reflected on scores of unseemly decisions that I had made through the years. But now my head was on straight … as straight as at any point in my life. For the first time since I could remember, life felt absolutely glorious. I was avoiding liquor bottles, while not avoiding mirrors. And the rungs of a corporate ladder no longer held any allure at all. So, of course, now was precisely the time I consciously would choose to become a white-collar criminal by maintaining my silence about Guenther and the others. Living life in perfect disharmony just came naturally to me.

My plan was to stay with American Service Companies for a few more months. When I was ready, I would give Wilson Delaney and the board a month's notice—the least I could do after twenty-two years. But first, I needed some time to settle the score with T. Albert Guenther. Though I had no intention of ratting him out to the authorities, he didn't know that. I still could gnaw away at his sense of well-being. With any luck, I could force him to leave the corporation before I did. One way or the other, Guenther should be taught a lesson. ASC may never set the standards of corporate excellence, but it would be a much better place without the likes of T. Albert Guenther and his trusty Wire Rims.

The last time I had laid eyes on Wilson Delaney's deep-tanned countenance was when he delivered his fatherly lecture to me in my conference room, at the urging of T. Albert Guenther. According to Edna, he'd been traveling about half the time since, which meant he'd been in the building the other half, which further meant he'd been avoiding me. But if Kirsten was correct, Delaney wasn't aware that Guenther and his minions had been engaging in criminal acts. So if Delaney really wasn't a party to the earnings manipulations, T. Albert wouldn't have risked going back to him with complaints that I had continued my quest by digging into their personnel files. He certainly wouldn't have shown him my e-mail exchanges with FriendInHighPlace. Guenther wouldn't want to call attention to where my energies were focused, nor to the fact that he and the Wire Rims had misappropriated their executive authority to gain access to my computer.

So either Kirsten was wrong about Delaney's involvement, or I had managed to do something else to alienate myself from our esteemed CEO. Unless he was angry with me, he couldn't have gone this long without tugging on my psyche for a few grins. Too bad, because I would have enjoyed the opportunity to introduce him to the new Milo Peters, the one who no longer cared about holding onto his approval. How liberating it would feel to be in his presence and not scrutinize his slightest gesture, not worry about his every intonation when he uttered my name.

It further dawned on me that the only people I'd recently been seeing around the office were Kirsten, Edna, and a smattering of corporate staff members who worked for me. I hadn't seen T. Albert Guenther or any of the Wire Rims for more than two weeks—not even in passing. Perhaps, like Delaney, they were avoiding me. But, then again, maybe this was paranoia on my part. It could be that I simply hadn't done enough to stay better connected—a situation I needed to rectify. After all, healthy relationships must be two-way streets. I vowed to reach out to these special gentlemen in whole new ways … certainly there must be all kinds of interests that we shared.

During the starts and stops of my career, I'd learned the best way for me to assure that I followed through on new resolutions was to commit them to writing. So before leaving the office on Monday, I sent FriendInHighPlace an e-mail.

"Received last night's update. Goldilocks still under spell of Big Bad Wolf; won't open up. Need to spend more time with story's other main characters. Wolfie has gone into hibernation. Three Little Pigs also in hiding … perhaps worried that their houses are made of straw …

would hate to see those cute curly tails caught in the door. Will journey deeper into their enchanted forest this week."

Okay, maybe I was mixing my fairy tales, but I figured there was a certain amount of creative license that went with corporate espionage.

~~

On Tuesday afternoon, I swung over to T. Albert Guenther's corner of the executive floor. His assistant didn't have time to react or warn him of my unscheduled arrival. I breezed past her workstation and opened the closed door to his office. I had no idea what I'd find behind it. Guenther could have been in the middle of some important meeting. For all I knew, he could have been hosting a séance with the spirits of Andrew Carnegie and John Jacob Astor. I didn't care because I was so sure he'd be glad to see me.

As it turned out, T. Albert's chair was turned toward the window and he was hunched over, clipping his fingernails into a wastebasket. Based on the way he jumped, followed by the distasteful look on his face, the man didn't like interruptions to his personal grooming regimen. Otherwise I'm positive he would have stood and given me a big hug or something.

"Good afternoon, Al, old buddy. I haven't been seeing much of you around, so I figured I'd pop in and say hello. I've kinda missed you."

He had regained his composure and positioned himself squarely behind his desk, eyes drilling into me. I waited for him to respond, but apparently he was too touched by my heartfelt outreach.

"T-Man, for weeks I've been meaning to tell you what an incredible job you do in making certain that ASC makes its earnings forecast, quarter after quarter after quarter. The way we never disappoint those analysts is almost eerie. Wilson sure knew what he was doing when he named you CFO and allowed you to build out corporate finance to your exact specifications. What you've managed to do is sheer genius."

I again paused, offering him an opportunity to express his gratitude for the glowing praise, or at least return the toothy grin I was flashing. The stony silence on his part could only be interpreted as midwestern humility, so I continued.

"You know, Big Al, I think it would be terrific if we took the time to become better acquainted … to develop one of those personal friendships like you have with Glickman, McCaffrey, and Schumacher. In fact, I was looking at the weather map this morning and noticed the snow in northern

Wisconsin hasn't thawed yet. This coming Saturday there are snowmobile races up in Eagle River … probably the last of the year. How 'bout you and I drive up and make it a weekend? You know … some guy-bonding."

His lips never moved. He just glared at me. If I didn't know better, his expression could have been described as almost hateful. Sad, really, when I'd come with such high hopes.

"Well, just think about it … you can get back to me. After you've finished with your fingernails."

I gave him a friendly wave and backed out of his office, closing the door as quietly as possible. I looked over to his assistant, who was glaring at me in much the same way Guenther had. So I flashed a big smile her way as well.

"That Albert, he worries too much about his corporate image … I bet he hasn't told you that he and I go way back. We used to do some serious party damage when he'd visit our field operations. That animal can really pound 'em down … surprised he has any brain cells left at all. And you wouldn't believe the legend he was with the ladies. The guy's insatiable."

I strolled back to my office feeling pretty good about my acts of kindness. T. Albert was unlikely to have many guy friends to pal around with … so at least I'd tried. Maybe he'd take me up on my offer for the coming weekend, but just in case, I decided I should make alternative plans with Kirsten and Danny.

◦⁀ℳ⁀◦

On Wednesday morning, the target of my attention was Robert McCaffrey. I saw him heading into the men's room and darned if I suddenly didn't hear nature calling me, too. Considering the Wire Rims' penchant for time efficiency, I figured he might appreciate how I waited until he was standing at the urinal before I initiated a long overdue chat.

"Hey, Bob, how's the family? I hear your wife's father does a lot of big deals down in Texas. He must be darned impressed with what you've been accomplishing up north since you joined ASC. I bet he wishes you were back down there working for him again … he probably didn't have any idea that you'd be so darned good at getting deals done and setting up all those fancy reserve accounts. I hope you haven't been modest about telling him everything you've been up to."

I waited for a reaction, but apparently he didn't have much to say. "Milo, I would appreciate if you called me Robert."

"Sure thing, Robbo, I always forget."

Either he had downed too many lattes that morning, or his kidneys weren't performing the way he might have hoped. He sure looked eager to get away from that urinal, but his bodily functions weren't cooperating. The least I could do was continue to keep him company.

"Bobby Boy, whatta you say we grab dinner some night next week? You bring your wife and I'll get a date. I'd love to have an opportunity to tell her how much you've meant to the company ... the countless ways you've been contributing to corporate earnings that we can't even begin to acknowledge properly ... the unique role you've played on T. Albert's hand-picked team."

Robert McCaffrey must have been overwhelmed by my deep admiration for his accomplishments. He practically ran out of that restroom. Since he hadn't responded to my invitation, I assumed he needed to check with his wife regarding their social calendar. Strange though, he forgot to wash his hands. He'd always struck me as such a clean-cut young man.

Thursday was reserved for Frederick Schumacher. With the colorful rumors about his not-so-secret lifestyle, I didn't feel comfortable approaching him in the men's room. No, I chose the first-floor lobby. I went down fifteen minutes before lunchtime and struck up a conversation with Tony Scarpaletti, the security guard. By the time Schumacher got off the elevator at ten past noon, I'd lived through three generations of an Italian-American saga. Definitely a nice family, but I was glad I hadn't come across any of Tony's sisters or female cousins in my younger, more social years. Some of those Scarpaletti uncles sounded a little overprotective.

I waited until Schumacher was out on the sidewalk. "Freddie, my good friend, mind if I walk with you?"

He didn't bother to look my way. Funny, it was almost like he was expecting me. "That's Frederick, Milo."

"Sure thing, Fred. Where ya headed ... anyplace you wanna talk about? I'm always curious about what aspiring young executives do when they're away from the office. You know ... that whole 'all work, dull boy' thing."

"Just going out to grab a bite ...." As soon as he'd said it, he caught himself. "A bite to eat, Milo."

"Of course, Fredo, what else would you mean?"

I started laying it on thick about his many unsung heroics as treasurer and how I was sure he had contributed to corporate earnings in ways our investors couldn't possibly imagine. I was just hitting my stride when he remembered he had an important errand to run. Before I could offer to accompany him, he was out in the middle of Michigan Avenue hailing a cab. Too bad, because I'd wanted to ask him if he might be interested in starting up a Monday evening book club with me. I had this hunch that Frederick Schumacher might be able to suggest some unusual literature to a group of curious readers looking to expand their minds. In fact, I followed up with an e-mail to that effect as soon as I returned to my desk.

Since I'd started with Christopher Glickman at the beginning of my secret investigation, I'd saved him for last on this particular cycle. I wasn't worried that he and T. Albert would go running to Wilson Delaney again.

Friday morning I plopped into a chair and put my feet up on his desk. As usual, he was fixated on his computer screen.

"Got big plans for the weekend, Christopher?"

"That's Chris …." He trailed off in mid-word, surprised that I'd addressed him properly. "No, Milo, not really." He quickly typed something on his keyboard.

"Ah, too bad, Chrissie, my lad. A young stud like you should always have big plans. But then I guess those plans can come with a price tag if you're still married … a hefty price tag if you're not careful."

"I suppose so." He'd pulled his eyes away from his computer monitor, but he wasn't looking at me. He seemed much more interested in watching the doorway, as though he expected someone to appear there.

"Well, C-Man, you're probably wondering why I stopped by."

"Uh, I guess so."

"No particular reason … just wanted to say howdy and let you know how much I've missed our little chats. Catch you later." I was out of the chair, out of his office, and heading down the hall before he had a chance to tell me how much he appreciated the visit. Walking briskly toward me was none other than T. Albert Guenther.

"Al, my main man, what an unexpected pleasure … twice in one week. I believe Christopher is expecting you. You and those boys sure seem to have a special relationship … but then I guess you all knew each other before they started working here."

Strange how the whole genetic lottery works. In addition to being dealt a really odd physical appearance, T. Albert Guenther also must have suffered from a hearing problem. The poor guy walked right by me like he hadn't heard a word I'd said.

If my computer was being monitored dutifully, T. Albert wouldn't have been surprised that I was aware his ties to the Wire Rims had predated their arrival at ASC. Thursday night I'd discovered but another Internet café—this time in the River North area. And this one quickly became my new favorite because it had a soda fountain. If a rapidly changing world was going to force me to make regular trips through cyberspace, then I might as well be carrying a root beer float. On Friday morning, an e-mail from FriendInHighPlace hit my inbox.

"Connection established. Once upon a time (2003), Big Bad Wolf, Three Little Pigs and Goldilocks attended accounting seminar in New Jersey. Third-party confirmation that they spent much time together, often alone.

"Separately, looking into BBW's relationship with lead partner at ASC's accounting firm. More soon; gaps filling rapidly."

By the time Friday evening rolled around, I felt like I'd put in an exceptionally productive week. It was funny how some weeks just flew by. Though eager to move on with my life, I looked forward to staying put a little longer and tormenting Guenther, McCaffrey, Schumacher, and Glickman. I doubted the Wire Rims would last too long before abandoning ship. T. Albert Guenther, on the other hand, would need to feel the water around his shoulders before he went looking for an escape hatch.

As I was packing up my briefcase, Edna entered my office and picked up on my upbeat mood. "Mr. Peters, do I discern a new lilt in your step? This can't be the same gentleman who barely could walk this past Monday morning. I wouldn't imagine that such a marked difference can be attributed solely to the affections of a good woman,—"

I interrupted her before she could continue. In an exaggerated fashion, I tossed down the file folders that were in my hands and fixed my eyes upon hers. "Why, Edna, I knew we'd grown rather friendly, but I wasn't aware that you'd fallen in love with me. If you're intent on following through with any lustful desires, we're going to have to keep it to ourselves …

things could get kind of awkward, seeing as how I'm already dating Miss Woodrow."

She nailed me with one of those *Are you done?* looks—not the slightest smile in evidence. Here I was throwing my best stuff; yet nothing, no reaction. The woman had elevated deadpan to an art form.

"As I was saying, Mr. Peters, your abnormally high spirits might suggest you have more going on in your life than recent romantic interests. Based upon a few casual observations, I might go as far as to infer that you're up to something. Perhaps someone has needed to look behind the scenes here at corporate headquarters for quite some time ... but that someone should not underestimate the risks involved. I do hope you'll be careful. Have a nice weekend, Mr. Peters."

She'd said her piece, after which she turned and exited my life for another weekend ... probably to tend to some major global crisis that required her attention. I was touched by her genuine concern for my welfare, but in her own inimitable fashion she also was telling me not to back off. Why did it feel like the rest of us mere mortals were playing notes in a symphony being conducted by Edna Cutler? The woman's perceptive instincts were supernatural. For how long had she suspected inappropriate activities at ASC's corporate headquarters? For how long had she patiently gone about her business, waiting for just one overpaid corporate executive to stumble into what must have appeared obvious to her?

As far as Kirsten was concerned, my latest interactions with Guenther and the Wire Rims seemed to heighten the inner turmoil she was carrying. Whatever angst and guilt were building during her three years with ASC had come to a boiling point when she was compelled to tell me about the earnings scheme and the role she played in it. There may have been a momentary catharsis from finally admitting her complicity to someone she trusted, but that confession also had stirred a clawing desire to unload her full burden once and for all. She certainly didn't relish the prospects of public charges, a nasty trial, and a probable prison sentence, but at least she could wipe the slate clean and start over with her life. When I'd informed her on Monday that I had no intention of going to the authorities, I had stifled that hope. She would have to find a way to continue living with the strain of secrecy. Throughout the balance of the week she had sought me out with different ways of expressing her concerns, thinking she might change my mind.

"Milo, it's not bad enough what I have to carry around, but now I've caused you to compromise your own integrity."

I tried to assure her that she was in no way responsible for any compromises to my integrity. First off, I had done that so frequently in my career that there was little left to compromise. Second, the decision I'd made was mine and mine alone. It was I who felt manipulated by a lifetime friendship with Luke and the subversive bureaucrats to whom he was beholden. Screw them. In the long run, it was no big deal ... they could continue happily drawing their government paychecks by tormenting other corporations. There was plenty of greed out there to keep them busy. I was taking it upon myself to see that justice was appropriately served inside the headquarters of American Service Companies. I assured Kirsten that I could chase the Wire Rims out of the corporation and eventually get T. Albert Guenther fired by the omnipotent Wilson Delaney.

I don't think she understood how much at peace I was with my decision to blow off the authorities. I had no second thoughts whatsoever. My only struggle was how to deal with Luke. For an entire week I debated whether to go to Ashton's on Saturday morning. When my head finally hit the pillow Friday night, I'd settled on cowardice. I would take a pass on facing Luke and confronting his disappointment firsthand. After the prior week's breakfast, he certainly must have known where my mind was leaning. It wasn't like this was the first time I'd ever let Luke down ... hell, I'd made a hobby of it. Eventually he was bound to stop forgiving me, but at least this time my reasons weren't purely selfish. I didn't even bother to set my alarm clock.

I'm not sure if it was courage or guilt, but at 6 AM I was awakened by a subconscious rush. I threw on some clothes and headed for Franklin Street. I slid into the booth a few minutes before 6:30; Luke wasn't there yet. For once I could order a cup of coffee and wait for him to arrive.

At 6:45, he still hadn't.

More coffee.

7 AM. I was in disbelief.

Luke was standing me up. Apparently he, too, couldn't stomach the thought of watching me fumble with strained excuses and shrivel under his stare. So he'd made the easier choice on my behalf. For the first time in a lifelong relationship, I was the one on the short end ... I was the one left feeling incidental. I sat alone, recounting the many times I'd neglected our friendship out of pure self-centeredness. It was 7:30 before I fully was convinced he wasn't coming.

The rest of the weekend was another flurry of laughter, silly hats, and big city adventures with an inspiring kid and an incredible woman. On

Sunday, I again made the trip out to Park Ridge to visit my mother, but this time accompanied by Kirsten and Danny. For Winnie Peters, it was like hitting the Powerball. After I called to let her know we were coming, she found time to bake a pie and two kinds of cookies. With four people, we were able to play a decent game of hearts—at least as far as Kirsten and Mom were concerned. While they dueled for victory, Danny and I focused on sticking one another with the queen of spades.

The coup de grace of the afternoon was when Danny spotted a row of photograph albums behind the glass doors of some shelves in the living room. Over the hour or two that followed, the countless hours that my mother had devoted to organizing and captioning our family's stop-action memories were returned to her a hundredfold. The nostalgic journey proved rewarding for me, too. I couldn't remember the last time I'd seen one of those family albums … perhaps I never truly had. There was something heartwarming, a different bond or kinship that formed, when at age forty-four I could study and remember my dad and his brothers as they had looked when they were my age or younger. Through every broad smile and embrace captured on film, they were urging me to join them, to get my priorities straight and focus on matters that endured.

Paging through my own youth, I saw someone I recognized. An uninhibited kid who mugged for the camera at any opportunity, a kid surrounded by relatives and close friends who loved him unequivocally and whose love he returned in kind. A kid who had every reason to savor the years that lay before him. I liked and missed that kid in those pictures. I wanted to be that kid and believed I could be again. That kid inside had been reawakened since I'd moved back to Chicago, mostly due to the two individuals who sat on either side of my mother. Interestingly, the three of them seemed unable to contain their guffawing over the antics of that same kid in the pictures.

They might not agree, but Danny launched what I would describe as a merciless interrogation of my mother. He was dying to know what I'd been like when I was growing up. My older brother, Tim, always had been Mom's "big man," and I still was cool with that. However, I didn't understand why after all these years I needed to be referred to as her "little blondie." Kirsten thought the nickname "precious" and immediately took to using it.

As my mother responded to Danny's inquisition, I worked harder and harder to suppress my cringes. Occasionally, Kirsten would chime in with a question of her own, usually seeking clarification on some misdeed from my youth. I thought I'd read somewhere that mothers came equipped with an instinct to protect their offspring. Well, my mom must have been missing that gene, because she could have been a lot more careful with her word selection. Every time a phrase like *class clown, smart mouth,* or *principal's office* would slip through her lips, Kirsten and Danny looked over at me in unison and laughed. All I could do was shrug. It wasn't like I'd tried to keep my past a secret. Did they think I'd simply woken up one morning as a wiseass adult?

At least for some, that Sunday in Park Ridge was a virtual love fest. No surprise, Mom loved every minute with Kirsten and Danny; they loved every minute with her. And as a threesome, they loved every minute they could rip on me. Har-de-har-har.

As we loaded up to leave at the end of the day, they fawned all over each other about how much they were looking forward to the next get-together. I hoped someone would remember to invite me.

During our ride back to the city, the good times continued to roll—at my expense, of course. Danny felt this need to relive all of my most embarrassing boyhood nightmares. I couldn't comprehend why he couldn't just fall asleep in the backseat like a normal kid.

Chapter Sixteen

Two days later, all my best-laid plans were uprooted. I was sitting at my desk, mindlessly processing paper from one stack to the next, when Edna entered my office rather tentatively. That in itself was a bad sign, because Edna didn't do anything tentatively.

"Mr. Peters, you have two guests in the lobby."

I checked the open datebook on the credenza behind me.

"Edna, there's nothing on my calendar ... does yours show anything?"

"No, sir." She seemed almost sullen.

The woman knew everything ... why wasn't she being more forthcoming? The only people who showed up without making appointments were sales types who thought they might sneak in and introduce their companies ... convinced their well-oiled spiels were so powerful that any corporation would instantly hand over million-dollar contracts once they wedged their feet in the door. The two unspecified guests in the lobby were probably consultants or headhunters who figured I'd at least come out and greet them, and alas, they'd have their audience. I'd seen this ploy too many times.

"Edna, whoever it is, just tell 'em I had to make an emergency trip up to Iceland ... that the owner of some multibillion dollar company we're trying to buy is on his deathbed."

"Mr. Peters, they wouldn't give their names to the receptionist, but they did show her their badges. They're from the FBI."

"Oh, I see." This little detail caught me completely off guard. "Do you suppose they might fall for that emergency trip to Iceland?"

Edna didn't waste any body language dismissing my ill-timed stab at humor. I think she was too concerned about what kind of trouble I might have gotten myself into.

"You'd better show them in."

I felt a surge of nervous energy, so I hurriedly straightened my desk … even stacking the magazines on the coffee table in the seating area of my office. Our dress code was business casual, but I kept an extra blue blazer in my closet for emergencies. I figured an unannounced visit from the FBI might qualify. With sport coat properly buttoned, I started working on posture—shoulders back, stomach sucked in. Any moment, two men the size of SUVs would squeeze through that door, each trained to disable dangerous criminals in thirty, maybe forty different ways.

But when Edna escorted Agents Kessler and Davenport into my office, I thought someone was playing a practical joke. The two of them looked like they should be doing comedy in the Catskills. If first impressions meant anything, I figured these two must have been recruited into the bureau for undercover work. Not a soul on planet earth would ever suspect that either of them was a government agent. Some might even wonder if they had detectable heartbeats.

Victor Kessler was five-eight, tops; but he easily weighed in at more than 250 pounds. The dark bushy hair, sideburns, and mustache conjured up bygone images of barbershop quartets and ice cream socials. The chocolate brown suit wouldn't have been fashionable in any era, and it was obvious the man had purchased it during thinner days. In order to button the waistband, the front of his trousers had been shoved beneath his significant and protruding girth. His central totality was held snugly in place by a cheap leather belt that might snap at any instant. To Agent Kessler's credit, though, that belt and his wingtip shoes matched perfectly. Unfortunately, the color of both could only be described as baby-poop brown.

In contrast, Mitzy Davenport displayed the height and weight of a runway model. Six-one, maybe six-two … 115 pounds, soaking wet. Other than dimensionally, "runway model" was not a phrase that would come up in descriptions of this rather peculiar woman. If Washington Irving had wanted to give Ichabod Crane a twin sister, he couldn't have done any better than Agent Mitzy Davenport.

First they introduced themselves as government agents, then they showed me their badges, and finally each handed me a business card. Such prefatory overkill had probably resulted from so many people doubting that these two could possibly be with the Federal Bureau of Investigations. According to their cards, Kessler and Davenport were members of the FBI's Financial Crimes Unit—the FCU. If they were at all representative, we shouldn't anticipate a prime time series dedicated to this specialized unit anytime soon. Yet what the two of them might have lacked in appearance, they lacked even further in personality.

Following introductions, we moved into my private conference room where Agent Davenport took the lead. "Mr. Peters, I guess you know why we're here."

I tried to appear calm, as though I was accustomed to federal authorities dropping by for a chat. But this seemingly simple question already had me scrambling for an answer by which I wouldn't inadvertently incriminate myself for something. I tried to buy time with a proven stall technique ... responding to a question with a question.

"Are you selling raffle tickets for the FBI's annual fund-raiser?"

Okay, maybe attempting comedy wasn't the brightest idea, but I was nervous. When people are nervous, they tend to resort to their most basic instincts. In my case, that meant being a smart-ass. Fortunately, the approach didn't seem to make a negative impression on Kessler and Davenport. As I quickly came to learn, humor was a language they neither spoke nor understood. I could just as easily have been addressing them in Latvian.

Now it was Agent Kessler's turn. "Mr. Peters, we're here about the e-mail you sent."

No doubt, I'd forwarded my share of off-color jokes to friends via e-mail through the years, but I didn't think those actions merited a personal visit from the FBI. Certainly the government had better ways to spend taxpayer dollars. But for once I suppressed my sarcasm and played it straight.

"Agents, I'm sorry ... you'll have to help me out. I don't have any idea what e-mail you're referring to."

"The one you sent last Thursday to the Securities Exchange Commission." This time it was Davenport again.

"Oh."

I admit that this reaction lacked the insight and conviction that one might hope to convey in such a situation, but I was utterly baffled. My mind was racing for possible explanations and one alone made sense ... Luke. No wonder he hadn't shown up for breakfast on Saturday. He couldn't face me, knowing that he'd set me up. Problem was, I still had no idea what kind of e-mail he would have sent or what kind of predicament I might be facing.

Apparently FBI agents operated under a contract that required them to rotate their questions equally, because after a few moments had lapsed, it was Agent Kessler's turn to speak up. "Mr. Peters, that's all you have to say?"

I saw no alternative but to make a rather sheepish request. "Would one of you happen to have a copy of this e-mail that you could share with me?"

They reached for their respective briefcases like they were in a showdown. I barely had time to blink before two pieces of paper were slammed onto the conference room table. A dead heat. Without instant replay, declaring a winner would have been impossible.

The e-mail was from me alright, or at least it had been sent from my electronic address. I safely could presume that Luke had access to an army of techies who would know how to originate e-mails from someone else's electronic address. However, they'd cleverly covered their tracks. The e-mail was sent to "enforcement@sec.gov." Luke and his Washington playmates probably knew every SEC official on a first-name basis, yet this correspondence had been sent to the same general address that any run-of-the-mill whistleblower might use.

> "In accordance with my fiduciary responsibility as a corporate officer, I am notifying the Securities Exchange Commission that financial results filed by American Service Companies have been manipulated wrongfully over a sustained period. ASC's CFO and other senior finance officers have purposely and aggressively breached applicable accounting standards to misrepresent the true state of quarterly earnings. With great regret, I call these violations to your attention and request that the appropriate action be taken.
>
> Michael R. Peters
> President, Corporate Strategy and Support Services
> American Service Companies

This single paragraph was the smoking gun that Luke had needed and now he'd forced it into my hand. I reread the missive several times. His fingerprints were all over the damned thing. Who but a wannabe lawyer would construct sentences like that? The first required course at every law school in the country must be "Writing Like a Tight-Ass." Plus, there was the signature at the bottom. Who but Luke would know that my legal name never had been changed to Milo. As far as the government was concerned, I was "Michael R. Peters." And leave it to Luke even to remember the middle initial—"R" for Robinson, my mother's maiden name.

Agent Kessler spoke again, but I refrained from telling him that he'd gone out of sequence. "Does it look familiar, Mr. Peters?"

I swallowed and took a deep breath. "To tell you the truth, no. I neither sent this e-mail, nor had I seen it until a few moments ago."

Agent Davenport picked up her place in the rotation. "Then how do you explain the fact it was sent from your e-mail address?"

Another hard swallow and deep breath. "I would have to say it came from Luke."

On cue, it was Kessler's turn. "You mean somebody sent this as though it came from you?"

"Exactly."

Davenport again. "Mr. Peters, falsifying charges to the SEC is a serious allegation. If this is some kind of prank, your friend Luke could be guilty of a felony."

I warily eyed the two of them, wondering how forthcoming I should be. I decided it was time to go all-in. "I didn't say the charges were false … and besides, Luke is one of you guys."

"Excuse me?" I wasn't even sure which one had reacted so quickly … it might have been both.

"I said that the charges weren't false."

"No, not that … the part about your friend Luke." That definitely came from Davenport.

"Luke … Luke Papadakis … he works for the federal government. I'm not even sure which agency, but he's been part of your whole investigation into ASC."

"And what investigation would that be?" Agent Davenport seemed to be taking over full interrogative duties, as Kessler pulled out a small spiral notebook and began making notes.

"Ah, come on guys … why are we making this so hard? Certainly you know that the government has been conducting a secret investigation into ASC for earnings fraud."

"Mr. Peters, this is the first we've heard of it."

If my head hadn't been spinning enough, the ensuing ten or fifteen minutes put me over the top. Agents Kessler and Davenport had never heard of Loukas Papadakis. They indicated that once they got back to their office, they would run a check to determine which federal agency employed him ... so at least I might finally learn that. Likewise, they would put out an inquiry as to which agency or agencies might be looking into possible malfeasance at American Service Companies. But on this latter issue, they expressed doubts about coming up with anything.

Based upon the instructions the two agents had received to pay me a visit, they knew for a fact that neither the SEC nor the FBI was part of any investigation. After the SEC had received the e-mail on the previous Thursday, staff members had verified my position at ASC and compiled a dossier on me. Kessler tossed that fun little nugget out as nothing more than an afterthought. The man clearly had no concept of how unsettling it was for a normal citizen to hear that some powerful body in the nation's capital had made him the subject of an official dossier. I prayed that whoever pulled mine together hadn't seen fit to include my college transcripts. No one should be forced to look at grades like that.

The SEC staff members also had issued an internal alert, seeking information on any past or pending SEC investigations into ASC. With none in the system, they'd reached out to the FBI with the same request, and the same results. Late on Monday, the FBI's field office in Chicago was given the assignment of following up on my e-mail in person. Hence, the arrival of Boris and Natasha into my life.

The SEC and FBI were the two government agencies with primary responsibility for identifying and prosecuting corporate fraud. My two new friends couldn't imagine a different agency launching any type of investigation into ASC without notifying one or the other. But just in case, they would send out the query.

From that point, the agents only asked me a few basic questions regarding my "assertions" of corporate fraud at American Service Companies. Talk about a catch-22. No more than a week before had I finally decided not to bring charges against Guenther and ASC, yet Luke had seen fit to go ahead and do it for me. Now those formal charges were already being downgraded to mere assertions. Strangely, I felt insulted. The FBI's odd couple seemed to doubt the very allegations that I'd had no intention of making in the first place. I wanted to strangle one Loukas Alexio Papadakis.

With the possibility that another arm of the government was investigating ASC, Kessler and Davenport didn't feel comfortable probing too far into specifics about the manipulation of corporate earnings. They were worried about encroaching on another federal agency's territory. Or so they said. But such concern over turf and right-of-way wasn't remotely consistent with public perceptions about how the government operated. More likely, I figured this duo had stumbled onto an excuse to avoid any extra work on their part.

The agents promised to get back to me shortly—which according to government standards could have meant before the return of Haley's Comet. I escorted Sonny and Cher out to the lobby of the executive floor. As we waited for an elevator to arrive, Agent Davenport gave me her canned speech about the importance of confidentiality.

"You are legally bound not to discuss the substance of our meeting with anyone other than your attorney. You could be held liable for unfounded speculations that might impact ASC's publicly traded stock. You should ..."

There were other assorted warnings, but I missed most of them. She'd kind of lost me with that attorney comment. Hiring a lawyer immediately jumped to the top of my to-do list.

Agent Kessler felt a need to insert his own punctuation. "Mr. Peters, I'd go further and advise you not to acknowledge that you've even met with the FBI."

At that precise moment, the elevator doors opened and I gave my guests a halfhearted wave—choosing to keep my immediate reaction to myself. *Thanks for that spectacular advice, Victor.*

I turned and looked over at the reception desk. There sat Lynette Carrigan, speaking into her telephone headset in a low voice. Dear, dear Lynette. How thoughtful that Agents Kessler and Davenport had felt obliged to show the bubbly Ms. Carrigan their very impressive badges when they'd arrived. By dinnertime, field technicians across twenty-nine service lines and fifty states, plus licensed franchisees in four Canadian provinces and six Latin American countries, would know that the FBI had paid me a visit at corporate headquarters. But I wasn't supposed to acknowledge that fact to anyone. Brilliant.

On the return trip to my office, I stopped by Edna's cubicle long enough to ask her to track down a bottle of aspirin. "And while you're at it, maybe some arsenic and a syringe."

⌒⁊ℓ⌒

The balance of that day was a slow crawl. I tried to make sense of the various pieces, so I did what had become a routine practice. I plopped onto the couch in my office and stared at the ceiling.

My best friend in the world had set me up as a reluctant whistleblower. Maybe Luke had done so out of concern for the legal jeopardy into which I otherwise might have placed myself. Or maybe he had done it out of a personal interest to advance his investigation and career. Knowing Luke, I was betting on the former. Regardless, there was no turning back.

In short order, I would become the pariah of ASC headquarters. Hundreds of staff members who had no awareness or involvement with the fiscal misconducts would soon see their reputations besmirched by the mere fact that they worked for a tainted corporation. The net worth of thousands of associates would take a nosedive as our stock price sank; plans for retirement would need to be rethought, in some cases shelved.

By now, T. Albert Guenther and the Wire Rims would have heard that I'd been in a closed-door conversation with two FBI agents. Who knew what plans they might be making? Fake passports and chartered flights to some remote Mediterranean island? Or perhaps the easier alternative … a package with unmarked bills and a photo of me, sent to the post office box of some underworld assassin.

Any minute I could expect Wilson Delaney to descend upon my office. The man would turn catatonic once he got word that federal authorities had come to see me. The impact on Delaney's wealth and reputation could be calamitous. But his overriding anger would stem from the fact that I somehow had gotten entangled in activities outside of his purview and control. An anarchist, a renegade operating freely inside his royal court was intolerable.

To say the least, my plans of tormenting Guenther and his boys for a few more months were shot to hell. I also could forget any thoughts of quietly serving notice and easing into a less complicated, less compromised lifestyle. No, my imminent exit from ASC was likely to be featured in newspaper headlines and debated by cable TV panels. By the time the legal proceedings had run their course, I might have to change identities and move into witness protection.

Whatever the array of complications, they were incidental compared to my concerns over what the eventual revelations would mean for Kirsten and Danny. Reluctant or not, my whistle blowing was about to turn their lives upside down. Complicating matters further, Kirsten was back out in the field for a few days. The last thing I wanted to do was deliver such ominous news to her over a telephone. Besides, I couldn't even take that risk. Kessler and Davenport had stressed the absolute confidentiality of our meeting, and for all I knew they might already have tapped my phone lines.

Chapter Seventeen

Someone from HR had sent me the latest book on organizational theory off the *New York Times* best-seller list, so I tried reading that. Three chapters into it and no results.

I turned on the television in my hotel suite and ordered an artsy Italian movie with subtitles. An hour later, my eyes were still wide open.

Activities that normally put me to sleep were having no effect. Eventually I stole a few hours on Tuesday night, but even those were restless. Surely the whole situation wouldn't appear so dire in the sunlight of a brand new day. On Wednesday morning, I pulled back the curtains and raindrops were pelting the window. Optimism was overrated.

By nine o'clock, one of Chicago's most prominent attorneys had faxed back a signed contract. The esteemed Garrett Bedford Ross had agreed to represent me. In the wind-down phase of an illustrious career, the seventy-something Ross had stopped taking on new clients, but for me was making an exception. Actually, it wasn't for me ... he had no idea who I was. He was doing it for Edna, with whom he'd been playing poker on Thursday nights for more than twenty years.

Sometime around ten, Edna was notified that Agents Kessler and Davenport were back in the lobby. It had been less than twenty-four hours. Apparently Chicago's Financial Crime Unit was low on cases.

As soon as they entered my office, I anticipated some rough waters ahead. There wasn't that same spring in their steps or gaiety in the air as when they'd frumped in the day before. If anything, I sensed frustration, maybe a touch of anger—which I didn't read as a particularly good sign. We took our positions in my conference room.

"What a pleasant surprise, Agent Davenport … Agent Kessler. I hadn't expected to see you this soon."

Victor Kessler kicked off today's festivities. "We've run into a few surprises of our own, Mr. Peters."

Yup, that definitely was anger I'd sensed. Even a professional smart-ass knows when to shutdown his engines.

"I guess I'll just sit here quietly while you tell me why you're here."

Their expressions reflected the soundness of my decision. Kessler leaned back in his chair as Agent Davenport leaned forward and spoke in a soft monotone. "Mr. Peters, we've contacted every agency within the federal government that might possibly have reason, and we can report with absolute certainty that there are no ongoing investigations into the financial activities of American Service Companies, nor have any been contemplated in recent years."

She leaned back into parallel position with her partner and they awaited my reaction. I didn't know what to say and with my anxieties mounting under their stare, I started spewing random thoughts.

"Maybe it was my mistake … could be that I somehow heard him wrong. Maybe I made the assumption that Luke still worked for a federal agency. Maybe he works for a state agency or some private watchdog group. I'm sure there's an explanation … I just need to talk to him."

It was Kessler's turn to lean forward. "The only record we found of a Luke Papadakis working for the federal government was a gentleman who started with a division of the commerce department here in Chicago back in 1989. He put in more than fifteen years with commerce."

I grew excited. "Bingo, that's him … that's Luke. So what department or agency did he move onto?"

Davenport leaned forward to speak, but Kessler didn't drop back. It felt like they both were on top of me. "Mr. Peters, are you sure you want to do this? You're going to get yourself into a great deal of trouble if you continue playing games with a government investigation."

"What games? I just want to know who Luke works for."

Davenport was shaking her head this time. "Mr. Peters, we believe you're fully aware that your longtime friend, Luke Papadakis, died in 2005."

For all I knew, Agent Victor Kessler might have hit me with a tire iron while his partner had been speaking. The impact would have been the same. I blanked out, suffering some sort of temporary breakdown. My eyes may have remained open, but I was drifting back and forth between conscious and unconscious. My brain froze, as did time and life as I'd ever known it. I have vague recollections of the two agents practically carrying me out of that conference room. Some minutes later, I know I was sitting on the couch in the main part of my office, Kessler and Davenport hovering over me. Standing with them was Edna, looking anything but stoic. A towel soaked in cold water had been placed against the back of my neck.

The first person I remember speaking had been Edna. "Mr. Peters, please drink some more water." There was a glass in the hand she extended toward me.

"Would you like us to call an ambulance?" That voice had sounded like Kessler's.

I looked from one face to the next, not knowing how to react, not even sure I could get any words out. Little by little, I regained my senses—but that only made the whole situation worse. Now I could remember what had been said in the conference room. I felt a tear sliding slowly down one of my cheeks. Then the other. I looked down and saw that my hands were shaking uncontrollably.

"Mr. Peters?" It was Edna again.

All I could do was move my head from side to side, looking at her and then the agents and then Edna again, with what must have been an extremely pained expression. Finally, I was able to string together a single sentence.

"I should talk to my attorney."

As I sat there wilted and weakened, more and more of the forgotten details came rushing into my head. Painful memories were racing out from their locked-away hiding places.

Chapter Eighteen

In the summer of 2004, I had the world by the balls—or at least what parts of the world I cared about in those days. I lived in a luxury condo and belonged to a handful of elite clubs in Louisville, Kentucky. I'd been president of EverGreen Yards for nearly three years, during which time our annual revenue crossed the two-billion-dollar mark. Sales continued to set new records with every passing month and I finally had my own team of field managers solidly in place. This was the third and largest ASC company I'd run successfully. I was confident that Wilson Delaney would make me a group president sometime in the near future.

My performance bonus alone for the previous year had exceeded three-quarters of a million dollars. As a result, my total compensation was now among the highest across all of American Service Companies, and SEC regulations stipulated that public companies disclose the top five compensation packages in their annual proxy statements. Thus, anyone who bothered to read ASC's proxy would see my name and the staggering numbers next to it.

When friends made reference, I pretended that this public disclosure was awkward for me—working extra hard to project a humble embarrassment. Inwardly, I couldn't have been more thrilled. The measure of my business success was out there for anyone who'd ever known or doubted me to behold with awe and wonderment. Me, the good-time guy. Me, who hadn't been voted most likely to do anything. Me, who skated through college by the narrowest of margins. I was making what the big boys made.

I'd grown rather full of myself during those many years with ASC. Unquestionably, the summer of 2004 was the pinnacle of that self-enchantment. And as I basked in my own importance one August morning, my assistant buzzed to tell me that a man claiming to be a close friend was on my private line. Very few people had that number, so I picked up the phone assuming it was one of my local drinking buddies making plans for another summer weekend.

"Whoever this is, let me forewarn you that I'm booked through the end of the year ... unless you happen to be suggesting something that involves distilled liquids and an abundance of good-looking females."

"Same old Milorad ... always looking for someone else to fix you up with women."

It was great to hear his voice.

"Loukas, why the mystery? Why didn't you tell my secretary it was you?"

"I wasn't sure you were taking my calls anymore ... or if you even remembered my name."

Ouch. He'd left a message the previous week, but I hadn't gotten around to calling him back yet.

"Sorry, Luke ... I've been swamped. But I figured you were probably pretty busy, too ... working crossword puzzles, playing solitaire on your computer, whatever it is you do on the taxpayer's time."

"Yeah, I know, big shot. Assuring that the underlying infrastructure of American business continues to power the strongest economic engine in the history of civilization may not sound as important as controlling the spread of dandelions in our nation's suburbs ... but we all do what we have to do, Milo."

The words were there, but not the spark. Luke was going through the motions, not really into the verbal jousting.

"What's wrong, buddy? Too many dolmades last night?"

"I wish it was that simple, Milo ... I called because I have some tough news."

My first thought was that something had happened with one of his parents—both were getting up there in age. I hoped it wasn't anything between Natalie and him, or worse yet, one of the kids.

"Luke, what's wrong?"

"Remember when I called last week ... well, I'd received a preliminary report from my doctor. He sent me to some specialists for additional testing, and this morning they shared more conclusive results with me. I'm afraid it's not too good, Milo."

"Luke, what is it?" With the phone in my right hand, the left was pressed against my forehead. I could feel the veins throbbing from my racing heartbeat.

"I have pancreatic cancer."

"That can't be … you've always been so healthy … taken such good care of yourself. Are they sure? Maybe it's something else." I was saying every trite thing that probably shouldn't be said. Of course, they were sure.

"There's no doubt … it's pancreatic cancer, Milo."

I was looking for good news; there had to be a bright side. "But they've caught it at an early stage … they'll be able to treat it, right?"

"Officially, they've classified my particular cancer as stage III, meaning it has moved into the lymph nodes that are near my pancreas. But it hasn't spread to other organs, which would be stage IV."

"So that's gotta be encouraging. They can operate … you can have chemo and radiation." I was grasping for anything.

"You bet, Milo … I'm going to use everything possible to beat this. Hell, I still have four kids to raise … you know, my three with Natalie, plus you."

I was so busy processing the hard realities that I'd kept my deeper emotions in check. At least until Luke made his little joke. Now my eyes filled with tears, and I worked hard to mask the tremble in my voice.

"How is Natalie taking the news? And your parents?"

"Natalie's amazing … she's 100 percent convinced we're going to beat this thing. My parents … I've been struggling with how to tell them. Nat and I are going to go have dinner at their house tomorrow night."

"Luke, what can I do? How can I help? Do you want me to get up to Chicago this weekend?"

"Milo, you don't need to do anything other than root for me … say a few prayers now and then. As my closest friend, I just wanted you to know."

The phone conversation lasted a few more minutes. We made some small talk. I made several more attempts at offering up encouragement but couldn't find the words to say what truly was in my heart. I wasn't sure those words existed.

Right before I hung up, Luke stopped me. "Wait, Milo, I forgot to say thanks."

"Thanks? What could you possibly want to thank me for?"

"Today, probably more than any day I can remember, I really needed to hear your voice."

As soon as I put down the phone, I started searching the Internet for details. I'd known pancreatic was one of the deadliest forms of cancer, but the statistics were far more discouraging than anticipated. Less than four percent of adults survived five years. Less than thirty percent made it a year. At stage III, Luke's cancer was advanced. But this was Luke. If anybody could beat pancreatic cancer, Luke Papadakis would.

I beat myself up for not having returned his call from the week before. Upon hearing the preliminary prognosis from his doctor, he'd needed to hear my voice then, too—yet I'd been preoccupied with endless meetings and another week's profits. I at least could have picked up the phone over the weekend, but I'd been too busy being seen in all the right places with all the right people. How could I have pushed our lifelong friendship so far down my priority list?

After the phone conversation, I vowed to put Luke first. In the coming months, nothing would be more important than helping him through his toughest ordeal.

For the first few weeks, I did phone Luke frequently. Each time he would remind me that the road ahead would be long and I needn't check on him so often. He would tell me how fine he was doing. But each time, I could hear how glad he was that I'd made the effort to call, if only for a minute or two.

As we moved into autumn, ASC's planning cycle for the next fiscal year kicked into high gear. That was my busiest season, so the calls to Luke slowed to once or twice during the workweek and once on the weekends ... or sometimes, just the one time on a weekend. I'd meant to fly up and see Luke over one of those weekends, but when I'd become president of EverGreen Yards, I instituted mandatory Saturday work sessions for my senior staff during annual planning periods. I hardly could skip one of my own mandatory meetings ... what kind of example would that have set? Besides, Thanksgiving was just around the corner and I intended to spend four whole days in Chicago. There would be loads of time to visit with Luke.

By the time Thanksgiving arrived, I still was calling Luke once a week—at least, most weeks. Plus, I would send him funny cards as I was rushing through airports ... or occasionally e-mail him some goofy picture that I downloaded off the Internet. In every conversation, he assured me that his condition hadn't worsened. He was lying.

On the Tuesday before Thanksgiving, Wilson Delaney notified all our unit presidents that 2005 business plans needed to be revised in order to generate more dollars on the bottom line. It was typical Delaney to wait until the eve of a holiday weekend. I postponed my Wednesday morning flight to Chicago until Thursday afternoon, in time to catch the pumpkin pie portion of Thanksgiving dinner at my mom's house with all the relatives. Unfortunately, I now would need to be back in Louisville on Saturday, for another work session with my staff. But that still left most of Friday to spend with Luke, Natalie, and the kids.

I showed up at Luke's house in Wicker Park with a bagful of gifts for the kids and a jug of mint juleps for Natalie and Luke. The least I could do was export some Louisville hospitality to a couple of northerners. I envisioned a grand day with good friends, old memories, and plenty of laughter. What I hadn't envisioned was the toll that cancer already had taken on Luke.

When Natalie met me at the front door, she didn't seem particularly receptive to my hug, and her voice lacked its usual warmth. The stress of a holiday weekend, I figured. Then she showed me into the living room where Luke slept in an easy chair, wrapped in one of the familiar afghans his mother liked to knit. He couldn't have weighed more than 120 pounds. Last time I'd seen him, he'd been a solid 170-plus.

His facial features were sunken. The skin that clung to his bones was paler than white … almost transparent, with no color whatsoever. Atop his head was a tattered ball cap—the Cubs. No evidence of hair beneath. I wondered how many chemo treatments remained. Or if they'd stopped completely … a lost cause.

Why hadn't Natalie warned me at the door? I looked over to her and saw coldness in her expression. I then knew that her chilly reception hadn't been fatigue; the coldness she exhibited was a direct result of my presence. For some reason, she resented my being there.

I asked her where the kids were.

"They went home with Luke's parents last night. I thought you two might prefer to catch up with less commotion in the house … Milo, how long has it been since you've had that chance?"

It wasn't a question, it was a dart. And it wasn't resentment she was feeling toward me, it was deep-seated anger.

"I'm sorry, Natalie, I had no idea—"

She cut me off. "I know … there's no way you could have." But her comment wasn't meant to let me off the hook.

The sound of our voices caused Luke to stir. We both moved closer to him. When he opened his eyes and saw me, he broke into a broad grin.

Even in his weakened state, no smile could light up a room like Luke's. He glanced over at Natalie and pointed my way, as if to say, *"See, I told you he'd come."*

"I'll leave you two alone." Natalie scurried off to the kitchen. Given her druthers, she would have returned with a sharp knife from one of the drawers.

After Luke and I watched her disappear through the swinging door, we looked back at each other. I was still in shock, trying not to gawk at his appearance. I think he sensed my discomfort. He grabbed the brim of his hat and tipped it slightly forward.

"Like we've always said, Milo, Cubs fans to the bitter end."

"You didn't need to go to this extreme to prove your point, you crazy Greek."

I leaned down and circled my arms around him as he sat in the chair. He found the strength to reach up and wrap his frail limbs around my back. We hugged tightly for several minutes, neither trying to hide the tears. Finally, I pulled away.

He reached for a Kleenex on the table next to him. "Okay, I'm glad that's over." He wiped his eyes and the side of his face. "So what have you been up to, you big crybaby?"

He sounded exactly the same as he always had. The strength in his voice, the joy in his voice, the love in his voice. If I closed my eyes, Luke hadn't changed a bit. If I closed my eyes, Luke never would change. Perhaps that's why I'd been misled by our phone conversations ... the comforting familiarity of his voice. At least I could pretend that was my excuse for not hurrying home sooner.

I stayed with Luke for the entire afternoon. Natalie came back into the living room several times to give him his medicines and once to bring us a lunch of leftover turkey sandwiches. She tried to appear pleasant and polite in Luke's presence, but she avoided eye contact or any direct conversations with me. On two occasions, Luke nodded off and I was content to simply watch him sleep. When he awakened, he said the same thing both times.

"I'm sorry, Milo ... but God knows, you Serbs are dreadfully boring."

The third time he fell asleep, I decided I should go. I didn't want to exhaust him. I went into the kitchen to find Natalie, who was sitting at the counter thumbing through magazines.

"Thanks for telling me you're leaving, Milo. I'll call Luke's parents and ask them to bring the kids home for dinner."

She immediately reached for the phone and started punching numbers into it. It was obvious she hadn't wanted me to spend time with their children. I let myself out the front door.

How could I have allowed my priorities to get so screwed up? My best friend had been dying rapidly, yet I'd been too preoccupied to check with anyone else about the severity of his situation. Luke's wife barely could stomach the sight of me and I understood why. No doubt, Natalie Papadakis had heard her husband stick up for me many times over the years, despite the disproportionate energy our friendship required of him. Facing certain death, Luke had continued to defend me, his body atrophying while I was nowhere to be seen. How had I been so blind? How had I become so consumed with such trivial, fleeting ambitions?

I vowed, once and for always, to get my life turned around and headed in the right direction. It was the least I could do for Luke, out of gratitude and respect for his unmatched friendship, his positive influence, his unwavering belief in me. For everything he'd always meant to me.

I returned to Louisville with newfound conviction, like so many times before. But this time was going to be different. If watching life slip away from the man I loved like a brother wasn't enough to alter my self-serving ways, then I should declare myself a lost cause.

Less than two months later, I did just that.

For a solid week after Thanksgiving, I remained true to my vows. I called Luke daily, sometimes two or three times. We lamented the Bears and the Bulls. We relived memories of our youth. We filled the phone lines with banter, comfort, and admiration.

In early December, I got a call from Wilson Delaney. He still wasn't convinced that some of ASC's business units were doing all they could to tighten up the costs in their business plan submissions for the new year about to start, which would be his first full year as CEO. He wanted me to visit a number of other presidents and show them how to turn the screws. I was the only executive Delaney could count on to get the overall corporate plan to where he needed it in a matter of weeks. He told me just that—in no uncertain terms. He gave me full access to the corporate jet for whatever amount of time it might take. I couldn't turn him down; I had no choice. I packed my suitcase.

I lost track of the cities, the conference rooms, and the days. I still tried to phone Luke whenever I remembered. Some days, I was forced to keep the calls shorter than I would have liked. Other days, I couldn't work in a phone call at all. The budget work sessions usually started early and ran well into the evening … there was only so much time available. I figured Luke wouldn't notice much of a difference … it was only a few weeks. Besides, I'd be seeing him at Christmastime.

Unfortunately, Luke had taken a turn for the worse shortly after Thanksgiving. The doctors had concurred that he was unlikely to live through the end of the year. But Luke always loved the Christmas season; he wasn't going to ruin the holidays for his kids. He made a brief comeback. He regained enough strength to sit in his recliner while Natalie, his parents, and the kids opened their presents. Friends from his office had traveled to a farm well outside of Chicago and cut down a tree that took up half the living room; neighbors had weighted the branches with hundreds of lights and decorations. No one could stop this Christmas from being Luke's last, but those closest to him had done everything possible to make it one of his best.

I saw Luke twice while I was home for the holidays. My visit late in the afternoon on Christmas Day was the most telling. Receptivity to my arrival was mixed. On one end of the spectrum was Natalie's pronounced silence; on the other, Luke's electric smile. In between was the welcome embrace of Luke's parents, who could look past their disappointments in me and instead focus on what their son and I had meant to each other in our youth. The reactions of Luke's two daughters and son were definitely closer to their mother's. I'd met them on numerous occasions over the years, but I didn't really know them. Nor them, me. I hadn't taken the time; I probably had been too busy trying to impress Luke and Natalie with my latest accomplishments. To the Papadakis kids I was "that man"— that name their father forever was mentioning. Seeing me again in person, I almost could read their minds. *What's the big deal about this guy?*

On the day after Christmas, Luke and I sat alone for several hours. They were the most serious hours we ever spent together. No sparring, no repartee. No hiding from the fact it would likely be our last opportunity to share a uniquely special bond—the way that only two people who completely understood each other could. We had much to say, but far more that didn't need to be.

Luke realized his days were limited and was prepared to die. He was grateful for the life he'd been granted, the girl of his dreams, and the knowledge that his presence would continue to be expressed through the lives of his three greatest achievements. Like my father, no regrets. What better testament could there be to the quality of one's life than to die with no regrets? And better yet, to have lived with none.

We spoke in great detail about Natalie and his optimism that she would do fine without him. He wanted her to find new joys, new happiness, and even had told her she should marry again. She deserved the contentment of a soul mate in the years ahead … some other lucky man should share the love of the one perfect woman he'd ever known. After relating those hopes to me, he paused and chuckled.

"Milo, a word of advice … you may be my best friend, but in this particular area I don't think you can be much help. Let's just say that you and Natalie wouldn't have any fun on a date."

"Believe me, Luke, I know … not unless I handed her a bullwhip and strapped myself to a tree."

During the course of our conversation, he did ask me to reach out to his parents from time to time. We talked openly about my failures to stay better connected. Luke never had let those shortcomings bother him, insistent that the foundation of our friendship was too strong to worry about scorekeeping. He was convinced his parents took the same long-term view and would appreciate whatever future contacts I could manage.

"I'm sure my folks will carry a sadness for the years they have left, but I don't think they'll be the types to seal off the happy memories. The more they see Natalie and the kids, the more they can relish the time we did share. The same goes for you … please don't be a stranger to them."

The final few minutes of our time together were something sacred. To this day, I choke up when I remember those parting sentiments, but at the time we were able to express our most heartfelt thoughts without tears. Not a word was hurried or mumbled.

"Milo, I'm afraid we should wrap it up … I don't think I can stay awake much longer."

I leaned forward from my chair and clasped the top of his left hand. "I understand … you need your sleep. But, Luke, before I leave … I want you to know that I've always loved you like a second brother. More importantly, that won't stop … I always will."

He placed his free right hand atop our clasped hands. "Milorad, we are brothers in every way possible except blood. I don't know what's around the corner for me, but if there's any chance I can keep an eye on you, you can be sure that I will."

"God knows, you've had plenty of practice. Loukas, you've always been there for me … even when I haven't been there for you."

"As I said earlier, I've never cared about that. I worry more about you being there for yourself … about you finding yourself … about finding the

Milo Peters that's still inside you—the spontaneous, unpredictable Milo Peters who made people feel better about themselves, the Milo Peters to whom others were drawn, the Milo Peters who didn't hold back, who never was afraid to show people that you cared."

"Luke, you give me too much credit. You saw those traits only because you brought them out in me."

"Then let's simply agree … we have both been blessed. You are the best friend that any man could ever want."

"Indeed, we have been blessed. Loukas Papadakis, you're the best man I'll ever know."

A week after New Year's, Luke was moved to a hospital. Two weeks after that, he passed away in his sleep—Natalie and his parents at the bedside, along with sixteen-year-old Alexandra, fourteen-year-old Vanessa, and eleven-year-old Gregory. I was in Boca Raton, presiding over EverGreen Yard's annual convention.

However, I had seen Luke one more time. His father had called to inform me that the doctors were calibrating days rather than weeks. My company convention in Florida was still two days off. I needed that time in the office to make final preparations for the convention, but I was able to wedge in a flight to Chicago. I couldn't even spend the night. I arranged for a town car to take me directly to the hospital, wait, and then return me to the airport. It's hard to say whether I made the trip for Luke or for myself, to assuage the guilt. Either way, I'll always be glad I made it.

Luke was unable to speak. He was so heavily medicated with morphine that the attending nurse wasn't sure he had any awareness at all. She wanted to page Luke's family members, who were sleeping in a nearby lounge. They'd been holding vigil since Luke's admittance. I instructed her to let them rest.

For forty-five minutes I held Luke's hand, remembering how to pray and weeping most of that time. He wasn't yet dead, but I already missed him. I missed the mischief of our childhoods, the camaraderie of our teens, our progression into adulthood. This incredible presence in my life no longer would be there. I wept over the missed opportunities … the grief and guilt inseparable.

When it was time to leave, I bent down to kiss Luke's forehead, still clutching his hand. The moment my lips grazed his skin, Luke's hand squeezed mine. He gripped tightly for five or six seconds, as long as possible in his medicated state. Then he was asleep. I reached into a paper bag I'd brought with me and gently placed the new Cubs cap atop his head. Luke had always had a thing for hats.

The funeral was in an old Greek church, the same one where Luke had been christened as an infant and married as a man. Every pew was filled, the overflow standing in the rear. Gordie Hilpert and Rich Jenkins sat in the front row next to the four other pallbearers. I hadn't seen either since our last reunion at Ashton's—at least three or four years. Several rows behind them, I spotted someone else I hadn't seen in more than a dozen years. I stared until I caught her attention and we exchanged smiles from a distance. Carly still looked spectacular. She'd driven up from Cincinnati with her husband and, to me at least, they exuded the aura of two people who belonged together. I couldn't help but feel both happy and sad, knowing she'd been so much better off without me.

I recognized most from the throng of Luke's relatives, who sat in a reserved section of pews just to the side of the altar. Scattered among the rest of the assembled crowd were familiar faces from different phases of Luke's life—teachers we'd shared, fellow classmates and teammates, neighbors, and coworkers to whom he'd introduced me. Sitting in the front of the church, looking out across the many who gathered, I also studied faces of strangers and wondered how their lives had been touched by Luke's charisma and compassion. By the time it was my turn to speak, none of them seemed like strangers any longer. Luke was drawing us tightly together; some of us merely hadn't met one another yet.

The eulogy ran close to twenty-five minutes—much longer than allotted. The three or four times I'd practiced, I had worked it down to under ten, but that hadn't allowed extra time for people's reactions to the various stories I chose to tell. None of us really had finished our crying when we'd shown up for the funeral service, so sharing a few poignant remembrances of Luke allowed us to get a few more tears out. But mostly I recounted memories of an irrepressible Greek that evoked smiles, in many instances laughter. Of course, those reactions and the looks on the faces staring up from the pews had prompted me to throw in a few more stories, and then a few more. Luke's was a life that called for celebration rather than time limits. No one seemed to mind.

During the months Luke was dying, he had provided very little direction as to his funeral. He wasn't avoiding the inevitable, he simply chose to focus on matters he gave higher importance. He trusted Natalie to make suitable arrangements. The only detail he had specified was the eulogy. He'd been adamant that I alone must deliver it.

In keeping with Greek custom, almost everyone returned to the church basement after a short gravesite service at the interment. Amid cheeses, bread loaves, olives, platters of fish, pastries, and endless shots of brandy, we continued to share our favorite recollections of Luke. The stories I found most intriguing were the ones from acquaintances or coworkers who'd only known him in more recent years. I marveled at their depictions of Luke, even the word choices, because they were no different than those from family and friends who'd known him since childhood. Loukas Papadakis had remained unequivocally true to himself.

Just as he did in person, Luke's funeral brought out the best in people's behavior. Sure, there was sadness. But there also was a pervasive feeling of goodness that blotted out any negative energy. Whatever mistakes and conflicts that may have occurred in the past were forgiven, forgotten, or at least tabled for a day. The gang from Ashton's hugged and promised how we'd all do better at staying in touch—whether we meant it or not. Carly and I smoothed any awkward feelings that still might have lingered, and the wishes I extended for her continued success and happiness had been sincere. During a brief exchange, I even got the feeling that Natalie was softening in her attitude toward me. But that must have been the brandy temporarily at work, rounding her sharp edges or numbing my sensitivities.

A week after the funeral, I called Natalie to see how she and the kids were coping. I was committed to start clean, to develop and sustain a much deeper interest in their lives going forward. But before I'd even had the chance to unveil the new me, she took control of the conversation.

"Milo, we'll do fine. You needn't call and check on us … in fact, I insist that you not. I'm sorry to be so blunt, but I can't disguise my resentment over how many times you let Luke down … not just when he was sick, but ever since you moved away. He never would say it … all he would do was make excuses for you. But I saw it in his face and heard it in his voice whenever we spoke about 'his best friend Milo.' He would tell me how busy you were and that he understood, but I know he had expected so much more out of your friendship. And he had every right to; you had a real brother, Luke didn't—you were that brother. He wanted you two to play bigger parts in each other's lives, like you always had … but you became too damned important, I guess. Even after he told you that he was diagnosed as terminal … for God's sake, Milo … how could you remain so distant? Do you think an occasional phone call or a funny e-mail was all you meant to Luke? Is that all he meant to you?"

She paused to compose herself, but she wasn't done. "I know Luke wouldn't want me to say these things to you … he'd want me to reach out and stay in touch with you in every way possible. But Milo, I can't. I can't forget those looks on his face during his final months. You didn't have time then, so don't bother to find the time now. The kids and I miss Luke too much … and will for a long, long time. So don't add to that burden by making us remember how you repeatedly let down the best friend you'll ever have. I'm sure you weren't expecting any of this … but it's been building inside me for a long time. Good luck to you, Milo … I don't wish anything bad for you … in fact, I hope you might someday figure yourself out. But please, don't call us again."

The line went dead. My heart went dead. I was crushed … not because of what she'd said, but because every word of it was true … there wasn't a single condemnation that I hadn't at some point flung at myself. I doubt she would have found any consolation, but I could have told Natalie that I'd been equally neglectful with my brother Tim and everyone else close to me. For the petty aggrandizements of a shallow career, I'd sold out friends, family, and personal values. Finally, someone had called me on it.

Of note, I collected another bag of silver that February, with my promotion to group president. December's whirlwind trip to the other divisions had done the trick … another obstacle course successfully completed for Wilson Delaney. I eagerly was jumping through circus hoops, while my best friend sat dying, watching an empty sidewalk through the curtains in his living room.

"Mr. Peters, we believe you're fully aware that your longtime friend, Luke Papadakis, died in 2005."

After Agent Mitzy Davenport uttered those words in the conference room, so many anguished memories had come roiling out of the crawl spaces of my soul. Freed from an inexplicable confinement, they had reentered my conscious reality all at once, filling my mind with more than it could absorb. For some period of time, I'd completely shut down … then slowly I started reentry.

Davenport and Kessler chose to play their cards carefully with me, unsure of what game I might be playing with them. Checking into Luke Papadakis, they'd read the newspaper notices in his file. They'd seen that I delivered the eulogy at his funeral. I obviously knew the man was dead. So why, after sending an e-mail to the SEC, would I suddenly claim it came from Luke … or that I was part of an investigation that never existed, headed by a dead government employee who'd worked for an agency that had nothing to do with white-collar crimes? Why would a corporate executive be playing such a game at all … why would he allege earnings improprieties inside his own company? Was this guy, Milo Peters, a lunatic? Was there anything really to investigate inside this respected corporation? And how do a couple of federal agents tactfully proceed without creating a bigger mess than the one I'd already laid at their feet? Of course, Davenport and Kessler were going to move cautiously.

Waiting for Garrett Bedford Ross to arrive, the two agents would have preferred to sit in silence. They knew better than to probe relevant subject matter with a questionable character before his requested attorney was present. No, I was the one who started up the conversation—not because I thought I could resolve anything. After my prolonged silence, I merely was starting to think out loud.

"Agents, as I sit here, I can't begin to explain why I forgot that my best friend, Luke Papadakis, passed away … let alone the vivid memories of those recent breakfast meetings with him and his requests that I help with an investigation. And though none of this must make any sense to you, I'm almost certain I didn't send that e-mail to the SEC."

"Mr. Peters, the only thing we know for sure is that your e-mail was sent to the SEC, but considering your current state of mind, we should talk about it later." Kessler was trying to get me to stop.

"I'm sure we will talk about it later, but I still don't believe I sent it."

Now Davenport spoke up. "But even if you didn't send the e-mail, you'll still contend that ASC has manipulated its earnings?"

"I wasn't planning to come forward, but yes … most definitely, our CFO and members of his senior staff have been managing our quarterly earnings illegally for a number of years."

"And you know this for a fact?" Davenport was trying to sound sympathetic, but her skepticism was evident.

Kessler picked up the pitcher of ice water, refilled my glass from the table, and handed it to me. "Mr. Peters, please … let's wait for your lawyer."

I had to admit, nothing that I said could have seemed very credible.

With the distinguished sounding name and bellowing voice I'd heard on the phone earlier that morning, I was expecting Garrett Bedford Ross to storm into the office like Theodore Roosevelt or Winston Churchill. Instead my renowned attorney practically tiptoed into my office taking baby steps, wearing cheap white running shoes, a burgundy blazer, and a paisley bowtie. He was pencil thin with a crew cut. I momentarily panicked, worried that I might be slipping toward another breakdown. Until I heard the familiar booming voice, I thought I was hallucinating clowns. I learned later that colorful blazers, bowties, and a crew cut were trademark shtick for the legendary Mr. Ross. The running shoes and ridiculous walk were attributable to recent bunion surgery.

Appearance aside, the man knew how to take immediate charge. He told me to sit tight and invited the two agents to join him in my private conference room. On a couple of occasions they came out and asked me a few questions, and by the time the disjointed meeting was over, they'd also conferred with my mother via speakerphone. Since I didn't have a wife, they wanted to cover off my most immediate relative on a recommended course of action.

Chapter Nineteen

"Mr. Peters, I'll leave you and your mother alone, as I'm sure you want to get settled in ... but I'll be back in a half hour, so we can go grab a sandwich."

"Thank you, Dr. Sunstrom, and please call me Milo."

"Okay, Milo, I'm looking forward to our first session."

Her voice resonated with professional calmness—like a dentist, right before he fires up the drill. But at least I'd finally found someone who was willing to call me by my first name. Then again, Melanie Sunstrom was head of the mental health facility I had just checked into ... she probably would have called me Benjamin Franklin if that's what I'd wanted.

As I started unpacking my suitcases onto the bed, I noticed that my mom was hurriedly opening all the drawers and closet doors in the room they'd assigned me. I think she was wondering where they kept the straightjacket ... and I was kind of curious myself. Braydon Counseling Center was no four-star hotel; but for a nuthouse, it was much nicer than anything I'd envisioned. I guess I shouldn't have expected anything less with Garrett Bedford Ross looking out for my interests.

On the prior day, following the meltdown in my office, I readily had agreed to enter a special clinic for observation. Not that turning myself into a lab rat for a bunch of shrinks ranked high on my bucket list, but the realization that you've been having imaginary interactions with a dead person tends to open one's mind to all kinds of new possibilities. A few days under the microscope seemed like a reasonable concession for having stirred up a dust storm with the Federal Bureau of Investigations and Securities Exchange Commission. Little did I know that I'd spend nine weeks in the land of perpetually smiling white uniforms and end up on a first-name basis with most of them.

Per the agreement struck by my venerable attorney, I wasn't to be released until the specialists in whichever department that handled my particular condition could reach consensus on a diagnosis and treatment. Three weeks later, when they'd yet to resolve which department that was, it became apparent that consensus wasn't going to come easily at merry old Braydon.

I've got to hand it to the folks who chose the name, "Braydon Counseling Center." Good marketing. The name, which was plastered on everything in sight, suggested it was a stress-free, compassionate place that handed out friendly advice to those in need. More accurately, it should have been called, "Braydon Institute of Nonstop Intimidating Questions."

To begin with, when a person knows he's being analyzed for mental abnormalities, even the simplest queries are daunting … because somewhere in the building sits someone with a list of right and wrong answers. You worry about which dark sides to your personality are being revealed through the most innocent of responses.

"Good morning, Milo … how did you sleep last night?" What might they really hope to learn with that little jewel?

Or "Are there any particular magazines you'd like me to bring you?" Who wouldn't be a bit suspicious when a volunteer attendant stops by to ask such a loaded question? That is, if she really was a high school junior. For all I knew, she might have possessed the authority to transfer me into a padded cell on a moment's notice.

Then imagine twelve hours a day, being shepherded from one office to the next, room after room of soothing colors and pastoral paintings, where you meet with specialists that have enough pedigrees behind their names to spin off their own private alphabets. And, boy, did those docs like to ask questions. In fact, I think it was a game they liked to play among themselves … testing each other's ability to go entire days speaking only in questions.

"Well, hello Milo … it's ten o'clock, we have an appointment this morning, don't we?"

"Would you like to come in and take a seat, so we can get started?"

"Should we pick up where we left off last time?"

"Are we getting more comfortable expressing the true feelings we've been carrying inside?"

In scoring their little contest, bonus points must have been awarded for using the universal "we" as much as possible.

Day in, day out, we tore apart and reconstructed my life for as far back as I could remember, as though there was some standard formula that explained how people wound up having weekly breakfasts with figments of their own imaginations. Eventually, two of the white coats emerged as my main interrogators.

Over the course of eighteen years, Dr. Henry Tann had become a fixture at Braydon. Though his appearance and physical features reflected Korean descent, his family could just as easily have come over on the Mayflower. There was a photo on his desk of a smiling wife and four teenaged kids sitting on the dock outside their lake house in Michigan. An array of diplomas on his wall revealed that he'd attended exclusive schools up and down the East Coast. And strewn about his office was a lifetime of New York Yankees memorabilia, which would have been troubling to any Chicagoan. But once I got acclimated to the New York accent that explained his penchant for the most revolting team in the history of baseball and perhaps all of sports, I found him easy enough to talk to.

With Dr. Estrella Guzman, I needed to work through other obstacles before I could get comfortable opening up to her. First, the dark porcelain complexion, penetrating eyes and soft Mexican accent made it difficult for me to focus on any of the actual words that seemed to float out of her mouth. Then there was the way she kept crossing and uncrossing those shapely legs as she sat in the chair opposite me. With my fragile condition, it was like a seductive form of hypnosis. Fortunately, she must have recognized my wandering attention and eventually took to wearing pantsuits for most of our sessions. If she had stuck to the skirts and dresses, I might never have gotten a cogent thought out.

Oh, the fun we had behind closed doors, traipsing across a landscape of memories. No stone unturned, as I waxed on about the happy associations of my youth and the careless manner in which I'd diverted my energies to less pleasant preoccupations in the years since. With each seemingly benign question, wellsprings of emotion came bubbling forth. Details that I never would have believed I remembered, that I never would've believed might matter, suddenly took on gigantic importance in the recounted stories about my father and mother, my uncles ... my brother Tim and Baba Milka ... Carly and the gang at Ashton's ... and certainly Luke. With each carefully paced question, it became clearer and clearer how the treasured interactions with these individuals had shaped my values and aspirations. With each of my eventual admissions, it became clearer and clearer how much I'd fallen short of expectations—not necessarily the expectations these pivotal people in my life had held for me, but the ones they rightfully could have held … the expectations they caused me to hold for myself.

The serious psychological issues had taken root with my leap into the real world after college—so I guess in one sense, those desires I'd harbored about freezing time and avoiding adulthood had been appropriate. Henry Tann suggested that I probably hadn't felt good about my career choice from the day I started working for Zero Bug Tolerance. Hardly a shocker to me. What kid grows up hoping to make a career out of killing cockroaches? I tried to explain to him about the bad grades and the need to collect a paycheck, but I think scholarly professional types find it difficult to relate to such pedestrian concerns.

"Milo, it is likely your early unexpected success within Zero Bug Tolerance created an emotional incongruity that you chose to placate rather than confront. That is, while you didn't feel good about what you were doing, you experienced a new form of fulfillment in the discovery that you could do it so well. Your solution was to suppress the discontentment and focus on the gratifications. Soon thereafter you started encountering other aspects of the company that accelerated this inner conflict … questionable business practices that you felt pressured to engage in if you wanted to continue progressing … internal politics … the domineering and manipulative personality of your Mr. Delaney. To counter the mounting angst with what you found distasteful, you focused even more intently on your personal achievements … a textbook example of cognitive dissonance and a natural means by which to compensate."

I have to admit that when you're in the throes of round-the-clock psychoanalysis, you start listening for the smallest kernels of normalcy. To me it was good to hear that when I'd gone about screwing up my mental well-being, I at least had done it by the book.

Dr. Tann went on to explain how the intense focus on my career achievements had become a fixation over time, and ultimately that fixation begot obsession. Meanwhile, though I'd been playing a prolonged game of hide-and-seek with my negative feelings toward ASC and the way we conducted business, I actually had remained highly conscious of a raging war within.

"Milo, most of us with careers are forced to recognize and deal with inconsistencies between required job-related behaviors and our ideal self-images … we learn to reconcile them as practical trade-offs. Perhaps yours were more severe than most … I'm not sure I'm in a position to judge. But either way, you were unwilling to accept the compromises. In your own mind, within your own psyche, you were unable to let yourself off the hook. You saw yourself as a coward, and the more success you gained, the more cowardly you saw yourself becoming. Hence, your disdain for the company and what was required to succeed transformed into a disdain for yourself."

According to Dr. Tann, I'd become a self-loather by the time I reached thirty ... and that's when things really started getting complicated. Like many self-loathers, I started distancing myself further and further from the people that were most important to me. Worried that they'd recognize me for what I was becoming, I wanted to avoid experiencing their disappointment or disapproval at close range.

Consistent with many self-loathing tendencies, I also started looking to alcohol as a means to hide from my darker and darker thoughts. And to the outside world, I became better at using my trusty wit and sarcasm as camouflage. The essence of what I really wanted out of life, out of myself, was trapped inside a veneer of glibness and upward mobility.

Drs. Tann and Guzman helped me reconstruct a timeline of my downward journey, taking great care to point out how the causes and effects of my self-loathing played on one another. A squandered romantic relationship with Carly. The missed opportunities to spend more time with a close-knit family that had once been so important to me. My inattentiveness to meaningful friendships—most notably Luke, but others, too. The avoidance of reconciling my patterned behaviors with my personal values ... the recurrent feelings of totaling abandoning everyone and everything that was important to me.

Estrella Guzman took special interest in my personal relationships. "Milo, as the self-disgust intensified, you assigned even greater significance to the role modeling of other key people in your life. As the gap widened between your self-image and the strength of character you ascribed to the people you most admired, the standards of comparison became unachievable for you. And with the downward spiral of your self-perceptions, these individuals took on even more heroic proportions."

She went on. "The loss of your father and your regrets over missed opportunities with him created new levels of guilt that further fed your deepening self-hatred. Then, a few years later with your friend Luke's death, both the guilt and self-loathing escalated exponentially due to a belief that you had failed to properly be there for him during his illness. And, in all likelihood, the dress-down you received from his wife Natalie was something you'd been craving for years."

Dr. Guzman surmised I had convinced myself that I lacked the strength to alter behaviors on my own, so my inner self had wanted someone else to expose me for what I'd become ... or, at least, what I thought I'd become. I had to question her on this one.

"Time out, Doc. The only person to whom Natalie really exposed me for what I'd become, was me ... and I thought I'd already known what I had become. So why would I have wanted or needed someone else to call me out to myself?"

"Because, Milo, you had become so proficient at hiding the distaste for where your life was headed, you longed for someone else to recognize that your shortcomings were as bad as you believed they were, that you really did need to reevaluate and redirect your life. If no one else was noticing or saying anything, maybe you didn't need to change ... maybe you were just being paranoid and should simply lighten up on yourself. But that possibility wasn't satisfactory to your inner emotions, to the extended state of unhappiness in which you felt entrapped. You craved a wake-up call, a jolt from someone close to you that would confirm you were every bit as bad as you thought you were ... that your self-loathing and guilt were justifiable. Then and only then, you might find the impetus to truly change."

Reflecting on all the wrestling matches inside my head over the years, I had to admit that what she said made sense. In fact, the experts at Braydon had a lot of fancy jargon for *concurrent emotional forces* and *pervasive behavior patterns* that sounded pretty familiar. I just hadn't known them by name when I'd been living through them.

The complication I hadn't recognized, or certainly expected, was the transition into delusions. Their hypothesis was that the grief, pain, and guilt I carried from Luke's death and Natalie's reprehension had kicked my self-loathing into overdrive. As negative energies festered inside, the challenge of containing them was more than I could handle. My last promotion and the required relocation to my hometown of Chicago had offered up a remarkably convenient convergence.

My subconscious went to work. In one fell swoop, I could return home, regain my principles, and recapture my dignity. The agonizing dissonance could be eliminated, the self-loathing could stop. However, so many past attempts to change directions in my life had fallen short. I still harbored serious doubts that I was emotionally or psychologically equipped to navigate those uncharted waters on my own. I needed help, encouragement, strong moral support ... and what person in my life had I always looked to? Who had always been there to steer me straight? Five years after his death, what void in my life remained gaping and unresolved … whose absence had I failed to accept?

"Milo, you'd been back in Chicago for several weeks, wrestling with your conscience, wrestling with whether you wanted to continue your ambitious climb to the top of ASC or leave the company completely."

It was like Dr. Guzman knew exactly what I'd been feeling during those first weeks in January.

"Then on a Friday night, you were the guest of honor at a gathering of coworkers. You became the center of attention … many complimentary things were being said about you and your career accomplishments. The man who held the ultimate position you coveted, but who epitomized everything you hated about yourself, was right in the middle, praising and toasting you. All of your struggles, all of your self-doubts, all of your hypocrisies, were right there on full display.

"You tried to bury your self-disgust in alcohol … but you'd already learned that drinking and partying didn't help for long. So the next morning you went to Ashton's, a place filled with special memories … memories of a simpler Milo Peters, the way you wanted him to be again. Memories of a group that accepted and liked this simpler Milo Peters. Memories of a lifelong friend, Luke, who was such a seminal part of this Milo Peters … and on a subconscious level, you wondered if you could become that person again without his help."

Now it was Dr. Tann's turn. "Milo, when you walked into Ashton's on that first Saturday morning, all that Dr. Guzman just described was spinning inside your head and you seamlessly slipped into a delusional state. At the time, it was out of your conscious control. These types of delusional disorders are a form of psychosis, a loss of contact with reality."

It was just like a Yankee fan to be the one to stick the knife in. He'd said it … the dreaded "p-word." My diagnosis was official. I was a card-carrying psychotic.

First off, I want to be clear. A psychotic is much different than a psychopath, which I was relieved to learn. Psychopaths are those severely unstable folks who can do serious harm if they go untreated, while a psychotic merely has difficulty discerning reality from illusions. We psychotics aren't the ones who run off and make lampshades out of Great-Aunt Doris. I prefer to think of my condition as a more benign, genteel disorder … as much eccentricity as insanity. But I may be a little biased.

Drs. Tann and Guzman, along with their minion psychoanalysts, concluded that I'd been exhibiting a number of "classic symptoms" for psychosis. My particular form of psychosis can be triggered by a whole litany of stressful life events. High on that list were two influences that scored a double bull's-eye with me—anxieties about one's career and the death of loved ones.

With my career, I'd been amassing twenty years of pent-up worries, frustrations, guilt, and self-doubts.

With regard to the death of loved ones, of course there had been my father. His sudden passing caused me to more deeply question the waste I was making of my life. Then with Luke's, just a few years later, I realized that I couldn't stop myself ... I didn't know how to get off the merry-go-round. From a clinical standpoint, I'd become a walking, talking petri dish filled with psychotic bacteria.

I wasn't the least surprised when the white coats started enumerating the various emotional burdens I'd been harboring. After all, I'd been working hard to dodge every single one of them on a daily basis for quite some time. But the docs, they were astounded that one outwardly successful business executive could have lugged so much baggage around for as long as I did. According to these well-pedigreed oddsmakers, I should have snapped much sooner. Prime time for an initial psychotic episode was usually during one's twenties or thirties, but I'd waited until my forties. I reminded the doctors that puberty also had arrived late for me.

They informed me that many psychotics tended to be highly perceptive and intelligent individuals, but the white coats may have been trying to schmooze me. Dr. Tann seemed especially intrigued with the intricate game plan I'd been able to strategize on a subconscious level. He didn't want to admit it, but I think he admired how I'd enlisted Luke's imaginary help to explore financial irregularities inside American Service Companies.

"From what you've said, Milo, you had grown increasingly suspicious about the earnings results that your company was posting."

"Dr. Tann, trust me, I'm no financial genius ... but after working with Wilson Delaney for so long, one starts to naturally assume some form of funny business is going on behind the curtains at headquarters. I'd wondered about our ramped-up reliance on acquisitions and reserves. For five years, I'd been wondering why Delaney and Guenther had been in such a hurry to centralize our financial functions and hire all new people."

In keeping with standard white-coat practices, he built on my comment. "Well, from the vantage of your lofty new position at headquarters, you figured you finally could take a look behind those curtains firsthand. But you lacked the conviction or courage to take on those demons that surrounded Delaney head-on … you subconsciously needed to enlist Luke's assistance. Upon resurrecting your old friend, you conceived a plausible situation by which he arrived with new government authorities. You even had him instruct you on remaining silent about his presence back in your life. Quite clever, I must say."

I blushed. "How do I know you don't say that to all the screwballs under your care?"

I didn't want to be rude by ignoring his compliment. And to be honest, it was hard not to admire my abilities as a "delusionist." I'd been extremely thorough in concocting all those details … and my subconscious had done one helluva job of keeping so many complicated secrets from my conscious awareness during those cold, wintry months.

Those docs taught me a lot. A delusion is defined as an unshakable belief that some implausible circumstance is undeniably true. And, believe me, I can attest. Hell, now that I know it never happened, I still can see Luke sitting across the booth from me.

I'll spare you the technical details … most broadly, a delusion falls into one of two categories. First, there's your garden-variety paranoid delusion. People with this psychosis actually believe that individuals or covert organizations are out to get them. They do all kinds of bizarre things to protect themselves from illusory dangers, which might include conjuring up an imaginary character or two. But thank goodness my delusions didn't fall into this category, because these folks sounded way too scary for my tastes.

No, mine could be classified as one of those "delusions of grandeur." And given the choice, who wouldn't prefer being lumped in among this group? The very designation emits a more desirable aura. These are delusions whereby people believe they obtain some imaginary power or authority. It's not uncommon for these psychotics to invent people or bring people back from the dead to help gain this power. Not only had I given Luke, my most trusted friend, new life, but I'd also empowered him with secret investigative properties so that he could ride to my rescue.

To allay any anxieties I might have had about being diagnosed as a deluding psychotic, one of the smiling white uniforms tried to suggest that I was in good company. She brought me a copy of *A Beautiful Mind* from Braydon's video library. This was that popular movie about John Nash, the mathematical genius from M.I.T. and Princeton who'd won the Nobel

Prize. He invented imaginary characters that tried to enlist his assistance in the formation of a new world government.

I appreciated her gesture but politely declined to watch the movie. I remembered it well enough ... Nash sneaking around campus, thinking all those people were out to get him. I was insulted by the comparison to a certifiable paranoid. The guy may have been brilliant, but his delusionary actions had demonstrated little, if any, grandeur.

As much as I might have liked the folks at Braydon, at times I felt the doctors were overly zealous with some of their theories. In addition to my delusions, they labeled some of my other, more endearing characteristics as psychotic patterns. Candidly, I think they were stretching.

For endless hours, they compelled me to describe my daily activities and interactions from the preceding months. Over and over, I recounted details about my cat-and-mouse games with Guenther and the Wire Rims, the building romance with Kirsten, the restored closeness with my mother, the chemistry with Edna, and my effusive admiration for Kirsten and Danny.

I thought the white coats might get a kick out of hearing about the extents to which I pushed myself to come up with crazy hat ideas for Danny or to find appropriate cardboard cut-outs that would go with take-out Thai food in Kirsten's dining room. Or perhaps they might appreciate the creativity in how I chose to torment T. Albert Guenther and the Wire Rims, including the fictitious e-mail exchanges I'd played out on their behalf.

Instead these alleged experts in the field of brain science concluded that I had been exhibiting radical changes in behavior, accompanied by frequent, often unprompted mood swings.

"Milo, most of these spontaneous, impulsive actions were direct manifestations of your poor self-image and reflected a desire to break free from the daily behaviors you'd grown to abhor. In your psychotic state, you lacked contextual insight ... you were incapable of discerning the exaggerated patterns of your own behavior."

Estrella Guzman had laid that one on me. I think they believed it would hurt less from a lady, but they were wrong. She may have been nice to look at, but what a killjoy. Some of those very actions had turned out to be the most fun I'd had in years. I made a mental note not to go partying with any psychoanalysts once I rejoined the human race.

But she wasn't done. "Your recent predilection for staring blankly into nothingness reflected an elevation of your emotional conflicts combined with a mounting state of depression. Milo, you became increasingly dependent on these periods of withdrawal as a coping mechanism for impaired functioning caused by confused or disturbing cognitive processing."

That might have been true, but I could trace my tendency to stare blankly into space as far back as eighth-grade algebra.

Amid the psychobabble, there were glimmers of encouragement. For example, Dr. Guzman let me read over her shoulder as she'd made notes following one of our more pleasant afternoon sessions—one in which she had probed into my sex life.

"The subject's ability, at age forty-four, to pursue, experience, and sustain his first balanced, mature cross-gender relationship, encompassing no unusual carnal proclivities and no reported incidence of physiological malfunction, is notable."

Somehow, the act of falling passionately in love sounded different when described by a renowned psychiatrist; but I chose to focus on the positives. What middle-aged guy wouldn't take pride in the affirmation of his sexual virility by an expert … an attractive Latin female, no less? However in retrospect, I may have gotten too caught up in the moment with my response to one of her questions.

"Yup, erections I could pound nails with."

Both doctors agreed that my willingness to pursue a romantic interest in Kirsten Woodrow had demonstrated that my positive self-image hadn't been depleted entirely. Granted, I'd used a fabricated investigation with Luke as a mental crutch to take the initiative with Kirsten, but I still had subjected myself to the possibility of her rejection, believing in the end I could prevail. So I hadn't yet become a total lost cause. Likewise, my desire to open two-way interactions with Danny had been a positive signal. Also, the instant chemistry with Edna.

One afternoon, Dr. Tann weighed in pretty heavily about my prior history with friendships. "Milo, over the years, more and more of your interpersonal relationships had become business related, which to you meant they could be characterized as artificial and protective. You were interacting with a limited social circle on a purely superficial level. But since returning to Chicago, you started seeking out more meaningful relationships. This was good not only because such actions reflected a genuine intention on your part to alter behavior positively, but these more genuine relationships also afforded you much-needed reinforcement."

He continued. "Through the comfort and candor of strong interpersonal relationships, we are able to express ourselves on multiple dimensions, which all of us need to do for our psychological health. More importantly, we also receive vital external cues that we need in order to counter our natural insecurities. Doubt in oneself is a normal part of the human psyche. We require trusted people in our lives to tell us that we're okay. Milo, in shutting off so many valued relationships over the years, you were giving your inner demons a huge home field advantage. Until you recently allowed yourself to get closer to people in your life, how long had it been since anyone you might believe could have told you that you were a decent guy? No wonder you needed your best friend back in your life."

With healthy new relationships in my life and a concerted effort to reconnect with my mother, I had started to grow more comfortable in expressing myself as the deep-down guy I'd always meant to be. And from those interactions, people whom I trusted and cared about were telling me they liked this deep-down guy. So before my meltdown with Agents Davenport and Kessler, I'd already begun nudging myself down the road to recovery.

There had been other positive signs. I'd stopped turning to alcohol as a means of escape. And whether right or wrong, I had decided to remain silent about the financial misconduct at ASC in order to protect Kirsten from prosecution. I had weighed the facts and ramifications from all sides before arriving at a conclusion based upon what I believed to be the most rightful outcome, not the most convenient. Concurrently, my subconscious had decided that Luke should miss our last meeting at Ashton's. So, on a subliminal level, I was shutting down the bogus investigation and preparing to handle the consequences of my decision without Luke's imagined assistance. On my own I had started the process of leaving my delusions behind.

Nonetheless, once the reasons for my psychotic episodes had been diagnosed, the fun wasn't over. I underwent batteries of tests and participated in countless therapy sessions. And of course many more days of infernal questions.

After nine weeks of living center stage under the bright lights of a psychoanalytic dissection, I was released with very little fanfare. No champagne. No Braydon Counseling Center certificate to hang on my wall. Not even a T-shirt. However, Estrella Guzman did give me a hug ... and since we'd moved into baseball season, Henry Tann told me that he hoped my Cubs might make it into the play-offs. That was probably as much intimacy as they were capable of demonstrating with a patient.

Though I showed plenty of signs of relative normalcy, they unfortunately couldn't declare me as cured. My file was sent to an outside therapist whom I was expected to visit on a weekly basis, per the terms set forth by my attorney. I also was put on an outrageously priced medication that had five capital letters and lots of hyphens in its name. Thank goodness for health insurance.

Apparently experts throughout the field of psychology have been debating the biological nature of psychosis for ages. Some maintain that every psychotic condition is at least partially explainable by body chemistry. Others argue that only a portion of psychoses are impacted by the subjects' physiology. In my case, there was no way to be sure, so to play it safe they put me on the drugs. The list of possible side effects was impressive—eighty-seven in all. The one I thought most interesting was, "periodic feelings of depression or insecurity may occur." With any luck the prescribed cure wouldn't cause me to become delusional again.

For the duration of my stay at Braydon, I'd been placed on an extended leave of absence from American Service Companies. For two whole months I'd been paid my full salary to read over a dozen books and watch more nighttime television than anyone should have to suffer in a lifetime. I'd not laid eyes on a business communication, paid a monthly bill, or received a single call from a telemarketer. I'd been served three balanced meals and several nutritional snacks a day. I'd worked out regularly in the fitness center and slept at least nine hours every night. By the time Braydon released me, I was exuding wellness and serenity from every pore. If I had better understood the advantages of ASC's medical disability program, I might have traveled through the looking glass much earlier in my career.

Of course, there were a few minor loose ends. I'd caused the SEC and FBI to launch an official and very public investigation into my employer. The woman I loved was edging closer and closer to possible prison time. A young boy in a wheelchair that I absolutely adored might well be separated from his mother and primary caregiver. And I still was clueless as to how I'd managed to send an e-mail that had set all these horrors into motion.

According to Braydon policy, visits from immediate family members had been permissible and, in fact, encouraged. My mother came downtown twice a week or more, and those times together provided very welcomed respites. Not so much for me, but for her. Alone in Park Ridge, it seemed like she worried almost nonstop about her youngest son's mental state. On two occasions my brother Tim joined her—driving over from St. Louis just to see me. Throughout our life, Timmy had done a better job of remembering the things that Dad taught us about family and priorities. Like Luke, my brother was able to look beyond the many times I'd fallen short of expectations, focusing instead on the deeper bonds we should strive to preserve.

Due to the litigious alarms that go off as soon as someone utters "my significant other" to an institution possessing targetable assets, Braydon offered no resistance when I suggested that Kirsten and Danny were the same as immediate family to me. Kirsten visited me every single day, weekends and holidays included. I wondered how she was able to stay in town that long without traveling on business, but I wasn't allowed to ask about anything connected to American Service Companies. The FBI had specified a host of subjects that were off-limits—which, of course, were the very topics I was dying to talk about.

On Saturdays, she brought Danny. Each week they hauled in a different-themed meal with all the attendant accoutrements. Not once did Danny fail to come up with some outrageous hat that either he had made for me or convinced his mom to buy. Their combined ingenuity was the talk of the Braydon staff. If Danny was sad or embarrassed that silly Mr. Peters was locked in a loony bin, he did a great job of hiding it. There was no doubt which day of the week I relished most.

According to the terms by which he'd agreed to admit me to Braydon, Garrett Bedford Ross or designated members of his legal team also could visit me during my stay. As could Agents Davenport and Kessler, for purposes of their investigation—with the stipulation that my legal counsel also be present. Only during these meetings was I allowed to discuss any aspect of the financial improprieties at ASC or the pending investigation. But even those conversations were decidedly one-way. I provided whatever answers I could about past activities; they offered me nothing in return related to how the case was developing in the outside world.

And lest I forget, there was one more person who visited me regularly in the cuckoo's nest. Edna. By no stretch of my imagination could I have come up with a clever means to designate her as another family member. She came up with a better idea on her own. Edna Cutler was included on the list that her poker pal, Mr. Ross, had submitted to Braydon as his legal team. For a salary of one dollar per week, she was retained to messenger important legal documents between Mr. Ross and his client. If she ever brought such documents on any of her frequent visits, she neglected to give them to me. I don't think she'd ever admit it, but I suspect that the stoic Miss Edna found the executive floor a tad dull without me and my sophomoric sense of humor.

Chapter Twenty

My release was on a balmy June afternoon and Kirsten was there to pick me up, tanned and more beautiful than ever. After nine long weeks, I hoped she might be as eager as I was to see my hotel room again. After all, the company had paid a lot of money to keep a room that hadn't been used for over two months. Of greater significance, I'd never seen Kirsten with tan lines. But our conjugal reunion would have to wait; she wanted to talk. Women are wired so differently than men.

To my surprise, she drove to Ashton's and we planted ourselves in a familiar corner booth. I hadn't been that explicit in my previous conversations with her about Ashton's, so it was obvious that a lot must have transpired in my absence.

"Milo, there are two things I've been dying to get off my chest, but I wasn't allowed to discuss them when I visited you at Braydon."

I was all ears. "The sooner we do that, the sooner we can move our discussion to a more private location."

"Cool your jets, Romeo, we're going to be here a while."

"Okay, but if you feel someone groping you under the table, don't worry, that'll be me."

I'd earned my first playful glare since returning to the free world. It was comforting to know that I hadn't lost my touch. Ill-timed humor was like riding a bicycle.

Her expression turned serious. "Milo, you need to know that I was the one who sent the e-mail to the SEC from your computer."

I sat quietly, letting her admission sink in. I repeatedly had dismissed that possibility. Why would Kirsten have done such a thing without telling me? No, while I was in Braydon I'd convinced myself that my subconscious must have sent that e-mail while chasing down some delusional tangent.

She could see that I was processing the implications of what she'd just told me, but she couldn't wait to blurt out her second bombshell. "Also, Milo, I've struck a deal with the government … I've been terminated by ASC … and in a couple months, I'll be heading to prison."

God, how she must have been waiting to unload all of that. On the first revelation I'd gone silent, now I was dumbstruck—trying to project what life would be like for her, for Danny, for me.

After a prolonged silence that became uncomfortable, Kirsten spoke up again. "I thought you might have something to say about the fact that I used your name on an explosive e-mail to the SEC … or, at least, that I'm going to jail."

I shook my head back and forth a few times, jolting myself into the present. "Uh-h-h, I guess I didn't know that sending counterfeit e-mails carried such a stiff penalty."

At first she looked startled that I could be so clueless. Then her face relaxed into a soft smile, realizing that I'd attempted a joke. Yep, in response to two of the most complicated revelations that one person might ever have to make to another, I'd actually attempted a joke. I definitely hadn't lost a step from being out of action.

The smile grew bigger. "Peters, only you could make me laugh at a time like this … or even would want to."

"Yeah, gallows humor is one of my specialties." I leaned forward and placed my open hands on the booth's table. She placed her hands in mine and I brought them up to my lips. "Is there any chance we might go back to the beginning so you can fill in a few blanks?"

We'd arrived at Ashton's in the middle of the afternoon. By the time we left, it was almost dark outside, we'd ordered dinner, and the waitress had filled our coffee mugs more times than I could count. Indeed, a lot had happened while I was off frolicking with the white coats. We started with the e-mail.

"Milo, after you told me you weren't going to step forward about ASC's manipulated earnings, the next few days became a living hell. I'd been carrying my own heavy burden for three years, but now to protect me, you were going to place yourself in legal jeopardy because of what you knew as a corporate officer … just because I'd needed to get all that off my chest."

Kirsten continued. "That day at lunch, when you were asking me some very hard questions that led me back to the New Jersey seminar when I first met Guenther and the others, I could have avoided the whole subject … I could have shut you off and we never would have gotten into discussing the rest. But I needed to tell someone … someone I trusted … someone who might understand how I'd made such a mess of things. Then later, after you told me about a friend in the government who was part of an investigation into ASC, I figured they were bound to discover what had been going on with earnings … whether you helped them or not."

She became more animated. "From what I knew, you might have been forcing your closest friend to file charges against you … I couldn't let that happen. And even if you weren't charged, I couldn't let you compromise your integrity with either your closest friend or yourself. Since moving back to Chicago, you were doing everything possible to feel better about yourself. And you deserve that … you are such a good man. How could I allow you to bury your principles?"

"My God, Kirsten, the whole situation is so twisted. There was no investigation. My best friend was dead, so he couldn't have filed charges against me. As it turns out, the government had no suspicions at all about ASC. But because I'd gone off the deep end, you didn't know that. Everything would have been fine."

"Not really, Milo. There still would have been the issue of you knowing that the fraud had occurred and having to live with yourself for not coming forward."

"For you and for Danny, I could have done that. I'd already begun to deal with Guenther and the others in my own way."

"We'll never know how that might have turned out, but I wasn't willing to give you another emotional club to beat yourself up with. You've done too much of that already."

"That's one of the things the docs kept telling me … that I need to loosen up and feel better about myself." Yet even as I spoke these words, I inwardly was feeling more unworthy than ever—astounded that this incredible woman would make such a sacrifice on my behalf. "But, Kirsten, the ramifications for you were so severe … and for Danny."

The calmness in her response reflected an inner peace with her decision. "Let's not forget that I knowingly participated in financial fraud. My sworn responsibility as controller for a public company was to ensure that we obeyed accounting laws, not close my eyes as we skirted past them. I've been horribly ashamed of myself for way too long … the feelings were overwhelming at times. They affected my moods, and Danny often paid the price by watching me wrestle with a guilty conscience. You probably didn't see that, because the times we spent with you were filled with so much happiness ... when we were together, you kept me distracted. But the guilt was still there. When I believed you were planning to expose the whole earnings scheme to the authorities, I was relieved; it was why I willingly provided you more of the dirty details you needed. Then you changed your mind and I started dreading the thought of carrying that weight into the future."

"But Danny?"

"Danny will be fine ... in the long run, better. There no doubt will be a tough period while I'm in prison. The only place that makes sense for him to stay is with my parents in Wyoming, so he'll get to know them a lot better than he would have otherwise. I'll miss him terribly, but he'll learn from my mistakes ... that people must accept the consequences of their actions. He'll come to respect that when his mom really screwed up, she ultimately did the right thing. He already has dealt with a lot in his life ... and Milo, he's strong enough to deal with this, too."

I hadn't considered the possibility that Danny would be living a thousand miles away while Kirsten served her sentence. Very soon my life was going to feel a great deal lonelier again.

"Kirsten, how did you make it appear as though the e-mail to the SEC had come from me?"

"It did come from you ... or at least your computer. Thanks to T. Albert, I knew your password: 'Not2Late.' You never lock your office, so I just came back into the building one night and logged on to your computer. After I was done, I deleted it from your 'Sent Mail' folder so you wouldn't find out."

"You even thought to use my legal name, which no one ever sees. How'd you know it?"

"I'm the controller, remember. I have access to payroll records. You pay taxes to the government as Michael R. Peters ... so I wanted to make it as easy as possible for the SEC to verify that you weren't some crackpot sending in random claims about another public corporation."

The conversation then segued into what had transpired after I'd checked into Braydon and how it could be that Kirsten already knew she was going to prison. There hadn't been enough time for the necessary hearings and trial to convict her.

On the two days that Davenport and Kessler visited me in my office, Kirsten had been traveling on business. After my meltdown, Edna had called her and she flew back to Chicago that afternoon. She, of course, had known what the e-mail to the SEC said, so she also recognized the likelihood that she'd soon be facing criminal charges. She needed an attorney and Edna put her in touch with Garrett Bedford Ross. Mr. Ross normally wouldn't have considered representing two clients on matters related to the same proceedings, but Edna had convinced him to at least listen to what Kirsten had to say.

Under protection of attorney privilege, she fully disclosed the earnings manipulations effectuated by T. Albert Guenther and his direct reports— including her complicity. Kirsten explained to Ross that she believed I had become part of a government investigation, along with the fact that she'd sent the e-mail to the SEC under my name in an attempt to protect me. She was willing to cooperate with the government in making their case against ASC, but unwilling to confess that she sent the e-mail if that knowledge would cause the FBI to implicate me for not voluntarily executing my duties as a corporate officer. That was all the information Garrett Bedford Ross had needed to get to work.

Ross's first order of business had been to convince the government not to pursue charges against me. In so doing, he actively was advocating the best interests of his one established client in the matter—me. At the same time, he was laying the groundwork to help Kirsten, whom he could represent without a conflict of interest if I were to face no charges. On my behalf, he negotiated with Agents Davenport and Kessler and an attorney representing the SEC. According to Kirsten, the wily Mr. Ross offered a series of perspectives the three of them found convincing. He assured them that until a few days prior to the government's involvement, I'd possessed nothing but suspicions related to the alleged fraudulent activities at American Service Companies. Further, he reminded them that I wasn't an expert on such matters.

"Remember, Mr. Peters did not send the e-mail. From his perspective, he still may have been trying to determine whether the accounting irregularities had really occurred or not, and therefore whether he as yet was under a legal obligation to report them to the SEC until he could be more certain. The accounting principles involved in this case are hardly black and white, even for people trained in finance, which my client is not. Then please consider his mental state ... would you want to prove to a jury that Milo Peters was capable of rendering such judgment at the time ... or that he should be held accountable for his related actions?"

Ross carefully intimated that if the FBI and SEC took a pass on me, a pivotal witness might be much more inclined to come forward in a highly cooperative frame of mind. "I may be wrong, but making a case against American Service Companies could hinge heavily on whether someone on the inside is able to corroborate fraudulent intent by those involved. I'm sure the government would feel more comfortable with its case knowing you have access to such a pivotal witness before proceeding."

After a flurry of phone calls between Chicago and Washington, the government triad concurred and I was let off the hook. I was in the clear and no longer in need of legal counsel on the matters at hand. Thus Garrett Bedford Ross was unencumbered in his ability to represent Kirsten.

He was able to barter in earnest on behalf of his now "undisclosed client," who had sent the e-mail in question. This second client could confirm the allegations made in the e-mail by documenting numerous specifics for the authorities. As the SEC attorney showed increased receptivity on the government's part, Ross shed more and more light on how his client had been entrapped into participating in the fiscal irregularities at ASC. He also suggested there were personal hardships that an eventual jury would likely take into account.

Ross pushed hard for a suspended sentence and no prison time, but due to concerns about public opinion and the political climate surrounding corporate corruption, the government was unyielding. Kirsten would have to serve time. However, they settled on a minimally applicable amount. Kirsten would plead guilty, forgo a trial, and be prohibited from the practice of public accounting or serving as an officer for a public corporation at any time in the future. She received a one-year sentence, with the government attorney's assurance of a four-month reduction once formal charges could be filed against other ASC officers due to her cooperation. In her mind, she was guilty and a conviction had been inevitable, so she was relieved to accept the shorter sentence and avoid the lengthier legal entanglements of a trial. More importantly, by being forthcoming she finally was taking the ethical actions that she should have taken three years earlier.

Within a few weeks of her agreement, she'd given the government what they needed to bring charges against T. Albert Guenther, Christopher Glickman, Robert McCaffrey, and Frederick Schumacher. No formal charges were filed against Wilson Delaney, but ASC's board of directors had felt pressured to release a public statement—and Kirsten pulled a copy out of her purse to show me.

Delaney must have been seething on the day it was issued: "All circumstances surrounding the alleged financial improprieties at American

Services Companies will be investigated independently to determine how such egregious acts could have gone undetected by members of senior management for the length of time suggested in the government's filed charges."

In none of her daily visits to Braydon had Kirsten offered the slightest hint of how these events were unfolding. Her life was being turned upside down, yet she'd arrived every day as though being with me was her only concern. She and Danny had made every Saturday a celebration. Clearly, Kirsten's abilities for compartmentalizing were superior to mine. Even more amazing was her capacity for unselfish devotion. I'd previously assumed that her feelings for me couldn't have approached the love I felt toward her. Perhaps I'd been wrong.

I eventually got around to asking Kirsten something that had been bugging me since we'd pulled up to the curb outside of Ashton's. Why had she brought me there to debrief me for reentry into the human race? I assumed she wasn't trying to torment me, so maybe she was looking to make a few imaginary friends of her own. Or maybe the shrinks had convinced her to bring me to the birthplace of my delusions as some sort of outplacement therapy.

"So why'd we come here, Woodrow? Were you afraid Ashton's was another one of my delusions and you needed to see if it really existed?"

"No, I've already been here ... weeks ago, with Agent Kessler and Agent Davenport."

"This is where they chose to have you unload on Guenther and the Wire Rims ... didn't you think that was a little mean-spirited?"

"No, we did all that in their offices. After one of our meetings, they mentioned that they were headed to Ashton's. I asked if I could tag along. Once we got here, it was only natural that we talk about you. They told me what they could about the things you were revealing to them during their visits to Braydon ... the imagined breakfast meetings with Luke ... how he died ... how you'd felt like you let him down while he was dying ... the special memories this place holds for you."

"They must have taken an instant liking to you ... they wanted you to hear and see firsthand what a whack-job I was, so you could get as far away from me as possible."

"Hardly, Milo ... it was you they took a liking to. They described how difficult it was to watch you break down in your office ... how they could see the emotional pain pouring out of you. They were astounded that someone with your position and outward confidence could be harboring so much anguish. Then as they met with you at Braydon and heard you open up about all your memories and the guilt you carried, that made an even stronger impression. They saw this truly good man trying to live up to unattainable standards. They reminded me that in their line of work, they don't get to interact with that many truly good people ... so, Milo, they started caring about you ... what had happened to you ... and what might happen to you in the future."

I had sold Mitzy Davenport and Victor Kessler way too short. I'd been eager to write them off as a couple of bureaucratic amoebae ... just like I always did with people who worked in the public sector. This was but one more tendency I needed to correct going forward. Ever since Luke had dared to pursue his life's passion while I was selling out for a paycheck, the government had become a convenient receptacle for resentment.

"I'm speechless ... even more surprising, I'm jokeless. I had no idea, Kirsten."

"Milo, that's a pretty common theme in your life ... you don't recognize the positive impact you have on the people you touch. Just look at Edna ... I've seen a whole new side of her in the few short months you've worked together. And how can I begin to tell you what you mean to Danny and me ... the joy you've brought into our lives?"

I didn't know how to react to the praise; I never did. So I looked down at my fingernails until I thought enough time had passed for me to get back to my original line of questioning. "But why were Kessler and Davenport coming here in the first place?"

"They wanted to cover all their bases. The descriptions of your meetings with Luke were so vivid and real, they wanted to see the actual setting ... but also inquire as to whether anyone else might have joined you during any of your weekly breakfasts ... in case there were others they should question as part of their investigation. While I was with them, they asked to talk to any waitresses who worked on Saturday mornings."

"What did they learn?"

"There was this one waitress, a young Vietnamese woman, who usually took care of your table. Kessler showed her your picture and she immediately recognized you. She described how you would arrive very early each weekend, order your coffee and then just sit here for an hour or more with your eyes shut ... always in this booth. Occasionally you'd open your eyes to ask for a refill and finally the check, but otherwise you never said a word to anyone. At first she assumed you had an all-night job somewhere nearby and that you came here to grab a little sleep before heading home. But eventually she decided that you must be into some kind of meditation because of the odd expressions you would make with your face."

"If she only had known what I was seeing behind those eyelids."

"So, Milo, I guess you have some pretty special memories of this place?"

"All the more special now that I've been here with you."

"I hope so ... I hope we can keep coming here. I like being an important part of your life."

"Kirsten, there's no part of my life that is more important than you. I've had nine weeks to put things in proper proportion."

At this point I was reaching my quota on serious conversation. "Speaking of proper proportions ... any chance I can get reacquainted with yours by having a nightcap back in my hotel room?"

She blushed, but modesty didn't keep her from replying. "I believe a nightcap is definitely in order ... you can't imagine how thirsty I suddenly feel. Edna's with Danny, and she practically ordered me to stay out late tonight. And you know we should never cross Edna."

"Edna ... my guardian angel." I started to chuckle but quickly stopped—overcome by a sudden impulse. "Kirsten, I don't mean to weird you out ... before we leave, I've got one more important question. I was going to ask you later, but now I realize I have to ask it here ... while we're sitting inside Ashton's, in this booth."

Based on the look on her face, my clumsy preamble must have scared her. "What is it, Milo?"

"Nothing bad ... at least I don't think ... and, well actually, it's several questions that I have." I was stumbling around, looking for the words I'd rehearsed in my mind. After all these years, I still got tongue-tied with women. "Kirsten Woodrow, I was wondering if you would marry me ... if we could live the rest of our lives together ... and if you'd allow me to play an ongoing role in Danny's life?"

Time stood still. I've never studied the nuances of facial expression or body language as carefully as I did for the next few seconds. I didn't see anything that looked like disgust or fear. She didn't bolt out of the booth and restaurant. I read that as a good sign. But she wasn't hopping over the table and falling into my arms either. Finally, she spoke.

"Excuse me, Milo, I must have missed something." She paused long enough for me to notice that my mouth was completely dry and my stomach was on the verge of hurling. At last she continued. "Did you just start a marriage proposal by telling me you didn't mean to weird me out? Before telling you I'd be thrilled to become your wife, I think it important to call that to your attention."

Okay, I was an idiot. I'd accepted my clumsiness in talking to women … let alone, in posing the one question that I thought never would tumble out of my mouth. *But wait. What had she said? "I'd be thrilled to become your wife."*

I don't need to recount the details from the balance of a very special evening … they're rather personal and have no bearing whatsoever on my story. Suffice to say, we made it to the hotel room. And yes, it was incredible, spectacular, magnificent, and so forth … and, damn, we were good … in fact, we were epic good. But modesty and chivalry prohibit me from saying a single thing more. Not another word about newly explored variations, the inconceivable display of endurance, or the mutual arrival at our desired destinations. Trust me … epic good.

Though the timing may have been impulsive, the decision to ask Kirsten to marry me was anything but. During my restful weeks at Braydon, I'd had ample opportunity to reflect on my feelings for her. My devotion to her and Danny was absolute. Granted, I didn't know at the time that she'd committed herself to prison, or that I'd eventually be married to an ex-con. But this revelation hadn't altered my feelings in the least—after all, I was only a few hours out of the nuthouse myself.

However, I'd been totally unprepared for one aspect of the marriage proposal—her consent. How could this talented and gorgeous woman possibly consent to marry me, a goofball kid from Park Ridge who'd spent more than two decades wandering through an adulthood wasteland?

In younger years my imagination had been rather vivid, but never could I have conceived such a scenario. On the verge of a midlife meltdown, I would resort to an imaginary best friend and government investigation. Soon thereafter, I would start a romance with a woman about whom I'd fantasized for three years. Of course, she would have a seven-year-old son, in a wheelchair no less, who could run circles around me in brainpower and maturity. And together we would live happily ever after … that is, once she'd served her prison sentence and I was done seeing my psychotherapist. My life had become the pilot for a sitcom. How superbly fateful … me, the guy who'd forever been grabbing for easy laughs.

Chapter Twenty-one

My first day back in the office generated an interesting mix of reactions. To the casual observer, Edna projected her normal indifference, but the small bows atop the tall coffee cups, waiting for me in their usual place, told me privately how much I'd been missed. Eager well-wishers streamed by throughout the day—all of whom worked for me in one way or another. There wasn't a person on the corporate staff who wasn't worried about the personal impact of the SEC investigation that I'd managed to set into motion, yet still they grinned and gleamed for my benefit. A few even managed to come off as sincere, as though ASC's besmirched reputation and falling stock price were of no concern to them. Nonetheless, I was careful when I stood near windows, not wanting to give any contracted snipers an easy kill shot.

I'd been saddened to learn that I wouldn't be running into my old buddy, T. Albert Guenther. Following the SEC's press release announcing an investigation into earnings manipulations at American Service Companies, the CFO's presence proved to be a significant distraction. Thus, at the urging of the board, Wilson Delaney thought it wise to place T. Albert on unpaid leave. That had occurred during the early weeks of my absence. Since then, the SEC and FBI had announced the filing of formal charges against Guenther and four of his direct reports. Details of Kirsten's cooperation had been disclosed, as well as the terms of her settlement and sentence. The Wire Rims and Guenther were awaiting the date of their trial.

Since they'd not yet been found guilty, Glickman, Schumacher, and McCaffrey could continue to perform limited duties until suitable replacements were found. It was agreed that a level of continuity needed to be maintained on behalf of shareholders. However, their work product was monitored closely by government auditors who worked out of assigned offices at ASC headquarters, as well as an interim CFO appointed by ASC's board of directors. I chose not to pay any social calls on the Wire Rims upon my return. Their lives had turned into a living hell, with the only uncertainty being the duration of their looming prison sentences. Gloating was unnecessary. If anything, I felt compassion for these wayward lads and their families. According to Garrett Bedford Ross, Guenther's handpicked trio had fallen like dominoes once the government started pressing for incriminating evidence on the odd little man that had lured them into his meticulously planned scheme.

Upon admitting guilt to the SEC, Kirsten had been terminated for cause and would receive no severance from ASC. Additionally, the government imposed penalties on her various retirement and profit-sharing funds. She, of course, took all this in stride, accepting rightful penance for her "inexcusable lapses in judgment."

For me, the hardship of her termination was much more personal. How could I be expected to show up for work if there was no chance of catching a glimpse of that magnificent walk of hers? These are the considerations that so often tip the scales of history. I'd been undecided about whether to submit my official resignation on the first day I returned to the office or hold off until later in the week. Seeing Kirsten's empty office removed any doubt.

I waited until late afternoon, wanting to see if the Great Oz might round the necessary corners to welcome me back to his Emerald City. After twenty-two years of pandering to his ego and propagating his successes, Wilson Delaney must have decided that I no longer could be of use. Since I'd come to the same conclusion, I would go to him. He was sitting at his desk reading a magazine, opened to what looked like a two-page spread about sailboats. Upon hearing my footsteps, he instinctively removed his reading glasses. No one was supposed to see him with his reading glasses.

Everything around him screamed opulence. Why not? ASC shareholders had paid for it. The imposing mahogany desk had been shipped back from one of Delaney's business trips to South America. The expansive Herati rug had cost over a hundred thousand dollars, the oil paintings at least that much. The price for his three sets of antique bookends equated to the annual salary of an experienced branch manager—and the price tag on the custom-designed cabinet in which they rested could have covered a regional vice president.

According to the terms of Wilson Delaney's contract, ownership of these items would transfer to him upon his retirement—a nice little add-on to the multimillion dollar payments he was guaranteed for ten years. Among the thousands of associates who would spend entire careers with American Service Companies, only a few dozen might exit with a retirement plan worth as much as what the CEO would receive in office furnishings alone.

He flipped on the neon smile. "Peters, good to see you. I trust your head is screwed tightly into place again."

"As much as possible, Wilson ... but still loose enough so that you could get inside and try to mess with it some more."

"Very good ... very good, Milo. Obviously you've retained that charming wit of yours."

He chose to remain in his chair, which meant he didn't want me to stay long. Otherwise, he would have stood up, straightened the expensive silk tie, walked slowly around the desk to greet me with his manliest handshake, and invited me to sit down for a chat. Oh, how I had coveted those chats, the affirmation of his favor.

"I won't stay long, Wilson ... just wanted to stop by and tell you I was resigning. You can get back to me on whether you want me to stick around and hand things off for a few weeks, or if you want me to leave sooner."

He displayed no outward reaction. One of his special skills was demonstrating that nothing could faze him. Another was trivializing those around him, if the situation called for it.

"That's fine, Milo. Just work out the details with human resources ... whatever Cynthia Richards decides about your departure date is fine with me." He looked at his watch. "Was there anything else?"

"Nope, that was it."

As I turned to leave his office, I experienced an uncontrollable urge to whistle. Fortunately, I was able to constrain myself until I was out of earshot. Damned if I'd let Wilson Delaney hear that the anthem of my liberation was a Carpenters song.

Since shaking my hand at that first annual convention, this man had held a firm grasp over me. For more than twenty years I'd revered him, feared him, and loathed him, all at the same time. I'd seen through the veneer to observe both the depth and emptiness of his commanding presence. At some point in earlier years, there must have been positive aspects to his personality. Maybe with friends and family there still were. But within the ranks of ASC, one never heard praise for the man himself—

only his position, his authority. As he'd ascended through the corporation, the power had exuded from him, and like insects to a bright light we were drawn to it. We danced, juggled, and made rhymes for his attention and amusement. How many times had I hated myself for succumbing to the contrivances of his overblown ego? For sacrificing my own principles to advance his self-serving agendas? For craving his approvals ... for the endless angst, the wrenching anxiety over securing my standing with a man I never could respect?

As the years had passed, I'd channeled more and more resentment toward Wilson Delaney, finding the convenience in blaming him for what I became and what I didn't. Yet inwardly I knew the responsibility wasn't his. He hadn't changed; I'd learned all I needed to know about his true character when I first started working for him. With each new opportunity, I'd been the one who made the choice to conform to his standards.

Despite so much pent-up emotion, the actual severing of my puppet strings seemed anticlimactic. There was no rush of release, no cathartic celebration. Only contentment. Pucker-up-and-whistle contentment. I'd turned the page at last.

❦

Three days later, Wilson Delaney announced his retirement. He was quoted in the press release as saying he wanted to spend more time with family and philanthropic interests. Odd, since neither had held much interest for him for as long as I'd known him. Rumors were rampant about what had transpired behind the closed doors of the board room. The only thing I knew for sure was that Delaney wouldn't have taken early retirement voluntarily. ASC was in the midst of a public scandal, and whether he'd played a direct role or not, the buck stopped in his corner office. The editorial pages were hungry for blood and the prosecution of a few bean-counters wasn't enough to satisfy them. The board had no choice but to serve up the CEO.

At least a week would have been required for attorneys to nail down the countless details before an announcement of this magnitude could have been made public. So Delaney likely had known his fate during our final exchange in his office. In retrospect, the calmness he'd displayed, the calculated indifference in my presence, were even more telling, but not at all surprising. For me, the turnabout was sublime. Wilson Delaney could forever blame Milo Peters for his downfall—me and my delusional investigation. To whomever he spoke in the years ahead, I could be his culprit. In no way would this man accept the outward responsibility for a corporate culture in which greed and manipulation had flourished. But inside, he would know. Whenever he looked at a mirror, he'd be reminded.

To the outside world, Wilson Delaney would appear to have come out on the winning end. He would have his carefully crafted press release, lavishing praise for how much he'd accomplished during his career. There would be the requisite excess of retirement dinners and tributes, where his contributions would become more legendary as each speaker took the podium. He still would have his tens of millions, the houses, the country clubs, and probably a new and larger sailboat. No matter what, the guys at the top somehow seemed to come out on top.

But I understood what really made Wilson Delaney tick. Though his visible trophies were important, the winning was paramount. The one thing he ultimately couldn't tolerate was defeat. In the years ahead, when he might be sitting by one of his pools, teeing it up with his upper crust cronies, or dropping anchor from his latest toy, he always would know. And it would eat at him, it would gall and chafe, it would never stop plaguing him. The last move on his corporate game board, the arena that defined his lifetime, had been defeat.

Chapter Twenty-two

Our wedding day went miraculously well, considering the whole event was pulled together in less than two weeks. The hurriedness did give my mother momentary pause, as her Midwest morality kicked in. To Winnie Robinson Peters, a rush to the altar signaled premarital pregnancy and the associated stigmas of her generation. Strange that she'd be relieved to hear our expedience was driven only by the imminent prison sentence of her future daughter-in-law. My mom was so taken by Kirsten and Danny that she could look right past the felony conviction … after all, white-collar crimes carried a certain cache. Heck, since Mom long ago had given up hope that I'd someday be married, she might have been willing to ignore an armed robbery or two. Just as long as the bride wasn't pregnant.

We took advantage of the summer weather, which doesn't last long in Chicago, and held an afternoon ceremony in my mom's backyard. The minister was one of my brother's best buddies from high school. Tim and his family dropped everything and headed home for the festivities, as did uncles, aunts, and many of my cousins. Kirsten's parents drove in from Casper.

I couldn't count the number of times I'd fumbled the ball in my relationships with Gordie Hilpert and Rich Jenkins, but to my amazement both still wanted to attend, along with their wives. I think they were curious to see if I could handle the vows without getting tongue-tied.

I was surprised even more to see a few others in attendance. Agents Mitzi Davenport and Victor Kessler arrived together, as did Drs. Estrella Guzman and Henry Tann. The esteemed Garrett Bedford Ross came alone. I hadn't thought to invite any of them, assuming they all probably would prefer to be done with me. But apparently Edna had been working the phone lines.

To extend one special invitation, I'd paid a personal visit to a house just a few blocks from where I'd grown up. It looked much the same as when I used to swing by to pick up Luke and the guys in my mom's station wagon. For the wedding, Mr. and Mrs. Papadakis arrived early and stayed late, exactly the way Luke would have. They were especially elated to meet Danny because, just as I'd told them, his spirit and enthusiasm were so reminiscent of Luke's. But also there was the hat. Atop Danny's head rested a beaten-up ball cap with a Cubs logo on the front.

During the ceremony, Kirsten and I stood under a sprawling oak. Glancing up, I saw a few remnant planks from the tree fort that Tim had helped Luke and me build when we were in fifth grade. On such a joyful occasion, in a backyard so filled with memories, Luke, my dad, and Baba Milka definitely were in attendance. Not as delusions, but as a rich and permanent presence in my life. At my side was Danny, smiling from ear to ear … the best man by any definition. Next to Kirsten stood Edna, the maid of honor … and stoicism be damned, also beaming brightly.

Following much food, beverage, and celebration, our guests cleared out well after darkness. Fortunately, I'd remembered to make the appropriate arrangements for our wedding night. Danny would stay at my mom's house, which meant Kirsten and I could pick anyplace in Chicago to share our first entire night together. So with Danny in the guest room, we took my old room, the one right above the kitchen. Growing up, I'd fantasized about getting naked with any number of hot girls in that room, but I hadn't contemplated marriage as the prerequisite.

I pulled out all stops in my preparations for a memorable night. Some might have gone with candles, champagne, soft music, and the like, but I decided to stick with the boyhood bedroom motif. For mood lighting, I rooted through at least a dozen boxes in the basement before finding the lava lamps that Tim and I received one year for Christmas. Rather than an ice bucket, I opted for an old cooler we'd used on Boy Scout campouts, then filled it with cans of grape soda … perfectly chilled. Hoping Kirsten and I might work up an appetite, I laid out an array of Moon Pies, Cracker Jacks, and beef jerky—and not those measly versions from some corner convenience store, but the large economy packs. I didn't want Kirsten to think I'd skimp on our inaugural night as man and wife.

By the time Kirsten joined me from the bathroom down the hall, Van Halen was playing on a boombox and I was decked out in the brand new Star Trek pajamas that I'd rush-ordered via the Internet. Upon entering, she looked around, shook her head in disbelief, and then closed the door behind her. She remained standing by the door, smiling. But this wasn't that smile I'd seen so often … the one she used to humor my silliness. This was a wedding night smile.

"Milo, I hope you never grow up." She dropped her robe to reveal she was wearing nothing underneath.

I was spellbound by her sensuous beauty and the uninhibited way she allowed me to feast upon it. The lava lamps accented her skin with an iridescent glow. She stood there as the most erotic vision imaginable. Finally, I spoke, my voice cracking in midsentence.

"Mrs. Peters, I'm pretty sure this is going to be my best sleepover ever."

~⁄⁄~

A month later, Kirsten would report to a federal women's facility in Waseca, Minnesota, but we didn't have much time to fret about the impending separation. Our more immediate concern was Danny. Garrett Bedford Ross worked one miracle after another to get me appointed as a legal guardian for Danny—no small task, considering my recent stay at Braydon. Kirsten, Danny, and I were interviewed, in some cases interrogated, by more agents of the court than I care to remember. It didn't hurt that we'd made the decision to move in with my mother, as her influence was viewed quite positively. To say the least, Mom was thrilled.

I'd suggested the move to Park Ridge as temporary—just for Danny and me during the eight months that Kirsten would be away. But soon we were talking about making the move more permanent, for all of us. I had declared that I was leaving the corporate world to reorder my priorities around the people most important to me. Well, Kirsten took me at my word and put her brownstone up for sale. She'd grown close to my mom and was absolutely certain the arrangement would be fantastic for Danny. So I got busy with a local architect to adapt the old homestead for Danny's wheelchair and other special needs. Before long I was writing checks for added living space and a whole menu of upgraded amenities. Reordering life's priorities didn't mean we shouldn't pamper ourselves.

We enrolled Danny in a new school on what was a very happy day. Several weeks later we made the first trip to Waseca on what was a much tougher one. The countdown began.

Epilogue

In more than seven months of making the same trip, we've discovered a few shortcuts. We can cover 334 miles of Illinois, Wisconsin, and Minnesota highways in just under six hours—as long as we get out of the Chicago metro area before traffic picks up. That gives us a lot of time to talk about all sorts of things and I'm constantly blown away by the stuff he stores in that head of his.

This morning we tried a new route because of road construction ... and make no mistake, the kid also can read maps. We still arrived well before 2 PM, when visiting hour started. Today we'll be on the highway again by 3:15, so we can make it back home tonight. We've been going to church with my mom and Danny doesn't want to miss tomorrow's Sunday school lesson; they're talking about Noah's ark. The poor teacher has no idea what she's in for when the discussion turns to animals.

Our drives back to Park Ridge have been mostly upbeat, especially now that we're into the home stretch. Only one more roundtrip without her. In two weeks, Kirsten will be coming home with us and we'll finally be able to put the whole mess behind us ... at least the painful parts.

Like I mentioned at the outset, equating my experiences to other recent and more infamous corporate scandals may seem a bit far-reaching. Nonetheless, it's a roller coaster I don't need to jump onto again. Sure, the media may have covered plenty of other whistleblowers, but as best I can tell, none of them saw fit to turn in their girlfriend or spouse. And I'm 100 percent certain that no one else thought to resurrect any dead friends for moral support. My little journey stands alone. I only hope that others may have learned as much from theirs.

I'm hell-bent to get it right from here on out, and believe me, I'll have more than enough help. You should see the way my mother and Danny gang up on me when I eat too fast … I can only imagine if I started screwing up with my priorities again.

And let's not forget Edna. The Queen of Stoicism now has a standing invitation from my mom to join us for Sunday dinner and the woman never seems to miss one. She also drops by on other nights—except Thursdays, of course—to check on her "Daniel." Edna won't say anything outright, but I know she's worried about my influence on him. She's constantly reminding Danny that "one's sense of humor is better appreciated if used more sparingly"—but each time those words leave her mouth, she somehow ends up looking at me.

She and Mom have become fast friends—not a surprise, considering their shared concerns over how a certain boy grows up. That would be me. Both also happen to adore Danny, whose maturity appears to be much more evident to them.

Edna continues to work for ASC and reports that the executive floor has settled down again. The board named one of my group president contemporaries as the new CEO and he's doing an admirable job of restoring investor confidence. I'm happy for him, the company's many associates, and in particular, I'm happy that it's not me.

When Kirsten joins us, the house will be full … like it used to be when I was a kid. Importantly, the others are still there. Sometimes when I come downstairs, I can see my dad sitting in the living room, savoring Thackeray, Dumas, or one of the Brontë sisters. In the kitchen I'll see Baba Milka pulling a sheet pan of spinach pita from the oven. Or as soon as I turn onto our street when I'm walking home from work, I might see Luke's bike in the driveway or Tim shooting baskets at the side of the house. They're all present. They'll always be present inside me. The people in our lives stay with us, impacting us forever, if we allow them.

I came to this conclusion without the assistance of any fancy doctors. A heavy dose of good people in your life will keep things in proper perspective. Maybe that's why I so treasured those Saturday mornings at Ashton's back when we were in college. The clear message was sitting there at the table the whole time … I simply skipped right past it. That won't happen again. I've had a lot more opportunity to reflect on what's really important. People and time … and not wasting either.

The hardest tendencies for me to overcome are the ones dealing with time. I have to keep reminding myself that not wasting time is completely different than being in a hurry. In fact, being in too much of a hurry is often the biggest waste of all. I'd been in such an idiotic rush to climb the corporate ladder that I was tossing away years like candy wrappers. I don't mean to denigrate ambition and people who might enjoy successful careers ... it's just that my career hardly could have been considered successful in light of what I was sacrificing.

Speaking of careers, I guess I'd better come clean on my new one—because I'm sure Luke is splitting his gut over this one. I've taken over Noble Windmills. Yup, I'm in the rare book business ... me, my mom, and Danny ... Kirsten, too, very shortly. Danny gets dropped off at the shop after school and helps until closing. Not surprisingly, he's running circles around me when it comes to learning about the books we sell. His birthday is coming up in a few months and he's hoping for an early edition of *Huckleberry Finn*. Typical. When I was his age I only wanted books that came with crayons.

For now, my mom and cousin run the place on Saturdays, when we head over here to Waseca. After paying my cousin, my mom, and Danny, I'm not sure how much I'll be able to pay Kirsten once she starts, but I've agreed to cut her in on the profits. However, I've warned her about keeping her nose clean ... seeing as how we operate a reputable family business and she'll be an ex-con and all. Based on her reaction, that's one of those jokes I might want to toss out more sparingly.

Some afternoons, Noble Windmills seems to be crawling with customers. I guess they like the atmosphere ... and wait til they meet Kirsten. We've been adding more overstuffed chairs so folks can just relax and talk over a cup of coffee. A lot of these people used to do the same thing with my dad, and some of them probably haven't bought a book since before he passed away. But that's not the point. From my vantage, business is terrific before I even count what's in the cash register. I don't think I'm alone though. Everybody seems to need a special place, whether figuratively or physically. A place where we can go and feel good. A place where we can feel good about ourselves, our lives, and what it all means.

And there I go preaching again ... me of all people. But I gave you fair warning about what this cavernous visiting room does to me and, I bet, almost anyone else. It's funny what runs through our heads before the second hand completes that last lap and the buzzer sounds to tell us visitation is over.

ACKNOWLEDGMENTS

Special thanks to Bob Rothermel for his accounting expertise; Joanne Rothermel for her eagle eye in editing; Donna Cousins, a very talented novelist, for her insights and encouragement; family and friends for plowing through the early drafts; and, of course, Kris and the kids, for putting up with the imbalances of my career.

Novels by Mitch Engel

Deadly Virtues

Noble Windmills